CU00730605

THE GUESTS

CHARLOTTE STEVENSON

www.bloodhoundbooks.com

Print ISBN: 978-1-917214-22-3

To Thomas,
Happy birthday, gorgeous boy.

'He who controls the past controls the future. He who controls the present controls the past.'
—George Orwell

PROLOGUE

Everything happens in slow motion. I watch him fall. A monstrous tree being felled with no control over its path to the ground. A sickening crack reverberates around the room as his head collides with the kitchen counter, a brief interruption in his downfall. His body is limp and languid as he slides gracelessly to the floor, his eyes searching desperately for answers. I take a step towards him, my hands balled tightly into anxious fists, my blood a cocktail of adrenaline and fear.

He is still alive.

Confused, hurt, dying, but not dead.

Yet.

1

TAMSIN

The crying stirs me from oblivion. The crying that has woken me every day for more years than I care to remember. I don't sleep anymore. Sleep suggests rest and waking up refreshed, I simply stop being awake for a while. My head is throbbing, and I haven't even opened my eyes yet. I know that when I do, it will become a relentless pounding followed by roiling nausea in my stomach. I move my thick, dry tongue around my mouth. It tastes both rotten and sickly sweet – the after-effects of a bottle of Shiraz consumed before passing out last night.

I'm not sure why I feel so dreadful this morning. A bottle of wine is not unusual for me. Two bottles of wine are not unusual for me. I peel my eyes open and struggle to sit up, the stagnant room coming slowly into focus. The crying at the foot of my bed continues. It sounds louder than usual, intensified by my stabbing headache. I always try not to look at her right away. Perhaps she won't be there one day, but today is not that day.

I see her wriggling in my peripheral vision. At first, a nondescript shape followed by an arm shooting up into the air. My eyes dart towards her. As usual, she is covered by a blanket. A faded yellow and white blanket with baby elephants printed on it.

Her face is red, confused, and hungry. The noise escalates, moving through the usual trajectory of whimpering to sobbing and finally to screaming. She kicks ferociously, and her chubby pink legs spring free from the blanket, revealing a bulging nappy. I want to pick her up and comfort her. I want to soothe and sing to her, rock her gently in my arms and let her know that she is loved and cared for. But I can't.

I stand up and creep past her towards the door. I have never seen her sit or roll, and she is too young to be able to walk. These musings matter little as I know she will lie there crying until it is her time to stop. I escape the room and shut the door behind me. Sunlight streams through the curtainless landing window and burns my gritty eyes. The closed door muffles the baby's cries, but they still break my heart. I am sweaty to the touch but as cold as ice inside. A shower is definitely in order. And when I return to my bedroom, the baby will be gone. For today at least.

I stand looking at the bathroom door. Calming my rattled nerves and preparing for what I know comes next. Afraid to open it, afraid not to. In some ways, this one is easier to handle. For a start, she is silent, and her eyes are hidden. She's less intrusive and somehow less real. I open the bathroom door just enough to see through, wiping my eyes with the back of my hand and performing a quick visual sweep of the room. She sits, her back pressed against the bath, a thin pink nightdress barely covering her pale, delicate frame. Her head is bowed, knees pulled in tightly to her chest, holding herself together. She weeps, her bony shoulders pulsating, but no sound emerges. Her hair is lank, clumped like seaweed, and hanging over her face and shoulders. I guess she is around seven or eight years old, definitely no older than nine.

Some nights, she visits me in my nightmares. My dreams are haunted by her reaching out to grab my leg as I step into the bath, or worse, pulling the shower curtain back before attacking me with claw-like fingers. I watch her closely. I imagine her head

4

suddenly whipping up, staring through me with dead black eyes and charging at me while I am sitting helplessly on the toilet. None of these things have ever happened. She is consistent and never wavers. She will sit there, raw and needy.

Every day is the same. I could easily shower later, when she will be gone, but I don't. I come in here every morning to be with her; I owe her that. I'm the only person she has.

I sit at the breakfast table, nerves frayed and emotions running amok. My shaking hands grip a steaming mug of thick black coffee. It will take at least two of these coffees and my four morning tablets before I stop trembling. The distant beep of a phone alarm flows down the stairs. In nine minutes, it will sound again. And probably again nine minutes after that, depending on whether Summer hits snooze for a second time. Every day is the same. Painfully predictable. Summer will be downstairs sometime in the next fifteen to thirty minutes, and I will be calm and collected by then.

Summer is my seventeen-year-old daughter. In a few months she'll be eighteen. I'll have an adult daughter and can barely function as an adult myself. Her father, Alex, left us three years ago. Actually, that's not fair. He left me and wanted to leave me so completely that he left Summer, too. I scared him away. My haunted brain pushed him too far. Neither Summer nor I have seen him since he closed the front door on us. Alex's absence in our home has left a hole.

We weren't happy together, but I do miss him in some ways, and despite Summer's protestations, I think she does too. He was not a bad husband, and the end of our marriage was not his fault. To everyone but me, he is painted as the bad guy, the abandoner. But that's just not true. He left because he was terrified. Terrified of me. And he was right to be. Summer and I don't talk about him much anymore. I should probably try fixing that, but there's a long line of other things I should fix first. Nine minutes must have passed because I hear the alarm again. This time, it's followed by the sound of Summer's feet hitting the floor and the creak of her bedroom door as she opens it. She yawns exaggeratedly and thunders across the landing. I've talked to her so many times about how heavily she walks. It never changes and really doesn't matter alongside everything else.

I look down at my ashy hands, dried blood clumped in the corner of my left thumbnail. I suck it and gag at the sharp metallic taste. My hands may be uncared for, but at least they are steady. The coffee and tablets have done their job. I am calm, clean, appropriately dressed, and outwardly normal. All I have to do is keep this going until Summer leaves for the day. Summer attends the local sixth form college. Weekends are much more challenging for me than weekdays. Keeping up the charade of normalcy for a whole twenty-four hours is crippling. Thankfully, Summer is now at an age where she prefers to spend every waking moment with her friends or staring at her phone, and I can disappear into the background. Once upon a time, my home felt like a sanctuary. Now, it is a prison.

I wiggle my eyebrows up and down and puff out my cheeks. I smile and laugh, firing up my muscles, preparing my face ready for Summer's entrance and temporarily lifting my features back to where they should be. My face hangs off my skull these days, misery and exhaustion painted all over my dry, blemished skin. Expensive make-up is my saviour, and I've recently downloaded an app for face yoga. It's wholly ridiculous, but anything that helps me keep up appearances is worth a shot.

Summer enters the room, and I beam at her, then dial it down a notch from joker-esque grinning to something that resembles friendly and welcoming. With her slight frame and big innocent eyes, Summer appears much younger than her seventeen years. She smiles and yawns at the same time, which makes her look even more adorable. Summer twirls her hand through her long dark ponytail and drops into the chair opposite me at the table, the floral cushion slipping out slightly from under her as she does so. My eyes fill as I take in her pure beauty that shines from within. She has such a wonderful heart. I don't know how I ever had such an incredible, kind, selfless daughter.

Physically, Summer is more like me than Alex, although my dark hair is now styled in a no-nonsense bob, and my eyes are sunken and lined underneath the magic war paint. But aside from the packaging, Summer is nothing like me. The thought that one day she could be is terrifying. I can't let that happen to her. Alex was a buffer between my hideous thoughts and Summer. With another person in the house, I knew our daughter was safe. He could protect her from my darkness. I no longer care much about myself, but as I am the only parent that Summer has left, I have to be a good, strong, and most importantly, normal person.

I hear Summer's voice, and it shakes me out of my thoughts and back into the room.

"Mum. Mum, are you there?" She giggles sweetly as she speaks, but I can detect a hint of nervousness in her voice at my brief dissociation from the room.

"Sorry, my love. I was daydreaming. Such a beautiful day, isn't it?" I look out of the window, down our long, sloping garden. It may be the beginning of spring, but it is not a beautiful day at all. The view is dull and dreary, with not a speck of blue sky visible through the thick grey clouds. Neither of us comment.

I walk to the sink to fill the kettle and try to compose myself.

"Tea?" I ask Summer, and I am startled when she suddenly appears right behind me, her hand reaching into the fridge.

"I'll just grab some juice, thanks." She fixes me with her deep, caring eyes. "What's up, Mum? Why so jumpy?" I force a carefree laugh and attempt a cheery tone.

"Sorry, I'm just not quite with it yet. A cup of tea will sort me right out, I'm sure." I reach out and tuck a stray lock of hair behind her ear, marvelling at the softness of her skin as I do so. There's a brief moment of understanding between us, and I turn away quickly, feeling an overwhelming sense of guilt. I don't want Summer to understand anything about me. I want her to be happy.

"Sit down, Mum. I'll grab us some toast." She places her warm hands on my shoulders and squeezes slightly, steering me back towards my chair before I can protest. I continue my light-hearted approach despite the crushing sense of failure enveloping me. My daughter thinks I am too useless even to make toast, and that's with me pulling out all the stops to appear competent.

"That's very kind, sweetheart, but you sit down; you've got a long day ahead." I begin to stand up, but Summer comes over and wraps her arms around my neck, resting her head on my shoulder. Her ponytail swishes into my eyes, but I don't care. I breathe in the smell of her apple shampoo and pat her hands gently with my withered fingers.

"Just sit down, Mum. I know teenagers get a bad rep, but I can definitely do some toast." She turns her head and kisses me with a flourish, leaving a smear of lip balm on my cheek.

"Anything exciting at college today?" I say, trying to move the conversation to something that will get her talking.

"Not really, but remember, I have a football game after college. It's an away game, so Amma's dad will drop me home."

I hadn't remembered about the game, but it looks like I won't have to do anything anyway. "That's great, sweetheart. I'll have tea ready for us. Anything you fancy?"

"Pizza would be good," she mumbles with a piece of toast clamped between her teeth and puts a plate with two pieces of heavily buttered toast down in front of me.

I watch as a chunk of butter slips slowly off the side of one of the pieces and onto the plate. I can't eat this. I can barely look at it. Thankfully, Summer is too engrossed in gathering her belongings and devouring toast at an alarming rate to notice my initial reaction.

"Anyway, I better go, Mum. I'll see you at sixish." She glugs down the last of her orange juice and fixes me with her brown eyes before she goes. "Eat up, Mum. You're super tiny these days."

I pick up the least buttery-looking piece of toast. It sags in my hands. "Of course, this looks delicious. Just what I need."

Summer mimes lifting the toast to her mouth, encouraging me to take a bite. I follow her, taking a tiny bite of the corner and ignoring the instant nausea that hits me.

"Wish me luck!" she trills as she slams the door closed and hurries down the garden path.

I rush to the bin and spit out the mushy crust before returning to the table to retrieve the plate and tip the remainder of the toast into the bin. It slides slowly in, and I'm so relieved not to have to look at it anymore. I wipe my mouth with the back of my hand and click the kettle on to boil again, staring out of the kitchen window at the empty garden. When Alex was here, the garden borders were filled with beautiful fragrant flowers. Now, they are empty, apart from the occasional weed. The bottom of the garden was where Summer and Alex used to plant things together. Summer graduating from looking for worms and trying to dig to Australia, to tending to their flourishing crops with care and pride. They were so close when Summer was little. Much less so in the years before he left.

I focus on a particular spot towards the end of the garden. An utterly unremarkable patch of grass that looks no different than any other. There is nothing to see, but later today, that area of grass will be occupied by my third unwelcome guest.

My third shadow.

2

SUMMER

I close the door and run down the garden path as though I don't have a care in the world. In many ways, I don't, but when it comes to Mum, there is an ever-present worry that I can't shake. I stop when I know I'm out of sight. Our kitchen and living room are one open, supposedly modern and friendly living space. I don't get the idea behind this. All it means to me is that everywhere smells like food, and you can never hear the TV if someone is cooking.

I sneak around the side of the house and peer through the corner of the open shutters. As always, Mum is staring out of the kitchen window, wringing her hands and doing very little else. Her empty plate is beside her next to the sink. I knew she was going to bin that toast. Overloading it with butter seemed like a good idea, but she looked like she was going to puke when I gave it to her. She's getting more and more bony every day. Her tiny body needs calories. If it wasn't for all the wine and occasional biscuit or chocolate bar, I don't think she'd survive.

I know she thinks she's fooling me. She's always very well put together, and her make-up and clothes are beautiful, but I can see through all that. I can see it in her tired, darting eyes. I hear it when she stumbles out of bed every morning and rushes to the bathroom. She thinks I can't hear her crying in there.

I'm always awake before her. She needs the time each morning to pull herself together. I use my ridiculously loud alarms as a warning for her, not a wake-up call for me. I've come downstairs too early before, or met her on the landing, on her way in or out of the shower, and it hasn't been a good experience for either of us. She doesn't look like herself. The only word I can think to describe her before she puts on her make-up and takes her pills is… haunted.

I rest my hand on the window, wishing I could reach out and touch her. Comfort her and let her know that I'm here and I love her. She turns her head slightly, not enough to see me. I duck quickly, losing my footing and almost tumbling into the prickly hedge. I right myself as quietly as possible and, without looking back, begin my walk to college.

Mum has an appointment with a psychiatrist today. She lies to me and tells me she doesn't go to her appointments or take pills anymore. I don't know why Mum does this. For a start, she is the world's worst liar. But more importantly, why doesn't she trust me? A tiny P written in the corner of the date on our kitchen calendar is code for her psychiatric appointments. I was relieved to see the reappearance of the P this week. Unless she's forgotten to mark the calendar, I don't think she's been for a while. Her medication lives in a blue and white porcelain vase beside her bed, hidden underneath a massive bouquet of fake flowers. I sneaked upstairs once and watched from the doorway as she reached into it and retrieved them, the bright pink flowers dangling from her hand. She didn't see me. Sometimes, she's so far away from the world, completely disconnected from reality. At other times, she's so pent-up with worrying about every little movement she makes and every word she says. She's like a swinging pendulum that never comes to rest at a happy medium. I can't imagine how this must feel for her.

Amma is waiting for me outside college as usual. She is undoubtedly my best friend, and I feel so lucky to have found her. I adore Amma's family. Her younger brother, Charles, is sunshine in human form, and her parents are so lovely and welcoming. I think I've had more physical contact with Amma's mum than I have ever had with my own. Amma greets me with a beautiful smile, enveloping me in a much-needed hug. I fall into her, grateful for her presence in so many ways. She places her hands on my shoulders and pushes me away gently, focusing her eyes on mine.

"What's up, Sunny? Your mum again?" She raises a perfectly shaped eyebrow at me, and I have to stop myself from staring longingly at her impossibly beautiful face.

"Yeah, same old shit." I shrug as though it's nothing. Amma tilts her head and wrinkles her forehead, making it clear I won't get away with that answer, and our conversation is not over. "I just don't know how to talk to her anymore. She's being more and more weird. It's worse now than when Dad left." I break away from Amma's hold and turn my wrist to show her the time.

"Keep talking," she says as we walk through the throng into the building.

I only need to fill about three minutes. Amma and I haven't been in the same classes for a long time. She has always excelled at maths and science, whereas I favour literature and foreign languages. I have always thought she is much cleverer than me, but Amma assures me that we are simply different.

Sport is where we come together. Even as five-year-olds, we loved nothing more than running around in our back gardens for hours on end. My dad played football with us when we were small, before he lost interest in everyone but himself. Amma's dad would teach us everything we needed to know about tennis – never forgetting to tell us that he was regularly a championship winner when he was a teenager growing up in Ghana.

He would put us through drills and constantly exclaim,

"Strength! Power! Speed!" as we sprinted up and down the garden.

"Sunny?" Amma jolts me from my lovely daydream of playing in the Annans' back garden. I look up at her apologetically. "And you're always moaning about your mum being a total flake."

I know Amma is only joking, and I manage a small laugh and a self-deprecating eye roll. "I know. Look, we'll catch up later. I'm half asleep." I realise this is almost a carbon copy of my conversation with Mum this morning, and worry briefly that I'm becoming like her.

"We will." Amma's voice is authoritative, and she pulls me in roughly for another hug. "Now sort your shit out before Mr Howes kicks your butt for being away with the fairies." I nod and smile unconvincingly. "And stop trying to hide things from me. You know your poker face is non-existent, right? Meet me on the field at lunchtime. Tell me everything. Okay?" Amma blows me a kiss as she slowly jogs down the corridor away from me.

My poker face can't be as bad as she says it is. I'm pretty confident she has no idea how I actually feel about her, and I can't risk her finding out. I'm pretty convinced that Amma doesn't feel that way about me, and our friendship is undoubtedly the most important and secure thing in my life at the moment.

I can't imagine ever losing her.

3

TAMSIN

The events of breakfast keep running through my mind. Ridiculous really. Summer left happy and thinking that I was going to eat the toast. I untuck and lift my shirt and look down at my pallid, shrinking middle. The uneven skin is wrinkled and saggy. What is the point of losing weight if this is the result? I think I'd rather have my pot belly back. At least then, I wouldn't have spent a small fortune on clothes as one after another they began to hang from my frame.

In my wardrobe, I have clothes that span six different sizes. Some haven't even been worn. I look at the array of smart suits and dresses. I used to be an accountant. An actual functioning member of the workforce. I worked for a prestigious company and when Summer came along, I even had the confidence and the clients to set up a firm of my own. I used to be successful and driven. But over the years I let my client lists dwindle. I just sat back and watched it happen, until eventually it was just me and a bunch of smart suits I no longer needed. I kept promising myself I'd get back into it once Summer was a bit older. But who am I kidding, I couldn't go back to it if I wanted. My brain is mush.

Anyway, I'm not throwing any of these clothes away – I don't trust myself to stay the same size. I sigh and rub my fists into my eyes before letting out a strangled cry of frustration. I realise too late that I've made an utter mess of my eye make-up, and my palms are now covered with a mixture of black streaks and bronze powder. I roll my stiff shoulders back and shake my arms, trying to release some of the tension weighing down on me. I need to leave for my appointment in less than fifteen minutes if I don't want to be late.

I check my ruined make-up in the bathroom mirror. Thankfully, I'm alone in here now; the weeping girl has gone. Every day, I worry that her presence will expand into the day, and not just infect my mornings. I try not to think too much about the intrusion of the visitors in my life. The guests. My shadows. They don't hurt me. They are not affecting my ability to function, well maybe a bit, but not so much that I need to do anything about it. And I've managed to keep their existence away from Summer. I want her to enjoy as much of her childhood as possible before she realises how damaged I am. My biggest fear is that I will somehow pass this on to her, that her mind will eventually betray her as mine has. I can't let that happen to Summer. I don't want her to live like I do. Even I don't want to live like I do.

I arrive at the office of Dr Fergus McCabe with minutes to spare. I check my appearance in the rear-view mirror, and at least I look presentable. Smiling widely, I check my teeth for errant food particles, which is absurd given that I barely ate. I take a deep breath and exit the car, the wind trying to rip the door away from me as I do so. I barely manage to avoid my door crashing into the very expensive-looking Tesla parked next to me. My heart is thumping, and my hair is everywhere, sticking to my lips and obscuring my vision. The unexpected wind has unnerved me. There wasn't a hint of a breeze at home, and I've only driven three miles.

Today is my first appointment with Dr McCabe. He has

probably the most Scottish-sounding name I've ever heard, so I've imagined him as an enormous ginger-haired man, with a full, bushy beard. Possibly even wearing a kilt and greeting me with a bagpipe salute as I enter. I realise I'm being utterly ridiculous with this stereotypical image, but that's what my addled brain has conjured up. Until recently, I had been seeing a psychiatrist named Dr Pathirana, an elegant and astute South Asian woman who became too astute for my intentions. I stupidly thought that I could manage this on my own and tried to muddle through without the support of a psychiatrist. But waking up on the living-room sofa last week, face down in my own vomit and my pyjama pants sticking to my thighs with cold, pungent urine, I quickly realised that the only thing I can manage effectively on my own is getting completely wasted. Thankfully, Summer knows nothing about that night. I cleaned myself up and made an appointment with Dr McCabe's office the next day. I owe it to Summer to give getting better everything I have. And that's why I am here.

The waiting room is empty as I struggle through the door, the wind hampering my intention to enter elegantly. The young man at reception smiles at me sympathetically before averting his eyes and shaking his head rapidly from side to side to reposition his curly fringe. As I approach, I realise he is dazzlingly handsome, has beautiful blue eyes, and is probably still a teenager. The tips of my cheeks redden, and I clear my throat.

"I have an appointment with Dr McCabe. It's Tam... I mean Thomasina Cavendish." Saying my full name has always embarrassed me, and I've been Tamsin to everyone but my father my whole life. My father always insisted on calling me Thomasina despite my asking to be Tamsin from the moment I could talk. My sister, Hetty, is in a similar situation. Her name is Henrietta. What a very absurd and obvious way to say how disappointed you were at having girls rather than boys.

My mother insists that naming us was entirely down to my

father, which I can certainly believe, and she has always called us by the names we prefer. Overbearing is a very kind way of describing my father's behaviour and attitude towards his family. He was not pleasant to be around. He died when I was young, and I don't remember ever feeling much about it. To me, he was never really present, and I remember being happier when it was just me, Mum, and Hetty.

"Take a seat, Mrs Cavendish. Dr McCabe will call for you soon."

I instantly have choice anxiety over the numerous chairs in the waiting room and hover uncomfortably before finally sitting down in the corner, making sure I don't make eye contact with the beautiful receptionist again.

In a bid to feel less conspicuous, I pick up my phone and start scrolling. Only seconds pass before I hear my name called in a very subtle Scottish accent. I look up to see Dr McCabe standing in the open doorway of his consulting room, smiling. I'm immediately flustered and suddenly can't seem to get the clasp of my bag open to put my phone away. Rather than just holding the phone or taking the extra two seconds to open the bag calmly, I try to stuff it in the small gap at the top of the bag and drop it on the floor instead.

This is not the first impression I was hoping to make. Dr McCabe begins to walk towards me. I don't look up. Instead, I focus on the tiny scuff on one of his otherwise impeccable brown leather shoes. I feel like I am going to cry. Why do I have to make a mess of even the simplest of tasks? Dr McCabe stands in front of me, not saying anything. I eventually stand up, sling my bag over my shoulder, and hold my phone in my trembling hands. I roll my eyes and attempt to laugh good-humouredly at myself before meeting his gaze.

Thick tortoiseshell-rimmed glasses frame his brown eyes, and there is not a hint of facial hair on his slim, angular face. He holds his arm out and motions gently for me to follow him.

There's something about him that puts me at ease – an aura of calmness. My heart rate begins to slow, and my breathing starts to regulate.

Dr McCabe's room is plain and functional. There is no art on the walls, not even a plant. He has a well-worn black leather chair turned away from his desk. He gestures to the small blue sofa next to the window, and I sit, moving one of the oversized cushions onto my lap as I cross my legs. He pours me a glass of water and places it on the coffee table in front of me.

"Thank you." I smile and look down at the glass.

"No problem." He sits and crosses his legs before resting his hands on his knee.

There are a few seconds of silence. I look up fleetingly before returning my eyes to the glass of water, watching a bead of condensation make its way down to the table.

"I'm Dr McCabe. It's lovely to meet you." I look up, and his eyes gently crinkle at the sides. He looks genuine.

"It's nice to meet you too. I'm Tamsin. Well, I mean... call me Tamsin. It's the name I use. I don't like..." I let my sentence drift off, realising that at least half of my words were completely unnecessary.

"Of course. Tamsin. Well, let's get to know each other a little, shall we?" He uncrosses his legs and leans slightly towards me. "How has everything been?"

"Good. Really good." My answer comes out far too quickly, and I bite my lip to avoid any further words escaping.

"Excellent. Then I guess we're done for the day." My eyes widen and I straighten my back. Dr McCabe smiles widely at his own joke. "I'm sorry. I'm just trying to ease some of the tension. The first sessions are always like this. We don't know each other at all. Yet, somehow, you're expected to start telling me your most personal and private information."

I nod and manage to find a single word, my mouth suddenly feeling as though it is filled with cotton balls. "Yes."

"What I say is, let's lower our expectations for today. Let's just have a wee chat, shall we?"

I nod and stroke the soft cushion on my knee as though it were a pet cat. Dr McCabe taps his pen against his lip and creases his forehead before he speaks again. "Now, tell me if I'm wrong. But you strike me as someone who might respond better to questions rather than me just asking you to talk."

He is absolutely right. I wouldn't have a clue what to say. I nod gratefully. "Yes. Yes, definitely."

"Good. That works for me, too." We share a smile, and I start to relax again. "I've read your notes, and Dr Pathirana sent me a letter with your past history and the medication you're currently taking."

My heart drops at what Dr Pathirana might have said about me. She was getting far too close. "That's... um... good." I smile weakly again and wait for the question he promised me.

"Let's start there then, shall we? I'll tell you what I know, and you can tell me if I'm right. Deal?"

"Er... okay. Deal." He's definitely forgotten about the question-and-answer format we agreed on.

"Excellent." He claps his hands unexpectedly and straightens his glasses before reaching behind him and pulling a paper folder of notes out of the desk's top drawer. I feel a small swell of pride as I see that the folder is relatively thin. I'm sure he's seen folders overflowing with notes, even people who need two or more. He rests it on his knee and flicks through the first few pages.

"Okay, Tamsin. From what I can see, you're currently taking medication for generalised anxiety disorder." He raises his eyebrows at me, and I nod. "You've previously taken several different antipsychotic medications but haven't taken any for over twelve months."

I swallow audibly. "Yes, that's right. I was seeing and hearing things. People mostly. But that's gone now. I haven't had any of that for ages." I'm grateful that Dr McCabe doesn't look up as I answer him. I'm very comfortable and practised with this lie. But saying it to a new person always throws me off. The good thing, in fact the only good thing about hallucinations, is that nobody but me knows about them unless I tell them.

"Well, that's very good to hear. Hallucinations can be extremely distressing. I'm glad you're no longer suffering with them." He fixes me with a stare, and I fidget uncomfortably. I feel like a child insisting they haven't sneaked any chocolate whilst wearing a blatant chocolate moustache. He smiles, and I'm unsure if he believes me or is just deciding to let it go for now.

"You missed your last appointment with Dr Pathirana due to..." He flicks through my notes to the last page. "...food poisoning." He looks up at me with that stare again and raises one of his eyebrows spectacularly high up his forehead.

"Um. Yes." My mouth is starting to dry up and my words make a disgusting sticky noise as I speak.

"That's not true, though, right?" He smiles warmly. "You don't have to tell me why you wanted a different doctor, but the truth is always preferred. I don't need all the background information, so don't worry. We are starting afresh today."

My face feels alarmingly hot, and I wish there were something I could focus on in this barren room. There was always so much to look at in Dr Pathirana's office. I decide to tell a censored version of the truth.

"Yes, I made that up. I didn't want to go. Then I figured if I was dreading it so much, maybe I shouldn't go anymore. But... well, I still think I need to talk to someone."

He holds out his palms. "Great. And that's where I come in."

I give him a small smile and realise that I don't actually feel embarrassed, which is unheard of for me. My resting state is perpetually self-conscious and ill at ease.

"Okay then. Unless you tell me otherwise, I'll focus on your anxiety symptoms today. I'll run through a quick questionnaire to get a baseline. Then we'll have a think about your medication and future sessions. How does that sound to you?"

It sounds pretty good. I know the questions he's going to ask, and if I remember correctly, it's all multiple choice. Dr McCabe starts as expected by asking me whether I've been feeling nervous or anxious in the last two weeks and how many days I've felt like that. The answer to this is every day. The answer to all of these questions is every day. But I don't say that. I stick with answers like "once or twice" or "a few of the days", and I always say "not at all" for any questions about being annoyed or irritable. I don't want anyone to know that I have bad thoughts or feel pure rage sometimes. Not even someone who is trying to help me.

I'm a mother – a single mother. It's not okay to be annoyed or angry at any point. I can't have anyone worrying about Summer or poking their nose in and discovering my hugely substandard parenting. But feeling a bit worried or restless is okay, surely? In fact, couldn't that be seen as a positive thing? That I care so much about my daughter that I'm sometimes naturally worried and anxious.

"Tamsin?" My eyes dart to Dr McCabe as I suddenly come back into the room and realise that Dr McCabe must have been talking.

"Oh. Erm, sorry. I was just thinking." He tilts his head and raises both eyebrows this time. "I'd say several days to that one."

I can't remember which question we are on, and it really doesn't matter. Dr McCabe seems a little deflated by the end of the questions, and the atmosphere in the room is sombre.

"Okay, Tamsin. Thank you for answering those questions. I've recorded your answers alongside a note to myself that I'm not sure about the accuracy of your self-assessment."

I sit up straight, a natural instinct to protest awakening in me. Dr McCabe holds out a hand to stop me, and I gape at him, a look of injustice on my face.

"Please don't take offence, and it really doesn't matter how you choose to answer the questions. Your answers are subjective, and I can look at you objectively while you answer them. Otherwise, you could fill it in out there." He gestures to the waiting room.

I'd much rather be out there than sitting in here being scolded.

"Some people will exaggerate their symptoms and feelings; others will downplay them. Some people are right on the money. And none of those people are better than the others. It's just being human."

I still haven't spoken. I pick up my glass of water and take a small sip before clearing my throat. The outside of the glass is too wet now, and I wipe my hands on the cushion on my knee.

"Okay. Well, I don't like to make a bigger deal of things than I need to. I'm not lying." The tips of my cheeks flush pink, and I break eye contact with Dr McCabe.

"Good. That's good. That tells me you're a person who will try and get on with things, put people first, and perhaps suffer in silence rather than talking about your problems with family and friends."

I like the sound of that. "Yes. That's very true. My family, well, my daughter specifically, is very important to me. I don't want to put on her. I want to be there for her."

"That's very understandable, and staying well is the best way to be there for her." I nod and start picking at the pale pink nail polish on my thumb. "You know how on planes they tell you to put your oxygen mask on before helping anyone else, even your own child?"

"Yes, but nobody would actually do that, would they? Anyone would want to save their child first. Not doing that would be horrible."

"Ah, but you see. If you don't put yours on and you become unconscious, how are you supposed to be of any help to your child?"

I feel a rumbling of anger. He's being ridiculous.

"Summer is the name of your daughter. Correct?"

"Correct." I'm aware my tone is clipped, but he's suggesting I should let my daughter die and save myself. Completely absurd.

"And I can tell you want Summer to be happy and healthy."

"Of course I do. What kind of question…"

He holds up his hand in that annoying manner again. "Then all I'm saying is that you can't help her with anything without focusing on yourself, too. You need to make yourself a priority. Understand that to her, you are a priority. She loves you."

His last sentence knocks all the wind out of my sails, and I feel myself shrinking into the sofa.

"How can she?" The words escape my lips before I know it, and I'd do anything to take them back. They are loaded with meaning. With three simple words, I have completely ruined the image I wanted to portray, and instead, I now look like a selfish, entitled mess of a person. Tears prick my eyes, and I see Dr McCabe looming towards me, holding out a tissue.

I dab my eyes and look up at the ceiling to stop the tears from falling. They come anyway, and I feel them drip down my face and onto my neck. No doubt creating tracks through my make-up as they go. Making cracks in my disguise.

I don't dare look at Dr McCabe. I have no idea what I'll do if I see the pity I know will be all over his face. I can't handle that just now. The urge to run from the room is overwhelming. I don't have to see this man again. I can just move on with my life.

I wipe my eyes, cheeks, and neck with the tissue, leaving it stained and torn. I know I must look an absolute mess. I place the cushion gently to my side and begin to stand.

"I'm going to go home now." My voice is quiet and almost disappears entirely, replaced by desperate pants of breath. I look up and give a small smile to Dr McCabe. His face is twisted with confusion.

"Sure. If that's what you want. I mean, you've paid for another twenty minutes." He seems completely unmoved by my outburst. He doesn't look shocked, sad, embarrassed or anything really. "Personally, I thought we were getting on great. Early days, I know, but if you feel differently, I understand."

I sit back down slowly. I'm not sure why. Everything inside me is still screaming to leave this room and its horrible mess of swirling emotions.

"You're supposed to show your arse in here, you know."

Suddenly, I'm horrified and indignant. How dare he? "My what?" my voice is shrill and haughty.

Dr McCabe laughs, wide-mouthed and I have visions of slapping his face with the back of my hand. "No. No, you misunderstand." I should hope so. "It's a Scottish phrase. It means you're supposed to be at your worst in this room. You're allowed to be angry, unreasonable, upset, whatever the bloody hell you like. This is your time. If you come into this room all prim and polite, what are we even doing here?"

I try to take in his words, but I can't think clearly through the blood pounding in my head.

"I am not going to judge you, Tamsin. Nothing you say here defines you. Everyone has horrible, horrific thoughts sometimes. Everyone can be unreasonable. Do you honestly think that showing a wee bit of sadness about wishing you could do more for your daughter is something terrible? For me, it's been the best part of the morning. I was beginning to think you were some kind of robot or plant."

Despite my aching heart, this makes me laugh.

"Don't sugar-coat things for me. If you want help with your anxiety, then tell me about it. Warts and all." He leans forward and clasps his hands on his knees. There's not a hint of insincerity in his words or his appearance. I believe every word he is saying to me.

"Would you come back tomorrow? Same time? I think we need a do-over." I have an intense urge to apologise. Instead I close my eyes and nod briefly. "Great. I think we know much more about each other now, Tamsin, and I look forward to speaking with you properly. Leave your preconceptions about what you should say and what I want to hear at home. Just bring yourself, and let's talk. Okay?"

"Okay." I sniff and manage another small laugh. I'm surprised to find that I feel a little hopeful, a glimmer of something positive stirring at the back of my mind. Dr McCabe and I both stand, and he holds out his hand. I take it and he shakes mine.

"It's been lovely to meet you, Tamsin." He points at a door off to the side that I had assumed was a cupboard of some sort. "There's a wee bathroom in there if you need to…" He draws circles around his face with his fingers. I laugh embarrassedly.

"Thank you." I'm sure he knows I'm not simply thanking him for the offer of freshening up before I leave.

"Not a problem. There's another door from the bathroom into the waiting room. Make an appointment with Jackson on your way out." I nod my head. "He's a great receptionist, but sure makes me feel old and haggard." He laughs as he strokes his chin. "Take care, Tamsin, and I hope you enjoy the rest of your day."

"You too." I reach for the bathroom door, no longer wanting to leave and feeling like I've made a step forward, no matter how small.

I can't remember a time when I last felt like that.

4

TAMSIN

I drive home in a daze. Snippets of hope about the future jump into my brain before crushing negativity banishes them away. But the good thoughts keep trying to push their way through. It's a nice but exhausting process. My jaw aches from absent-mindedly grinding my teeth. I look at my watch before I get out of the car, and I'm not surprised to see it's 1pm.

My body always makes its way home for 1pm, and I've stopped trying to resist her siren song calling me home. I stand before my front door, my stomach in knots. A tiny spider dangles from the doorframe, and I watch him for a while. Anything to postpone what I know is waiting for me. I debate running straight upstairs and shutting myself in the bedroom, but I know that doesn't work. It only delays the inevitable. There is a sickness inside me that eventually draws me out and forces me to look. To face her.

I take a deep breath and push the door open. It swooshes over a small pile of junk mail, and I leave it on the floor – no more delays. I walk straight through to the kitchen and stand at the window, holding on to the cold stainless steel of the sink, the skin over my knuckles straining and stretching painfully.

I raise my eyes slowly, and as expected, she is there. She stands with her back to me. Her arms are wrapped tightly around her tiny waist, her feet completely bare. At least it's not too cold today; I worry about her in the winter.

A pale pink dressing gown covers her body, with only underwear underneath. On braver and stronger days, I've been outside and walked up close to her, but today is a day to stay in the kitchen. My mind has already hit its limit. We have never spoken, and I don't even know if we could. I focus on her tangled brown hair, fluttering gently in the cool breeze as she stands and stares out into the world. This woman is an adult, but her frame is so slight that from behind, she could be mistaken for a girl of twelve or thirteen. Of all the ghosts in my mind, the shadows that invade my days, she is the one who haunts me the most. I feel her beckoning to me. She is silent, unlike the crying children upstairs. And I feel as though she wants something. I have dreams about her face. Sometimes, it is a face I recognise but can never figure out why. Often, it is featureless, a horrifying smooth mound of pink skin. A chill prickles up my spine, and I let go of the sink, wrapping my arms around my waist, mirroring her. The scene continues as it does every day and I watch powerlessly as she falls to her knees and bows her head.

She draws her shaking pale hands up to her face, and I see her bony shoulders begin to quiver as her dressing gown whirls and whips around her. I close my eyes and breathe deeply, counting slowly to ten in my head, willing her to disappear, urging her to leave me and this world alone and find peace. My heart breaks for her. She is in pain. I can feel it deep in my soul, a crushing sadness coursing through my whole body. As I finish counting, I feel her leave me.

I open my eyes and blink rapidly. All I see is my empty garden – a typical garden on an average day. I stay where I am for several minutes, breathing slowly and self-soothing my rattled nerves.

Summer's football game means I have a lot of time to get

through before she comes home. I should do something. I feel wretched about wishing away the hours. What a waste of a life. But there is nothing of significance that I need to be doing. I could sleep, but then I'd be awake all night. Since Alex left, I have to spend less time hiding, but there is a gaping hole in my days and nobody to share it with.

My sister, Hetty, lives less than a ten-minute drive away. We now only see each other at family occasions, and things are horribly strained even then. Hetty gave up encouraging me to spend time with her. I let her down too many times. Too many last-minute excuses.

I love Hetty dearly, and I know she loves me too, but when we are together, I bring her down simply by my very presence. I know that I damage her, and I don't want to do that to her anymore.

Hetty's husband, Gavin, is the physical embodiment of the word jolly. He is loud, round and exudes good cheer. He regularly bellows things such as "splendid" and "marvellous", which suit him perfectly. There's something innately lovely when he envelops you in a big sweaty hug. Best of all, he loves Hetty dearly, and she loves him back just as fiercely and completely.

I am so glad she has him by her side. Hetty had a neonatal brain injury, and as such, she has had to cope with infrequent but still terrifying seizures throughout her childhood and into adult life. Walking is sometimes difficult for her, and on some days, it is worse than others.

Hetty loves life, and she is one of those people who is genuinely grateful for every day and for every person she knows. Her zest and positivity are not forced, they are a true part of who she is, woven into every fibre of her being. I feel like a dark force when I enter their house. She doesn't hold on to things the way that I do.

Not only was my father furious that he was unable to have a

son, but he was also outwardly shamed by Hetty's disability. I'm sorry to admit that this affected me way more than it did Hetty. His cheeks would flush when she stumbled at the park. I would watch him and feel guilty for the second-hand embarrassment that overcame me. None of this bothered Hetty, but it ate me up inside. She has an inner self-worth that I don't possess, and I am envious of her in so many ways.

I'm glad my father wasn't around to see Hetty give birth to her beautiful boys, Luca and Kai. He would have claimed them as his own and tried to distil his own brand of outdated and toxic masculinity into the boys.

I push thoughts of Hetty to one side and decide to call my mother instead. Mum has flourished since my father died. She always answers the phone after five rings. Never four, never six. I often imagine her staring at the handset, counting and waiting for the perfect moment to answer. If it gets to six rings, I always hang up. It means she either isn't there or doesn't want to chat today. Mum answers on cue.

"Hello." Her voice is high-pitched and welcoming. It used to be tiny and cracked from the years of feeling inferior. These days, she has a beautiful curvy figure, and whilst I can see the inevitable signs of age creeping up on her, she still appears youthful and vibrant. She has a penchant for colourful oversized earrings and red lipstick. Unlike with Hetty, I don't worry about my sadness and anxiety dragging Mum down. She is as strong as iron, and if anything, I take strength from speaking with her.

"Hello?" Her voice is impatient now, and I'm unsure why I haven't spoken yet.

"Sorry, Mum. It's Tamsin. Bad connection, I think."

"Tamsin, I've been expecting you to call since last week. Where have you been?"

She doesn't say this in an accusatory way and isn't trying to make me feel guilty for my lack of communication. Everything my mother says is meant precisely how she says it. No undertones of any kind. She wears her heart on her sleeve.

"Sorry, Mum. Nowhere really. Just, you know, busy with Summer and her college stuff. I've been meaning to call. How are you?"

"Don't apologise, beautiful girl. It's so lovely to hear your voice."

"Yours too, Mum." And I absolutely mean it.

"Right. First things first, we need a date in the diary to meet up. I'll come round, shall I? Yes, I think that would be lovely. I'll bring a lemon meringue pie."

I give a little chuckle, and a warmth spreads through me. I love my mum and how she can make decisions while still speaking.

"That sounds lovely. Summer loves your lemon meringue pie."

"Everyone does, dear; it's bloody delicious." She gives an exaggerated laugh of her own, and I smile. "What day is best? Saturday or Sunday? Actually, let's do Sunday. I've got Pilates on Friday afternoon and we usually go for a drink afterwards."

I never have any plans. Mum knows this but is kind enough not to say so. Summer has football practice on Saturday mornings and usually hangs out with her friends afterwards. I don't want her to come home earlier than she wants.

"Sunday would be lovely, Mum. I'll cook something nice to go with your dessert. Salmon, maybe."

"Perfect. And get some decent bottles of something white and crisp. None of that plonky red stuff you're so fond of."

I cast my eye to the corner of the kitchen counter. There is a third of a bottle of Shiraz next to two empty bottles. Perhaps I did drink more than I thought I had last night.

"I will, Mum."

"And how's my beautiful granddaughter doing? She must be a foot taller than when I last saw her."

Again, I have to remind myself these words have no passive-aggressive meaning.

"She's great. She's doing so well at sixth form. We're..." I stop myself too late realising that "we" don't exist anymore. "I mean, I'm so very proud of her."

There is a moment of quiet, and sadness falls over me – a creeping loneliness. Mum fills the silence quickly and effortlessly.

"Wonderful. I can't wait to give Summer a big squeeze from her granny. Are any boys on the scene? She's about that age now, but keep her away from them as long as possible, I say. Nothing but a nuisance at that age."

I realise this is the first time Mum has asked me anything about Summer's personal life, and I've never volunteered any information. I've always thought it was Summer's business, not mine.

"No boys. Summer has never had a boyfriend. She had one short relationship with a girl a few months ago, but nothing serious."

Mum doesn't miss a beat. "Good. Good. There's plenty of time for all that stuff once she's a bit older and has got her exams out of the way."

Mum doesn't have an ounce of prejudice in her body. Mentioning that Summer has previously had a girlfriend is received no differently than if it had been a boyfriend. Precisely as it should be. I can only imagine how my father would have reacted if he were still alive. I add this to the already overflowing list of reasons why I am glad my father is dead. Not all life is precious. Some people are poisonous.

"Anyway, I best get on. I'm meeting Cora for a coffee. Want to join us?"

I have no idea who Cora is. Mum has become such a social butterfly and has a myriad of friends and social activities filling her days. The idea of going for a coffee with a complete stranger fills me with anxiety, even when the rest of my afternoon will be nothing but loneliness. However, I love that she still thinks to ask me.

"Maybe next time, Mum," I lie. "I've got a few errands I need to get sorted before Summer gets home."

"Okay, love. I'll see you on Sunday. Midday? If the weather is good, we can eat in the garden."

My blood freezes as a vision of the woman in the garden flashes before my eyes.

"Actually, Mum, 2pm would be better."

"Not a problem. 2pm it is. And don't forget the good wine!"

"I won't." I laugh and feel a swell of love for her wash over me. "Bye, Mum."

"Bye, sweetheart."

I hear Mum blow kisses down the phone before hanging up. I give a quick glance at the empty garden. There will be no more shadows today.

I've stopped worrying that another one will materialise or that the three who visit will appear at different times of the day or somewhere new. They have been my companions for years, and nothing has ever changed. Perversely, I think I love them. I wish they would leave, but they also make me feel less alone. They belong to me.

What would Dr McCabe say if I told him about the guests? He's probably the first person in a long time that I've even entertained the possibility of sharing this with.

I scan the room for some inspiration on what to do with the next three hours, but there is nothing. I don't want to leave the house again, and there is nowhere for me to go in any case. Wandering around aimlessly, trying to fill my time, only adds to the hopelessness.

I grab the bottle of Shiraz and open the cupboard to get a glass. I choose a coffee mug instead. It seems like a more appropriate vessel for drinking cheap wine in the early afternoon. It's more fitting with the slovenliness of it all. I take my mug of wine upstairs and consume most of the bottle in bed before dozing off into a fitful sleep, my dreams only slightly less haunted than my waking life.

5

TASMIN

BEFORE

Hetty and I have been plonked in front of the TV by Mum. It's uncomfortably loud for me, but Hetty is gawping at it with a dribbly grin on her face. Hetty is seven years younger than me. How can Mum possibly think that I want to watch the same baby shows as her? I get it, though; keeping Hetty happy and sitting still is more important.

Dad is already annoyed, and if Hetty starts shrieking or falls off the sofa, he'll get really shouty, and Mum will get weird and start fidgeting and fussing around. Hetty is two, and I know that all two-year-olds are loud and throw tantrums all the time, but Hetty's are worse than any of her little friends'. It's like she's properly angry sometimes.

I wonder if it's because she can't walk properly like the other toddlers at the park. She's wobbly and doesn't seem to do it right at all. Dad gets annoyed with her and hates going out with us without Mum. He's stopped doing that altogether now. I can't say I'm sad about it. I know he's my dad, but he's not very nice. Even my friends think so. He's mean, and he doesn't act like a dad at all.

My best friend's dad is amazing. He's so happy and smiley. I'd live at their house if I could. I bet they'd let me. Her mum's lovely too. She's got a smooth, soft voice, and when she asks me a question, she always seems excited and interested in the answer.

The best way I can describe my mum is "not there". I remember Mum was so full of life and energy when I was younger. We'd roll around the floor, giggling and playing games. She would have lots of friends who'd come over for cups of tea. They'd bring cake, and I was always allowed a slice too. They'd throw their heads back and laugh until tears streamed down their faces. There was always music playing in the kitchen and so many happy voices. That seems like another life now.

Hetty giggles and bobs her head along entirely out of time to the three puppets singing a horrible song on the TV.

"They're not real, you know!" She doesn't listen and starts waving her arms around. I sigh and push her a little further back into the sofa. I don't want her to topple off. Hetty annoys me a lot, but I hate it when she gets hurt. The worst thing is seeing her big brown eyes water when Dad starts shouting and blustering around the room if she's clumsy.

Mum had started to get a bit quieter before Hetty came along. I reckon it began when Dad stopped working away so much. Dad used to be away all week and came home every weekend. He worked in a big bank in London and had to get a train that took hours. I would usually be in bed before he got home on a Friday night, so I only had to see him on Saturdays and Sundays. Now he works in a smaller bank a five-minute drive away. I liked it better before. I think we all did.

He wanted us all to move to London, but Mum has lived here in Manchester her whole life. They've had lots of fights about it.

He used to shout things like, "I'm not having my children growing up sounding like dumb northerners."

He would say that everyone is poor and stupid up here, and he couldn't believe that Mum convinced him to leave London in the first place. When Mum was bright and strong, she would fight back fiercely, defending us all.

She would tell him, "You know where the door is" and laugh without fear. Now she just sighs or looks away. I'm worried that she'll give in one day, and we'll have to move. She seems to have given in to everything else. I haven't seen a friend of hers in ages, and I can't remember the last time I saw her smile, never mind laugh.

The kitchen door is closed, and I can't make out any of the words they say. They sound like a pair of hissing, spitting snakes. I have no clue why grown-ups do this. Hetty has no idea what is going on because she's two and can be easily distracted by an interesting-shaped stick. But I am nine, and I know they are fighting.

I hear the back door bang and Dad's footsteps stomping to the car. I can see him out of the corner of my eye as he gets into his Land Rover and buckles his seat belt around his enormous stomach. He's got so fat recently. Fat and sweaty, with a horrible shiny face and bumpy nose. He smells too, like old trainers. I'm glad he never wants to hug me.

I stare straight ahead at the TV and pretend to be interested. The puppet programme has been replaced with a cartoon with talking cars. They aren't holding Hetty's attention as much, and she's starting to squirm. I relax as Dad drives away. It always feels like a dark cloud has lifted when he leaves – a dark, fat, sweaty cloud.

Mum shuffles into the room, her shoulders hunched and her eyes swollen. She sits down beside us; the cushions barely shift as she perches on the edge of the sofa like a little bird.

Hetty lunges for her, and Mum grabs her swiftly with one arm to stop her toppling off onto the floor. She pulls Hetty onto her lap and shuffles them both back into the sofa, before stretching her left arm out towards me to get me to cuddle up next to her. I nudge along towards them, and Mum kisses the tops of our heads in turn and sniffs our hair. She strokes my shoulders and I gently nuzzle my face into hers.

We sit together quietly for a while, even Hetty seems to understand that this moment shouldn't be disturbed. When I sense Mum is about to get up, I grab her hand and squeeze it. She squeezes it back fiercely, and I fight back tears.

"Mum." I see that she is crying, too. Silent tears cascading down her pale face. "I wish Dad didn't have to come home." She shuts her eyes tightly and looks at the ceiling. I'm frightened she's going to be angry with me, that I've said something terrible and wicked.

The tears continue to escape through her pinched eyelids. She turns and looks at me, stroking my face with the backs of her fingers. They are cold and shaky, but still beautiful to me.

"I wish that too, Tamsin. I wish that, too."

She leans forward and places a soft kiss in the middle of my forehead before heaving Hetty up onto her hip and leaving me in the living room alone.

6

SUMMER

"Don't worry, Summer. It happens to the best of us. What defines you as a champion is how you get up after you fall. Every failure is a stepping stone towards success!"

Mr Annan pumps his fist into the air to add an exclamation mark to the end of his sentence. Amma rolls her eyes.

"Dad, seriously, would you give the inspirational quotes a rest for once."

Amma is sitting in the back of her dad's car with me despite Mr Annan's protestations that an empty front seat makes him feel like a chauffeur.

"I will not! Success does not wait for anyone. You fall down, and you get back up. Simple."

"Daaad!" Amma draws out the word in an annoyed, petulant tone. She turns to me and mimes being sick, poking a finger down her throat. "Ugh, it's like he swallowed an Insta positivity account and just vomits up bits of it all day."

I laugh despite myself. "He means well." I find Mr Annan's eyes in the rear-view mirror. "Thanks, Mr A. Once I've had a shower and eight hours of sleep, I'll be right back on that pitch. Don't you worry one bit."

"That's the spirit, Summer. See, Amma. I told you. This is important wisdom I am imparting…"

Mr Annan continues his TED talk as he drives, and Amma and I turn towards each other, both stifling a small giggle and tuning out his voice.

"You really okay, Sunny?"

I take a deep breath in and puff out my cheeks before letting it out slowly. "Yeah, I'm fine. I didn't even want to take that penalty. Ref was blind. We shouldn't even have had it."

Amma whispers in my ear conspiratorially. Her breath is warm and gives me butterflies in my tummy. "Don't let my dad hear you say that. He'll give you ten verses of a song telling you why that means you missed it."

We both grin at each other, and Amma rests her head on my shoulder. "Anyway, all the girls were well pleased with a draw."

"Yeah, I know. It would have been nice to win, though."

"And if we had, you'd be sitting here feeling awful because you scored a penalty and won the match for us when we didn't deserve it. At least this way, you can feel rubbish and know you've earned it."

I punch her playfully on the shoulder. "Hey! That's not fair!"

Amma puts her hand on my forearm. "It's completely fair, one hundred per cent accurate. I know you too well, Summer."

She never calls me Summer. I put my free hand on top of hers and we sit in comfortable silence for the remainder of the journey. Mr Annan has even stopped talking.

Our hands seem to pulse and fizz with electricity. I wonder if she can feel it, too. I sneak a quick glance at her face, and she seems completely relaxed, just looking out the window as we pass through streets and streets of identical semi-detached red-brick houses.

We pull up outside my house. My heart sinks when I notice the shutters in my Mum's bedroom are closed, a sure sign she's gone for one of her naps, and I'm grateful when I glimpse her walking through the living room towards the front door.

I'm waiting for Mr Annan to make the customary joke asking for his fare for dropping me off, and he doesn't disappoint.

As usual, I reply with, "Just put it on my tab, Mr A."

"Goodbye, Summer dear. Get some rest now." He's such a kind man.

"I will."

"See you tomorrow, Sunny."

I reluctantly pull my hands away from Amma and get out of the car. We blow kisses at each other as always, and I have to stop myself from blushing. What was once a simple and innocent part of our friendship routine is now loaded with meaning for me.

Mum is standing at the door, waving with a huge smile on her face. From a distance she looks genuinely happy and bright, and it warms my heart. As I get closer, though, I can see the dark circles under her eyes and I notice the faint smell of wine emanating from her. The smile is obviously plastered onto her face. I put my arms around her shoulders and kiss her alcohol-flushed cheek. I know she'd like the smile to be genuine, I know she'd give anything to feel truly happy, and I am certain it would kill her if she thought I knew about her drinking.

I turn to face the car and wrap my arm around Mum's waist. We stand in the doorway and wave goodbye as Amma and her dad drive away. I feel an unwelcome prickle of annoyance as Mum sways gently against my body. It's not even 7pm, and she's clearly half-pissed. I swallow it down and walk past her towards the stairs.

"Need a shower first, Mum."

I don't look back. I know my feelings of shame and disappointment are written all over my face. Mum's voice is irritatingly bright, with a hint of slurring at the end of each word.

"Okay, sweetheart. Tea is ready when you are."

"Cool," I shout back. Hating myself for being so weak and running away.

I feel much better after a shower. Mum must have sensed something, as she now holds a mug, not a wine glass.

"So, how was the match?"

I exhale loudly and wrap my arms around myself. "It was a draw."

"But that's good, isn't it? You said they'd probably beat you."

I can't be bothered with explaining the rest to Mum. Her eyes are glassy, and I'm not sure she'd remember the conversation anyway.

"You're right. I'm just tired and hungry." I flop down onto the kitchen dining chair, pick up my knife and fork and mime eating from the empty plate in front of me.

"Okay, Summer. I can take a hint." Mum laughs and moves towards the cooker to pick up an enormous pot on the hob. It's clearly not the pizza I suggested, and judging by the meaty, garlic and tomato aromas filling the room, I'm hopeful it's my favourite spaghetti Bolognese.

As she picks up the pot, it tilts to one side, and I race towards Mum to help her straighten it. Thankfully, nothing spills, but she's clearly shaken and somewhat embarrassed. At that moment I notice that her mug beside the cooker is filled with red wine, not tea as I'd presumed. I look at it pointedly and then towards Mum and shake my head. I've never known her to hide her drinking before. Isn't that supposed to mean you're an alcoholic? It can't be good news, anyway.

I carry the pot towards the table, and Mum and I sit across from each other. I haven't taken my eyes off her, but she is looking down at her wrists and rubbing each in turn.

"Are you hurt, Mum? Have you burnt yourself?"

Mum looks up at me with glassy, dazed eyes but speaks surprisingly clearly. "No. I'm not hurt. I'm just weak, Summer. I need to be stronger." She drops her eyes and is still rubbing her wrists, which are starting to look red and sore. We both know that the strength she is referring to has nothing to do with her wrists.

"Mum?"

She flicks her head back up like a startled deer, as though she had forgotten I was here.

"I'm fine, Summer. Really. I know what I need to do. I've been putting it off for so long because it's easier just to continue with the way things are, and hope that everything will be okay somehow."

This is the most honest I think she's ever been with me about her drinking. Even though she hasn't said anything specific, her words are loaded with meaning, and I get a genuine sense of her desire to change things.

I stand up and grab two glasses from the kitchen cupboard. I fill them with water, place one in front of her and take a large gulp from the other before setting it down. I stand behind Mum, wrap my arms around her shoulders and kiss the top of her head. She reaches up and wraps her hands around mine.

"I'll fix this, Summer. I will. I promise. I don't want to be like this." I'm shocked by how melancholy she sounds, and I squeeze her harder.

"It'll all be fine, Mum." I realise this sounds naive, but I need to inject some positivity back into the room somehow. "I love you."

"And I love you too, sweetheart. More than you could ever know."

I give Mum one final squeeze and lift the lid off the pot, delighted to find the Bolognese I anticipated.

"Why don't we start with eating my absolute favourite dinner together?"

Mum puts on a forced smile but appears more sober, at least. I dish Mum out a small portion, I don't want to overwhelm her, and she smiles gratefully. I pile my plate high and dig in ferociously.

We eat in silence, with only the occasional clink of a glass or scrape of a fork. It's not an uncomfortable silence. It feels contemplative, and like the beginning of something. Something positive, I hope.

Mum insists on tidying up the kitchen and directs me towards the sofa. I lie down happily, stretch out my aching legs and close my eyes.

Mum did very well with eating the food, better than I've seen in a long time. I also saw her pour the mug of wine down the sink. I wanted to congratulate her, but it felt weird, so I just stayed quiet. The last thing I want to do is embarrass her.

I only realise I had drifted off when I'm startled awake and open my eyes to find Mum looming over me, her head silhouetted by the ceiling light. She is watching me, studying the features of my face.

"You should get yourself to bed. You drifted off."

"You scared me!" I laugh nervously.

"Sorry, you just looked so still and peaceful. It reminded me of when you were little. I was just watching you."

"Er, creepy, Mum." I laugh again and stand up too quickly, black dots and stars appearing in front of my eyes. I rest my hand on the back of the sofa, and the world comes back into focus. Mum reaches her arm out to me, an identical mug to the one she was drinking wine from earlier in her outstretched hand. I look at it distastefully.

"I made you some cocoa to take to bed with you." She notices the look on my face. "I can pour it away if you don't want it."

I yawn and take the drink from her. "That's lovely, Mum. Thank you. I just stood up too fast and felt a bit woozy."

She puts her hand on my shoulder, and I feel her body trembling gently. "Night night, Summer. I love you."

"Night, Mum." I walk slowly upstairs, ensuring that my legs have woken up fully.

The cocoa is very welcome. Despite the huge meal, I still feel like I need some energy. Running around on the football pitch straight after a long day at college is really hard work. I feel Mum's eyes on me, and as I look over my shoulder, I see tears falling down her face. She smiles wistfully at me before turning and walking back to the kitchen. A creeping sense of dread accompanies me up the stairs. There's definitely more going on with Mum than meets the eye.

I wake up with a horrendous sharp pain in my stomach. My hair is plastered to my face with sweat, and there is a horrible, almost mouldy taste in my mouth. The pain begins to subside, and I take several welcome deep breaths. I reach for my phone, relieved to see it isn't morning. It's 2.24am. The pain resurfaces with a vengeance. It crashes through my abdomen like a torrential wave, and I pull my knees up to my chest, whimpering.

I've never felt anything like this before. I'm terrified and in complete agony. The pain begins to lessen again, replaced by a rising fiery nausea. I scramble out of bed. My pyjamas stick uncomfortably to various parts of my body with sweat. I fling open my bedroom door and crash into the bathroom, barely making it to the toilet before a fountain of vomit escapes my mouth. I'm allowed only a few seconds of relief before another hideous cramp tears through my abdomen. It feels as though my insides are tearing apart. My mouth waters, and when another wave of nausea hits me, I'm thoroughly expecting to see blood or internal organs expelled into the toilet.

I spend several hideous hours alternating between kneeling over the toilet vomiting, until my stomach has nothing else to give, and writhing in agony on the bathroom floor as hot stabbing pains leave me incapacitated.

Cautiously optimistic that my body has expelled everything it's going to, I lie on my back, sweat coating my body and dripping down my face. I'm as cold as ice, and my body is shaking uncontrollably. My teeth are chattering so loudly I'm worried I'll wake Mum. I know she wouldn't mind, but I want her to be able to rest.

I sit up slowly and grab the hand towel, patting my face and neck. I crawl towards the bathroom door and grab my bath towel from the hook on the back, wrapping it around me and sitting very still. Some semblances of warmth and normality begin to return to my body.

What the bloody hell was that? I feel empty and more exhausted than I can ever remember feeling. Thankfully, I'm pretty sure I'm not going to be sick again, and I have a sudden urge to weep. I feel absolutely disgusting. My mouth is coated with my stomach contents, and my teeth feel furry and revolting.

I try standing, and despite a slight feeling of light-headedness, I don't feel too bad. I can hear birds starting to sing outside. Twilight is beginning to brighten the sky and cast some light through the bathroom window. I run the cold tap and cup some water in my hands, splashing my face and then rinsing my mouth and spitting. I would love to drink some, but I don't think my stomach would thank me, and the thought of going through that again fills me with terror.

I look at my face in the mirror, the low-level light means I can't see any colours, I'm simply shades of grey, which is fitting for how I feel just now. My eyes are dark and sunken, and my hair is sweaty and limp. A dull ache and a grumbling nausea have replaced the sharp bolts of pain. I fold the towel on the floor and sit on it with my back propped up against the bath. I'm not ready to go back to my room yet. I'll wait here until I become more normal.

The bath is cool against the skin on my back and shoulders. It's rather lovely. I watch the sky brighten through the bathroom window, the colours changing to a beautiful bronze and heralding the start of a new day. I will most certainly be spending all of this new day in bed. College is a definite no, and I hope Mum won't make me see a doctor. I want to rest and catch up on sleep.

I must have eaten something weird or overdone it on the football pitch and somehow messed up my system. I feel like I've been poisoned. The muscles in my legs are aching from the game, too. A long day in bed is most definitely called for.

The door to the bathroom creaks open slowly, and my neck aches as I raise my pounding head. Mum is standing in the doorway. Her eyes are wide and as round as saucers, and I watch her visibly trembling from head to toe. I have no idea where to start with telling her about the monstrous night I've had, but it's obvious she is not just worried about me but downright scared.

My mouth is dry, and my voice is quiet and croaky.

"Mum, you won't believe–"

But I can't even finish the first sentence before she starts shrieking hysterically. She lifts her shaking hands to her eyes as the ear-splitting screeches continue to burst out of her. I'm frozen to the spot, chilled to the bone by the scene in front of me.

I want to speak, to reassure her that I'm okay, but I can't find the words. I watch her, dumbfounded and horrified in equal measure.

Her screams morph into unintelligible words before they become a terrifying continuous chant of "No, no, no."

Her quivering becomes more violent, and she now appears as though she is jogging on the spot, her hands still clamped over her eyes, almost clawing at her face.

A sharp pain pierces my head as I move. I tentatively change position from sitting to kneeling and reach out a hand towards her. I'm panic-stricken, but I need to help her. My voice is barely a whisper.

"Mum?"

She flings herself violently out of the bathroom, stretching her arms out in front of her and turning her head away as though

I'm the most heinous thing she has ever seen. She's wailing and sobbing uncontrollably.

"Why won't you just leave me alone? Leave me the fuck alone!" Her voice is unrecognisable, filled with anger and repulsion. "Just leave! Fucking leave! Fuck off and die!"

I can't believe what I'm hearing. Not only the horrible words, but her voice has now twisted into a guttural snarl. I pull my arm back forcefully from her, wrapping both arms around my body.

This feels like a nightmare. I don't recognise the woman in front of me. This is not my mum; this is a monster. Mum runs into her room and slams the door. I can hear her wailing. I don't move. Instead I listen and try to comprehend what just happened. My mouth waters, and I gag painfully.

A sudden urge to run from the house, run far away, envelops me, but I am rooted to the spot. Completely unable to grasp the slightest understanding of what Mum just did.

I want to call Amma and get her to come and take me away, but I know I can't. Despite her actions, I can't leave Mum here. What if she hurts herself? I'd never forgive myself if anything happened to her.

Mum's cries slowly begin to quieten until they are a mere whimper. I start to pace the bathroom, trying to keep the blood flowing through my spent body. I thought nothing could make me feel worse than the unrelenting vomiting, but I was wrong. I creep tentatively towards Mum's bedroom door, my mind a hive of terrifying possibilities. Creaking floorboards underfoot make me wince. Fear prickles my neck, and my heart threatens to leap out of my chest.

The house is considerably brighter now. Dawn has long since broken and sunlight illuminates my path. I reach out, turn the handle slowly, and push the door. It swishes quietly over the plush carpet. Mum's completely hidden under her bed covers – a large mewling mound. I can't control the tears anymore, and all I want is a hug from my mother. A strangulated sob escapes from deep within me.

"Mum. Mum, please."

The mound of covers becomes still and quiet. The only sound in the room is my ragged breathing. A surge of emotion overwhelms me, and words begin to tumble from my mouth, mixed in amongst the tears and cries.

"Mum, what was…? Why did you scream at me? Mum! Come out, please."

I am unashamedly begging her. Her pale face emerges from the covers, her eyes wild, and her hair sticking out at every angle. Whatever that creature was in the bathroom has now gone. Her eyes have returned to normal.

She climbs out of bed and pulls me towards her, then holds me at arm's length, examining my face curiously as though seeing me for the first time. Mum whispers, as though afraid that someone might hear us, despite having nearly screamed the house down moments earlier.

"What were you doing in the bathroom?"

Irritation prickles at me. "Throwing up!"

Guilt washes over her face, and she pulls me towards her. "I'm so sorry, Summer. You scared me."

"Yeah, well, I think it's safe to say you scared me too."

I want to pull away and demand answers, but I find myself nuzzling into her neck. I lie down, adrenaline ebbing away and exhaustion crashing over my aching body.

Mum strokes my hair softly and makes shushing noises. I fall into her gratefully. Yes, I have a million questions, and I most definitely want a proper explanation for what just happened. That was not a normal reaction by any stretch of the imagination. But my body's fighting against me. My arms and legs begin to feel lighter, and I find myself drifting away.

7

TAMSIN

When I wake up, Summer has gone.

The side of the bed where she fell asleep is still warm. The baby at the bottom of the bed is crying as usual. I don't bother to look at her this morning. I have much bigger problems than this today.

The room smells revolting, and I remember Summer telling me that she had been vomiting in the bathroom. Hopefully, she's not being sick again.

I roll over and press my face into my pillow, careful not to disturb the covers at the bottom of the bed. I have no idea what would happen if I did, but it's not something I want to explore this morning.

I have no idea how to begin to explain my behaviour to Summer. I screamed maniacally and shouted obscenities at her. Completely unforgivable. I swore at her.

I told her to "fuck off and die".

No explanation can even come close to healing the damage I have done. And everything was already damaged to begin with.

I woke confused in the night, unusual noises emanating from the bathroom. Sounds of crawling and shuffling along the floor interspersed with pangs of pained crying. I listened for a while, my heart pounding, convinced that a new guest had entered my life. Or the bathroom girl had grown stronger, and her appearances would no longer be contained to each morning.

Why did I not even check if it was Summer in the bathroom? I should have looked in on her. If I had, then none of this would have happened. I wouldn't have terrified my daughter and be lying here feeling like an utter failure.

Something inside me broke when I saw Summer propped up against the bath. I knew immediately it wasn't the shadow girl who visits every morning, but she was in the exact same place, with the same posture. My brain fractured into a million tiny pieces and I had no control over my words or my body. I have learned to live with the baby on the bed, the girl in the bathroom, and the woman in the garden. I know they won't hurt me. But there is always the ever-present fear of the appearance of another.

I don't believe in ghosts. I know the shadows are a product of my polluted and damaged mind. Dr Pathirana was constantly looking for explanations and coming up with theories. That's why I had to start lying to her. She couldn't accept that I didn't want to pick at the thread of the shadow's presence. I just wanted the drugs that would make them go away.

Summer will have to stay off college today. I know that they have a rule about being off for a day if you've been physically sick. Plus, she's probably not well enough to go anyway.

I swing my legs out of bed. The baby's incessant crying has become background noise, and I barely glance at her as I leave the room.

The bathroom door is closed. I press my cheek gently to the door, but don't hear any sound. My timings are all off this morning. I'm late out of bed and late into the bathroom. I don't know what effect that will have on what lies behind this door, and I don't have the strength to find out.

I make my way downstairs slowly and unsteadily. There is a sharp pain behind my eyes, and my head feels heavy and cumbersome on my shoulders.

Summer is already sitting at the table. Head in her hands, her hair clumped together in bedraggled strands. The complete diversion from the usual sequence of morning events makes my heart thump uncontrollably.

Summer raises her head slowly. Her eyes are puffy and her complexion is almost grey. She looks really ill and hugely upset, and I know that the latter is almost entirely my fault.

I rush towards her, arms outstretched, desperate to take some of the pain away that I have inflicted. My heart drops as she unconsciously flinches away from me, and I stop, arms still raised. I feel my heart break inside my chest. My girl is afraid of me. All I have ever wanted is to protect her, not just from the world but from me and the wrongness that lives inside me. I'd do anything to keep it locked inside me and forever away from my beautiful daughter.

Sadness wells in her eyes, and I want nothing more than to hold her.

"Summer." Her name is all I can manage, and it comes out as a whisper.

"Mum?" She says my name as a question. Her lips begin to tremble, and tears fall freely down her cheeks.

The rushed apologies and justifications of earlier were a product of our combined exhaustion and relief, but that won't suffice for Summer this morning. She wants an explanation. She deserves answers.

I move slowly towards the kitchen table and lower myself quietly into the chair. Summer simply watches. She doesn't recoil this time. I take a deep breath, close my eyes, and steady myself. Summer deserves the truth. I am hurting her by trying to protect her. I reach my hand out towards her, stroking the polished wood before turning my palm up as a way of invitation.

Summer mirrors me and reaches out as far as the tips of my fingers before fixing her eyes on me. Imploring and full of questions. Her stare feels too intimate, and I have to force myself not to look away.

"I'm so sorry, Summer." I shake my head in disbelief at my actions.

"What… what even was that?" Summer's mouth crumples and she makes a choking noise and sniffs. Words are too hard for her. The emotion is sitting too close to the surface.

"I owe you an explanation."

Summer pulls her hands back slightly and mutters something under her breath before looking back up at me. "I'm listening." She folds her arms and leans back. Her strength is returning, and her defiance is growing.

I clasp my hands together in front of me. "When I was really poorly, I used to imagine that there was a girl in the bathroom." The words come out fast, and it's a relief to admit them out loud, even though they are not entirely true. Summer puffs out a breath and rolls her eyes. "I'm serious, Summer. I wasn't coping, and I used to see and hear things that weren't there. It didn't last very long, but it was an extremely scary time for me."

"That makes no sense, Mum." Summer's voice is filled with disdain and disappointment. I'm trying to be truthful, yet it's as though she thinks I'm trying to lie to her or fob her off with some farfetched story. "So you thought I was some kind of ghost, and you freaked out. Is that the story we're going with?"

Summer raises an eyebrow before pushing her chair back violently and standing up. "I'm not a fucking child anymore, Mum. I don't deserve to be fed bullshit like this."

Her swearing jars me. It's not like her at all. Irritation flickers inside me. I know that how I behaved must have been horrendous for her, but I am trying to put it right, trying to let her in.

"I'm not feeding you... anything, Summer. I am trying to explain."

"Yeah, well, I'm pretty sure you could come up with something a bit more convincing than that."

She turns away from me. I stay seated and look down at my hands. I am at a loss.

"Why can't you just admit you don't want me here?" Her quiet accusation knocks me sideways. How could she even think that? I open my mouth to speak, but there is nothing there. My breath has been stolen. "That's just what I thought, Mum." Her voice raises in volume, and she spits out my name as though it were disgusting to have in her mouth.

She storms out of the kitchen.

"Summer, come back, please. Please. We need to talk."

She turns back towards me and stands in the doorway, chest heaving and eyes blazing. "No. No, we don't." Her tone is sharp and vicious. "I told you I would listen, and you just take the piss. Well, now it's time for you to listen." She is breathless and wild, her face breaking into a grimace whenever she speaks. "You drink too much. You don't eat. You plaster your face with make-up and put on a fake smile for the world to see. You're a fucking mess, Mum. I have tried my best to be there for you, but you need to sort your shit out. And you need to start being honest. I know you'd swap me to have Dad back in a heartbeat."

A tidal wave of emotion hits me with such force that I feel physically pushed backwards. "That is not true!" I match the volume and ferocity of Summer's voice.

"Really? Well, that's how it feels. It's like you just want me out of the way all the time. You're always sad, and you're usually drunk. I keep out of your way every morning until I think you've got yourself ready to have to put up with me. Do you know how that feels? I've got nobody else, Mum. You've alienated my entire family. I barely see Grandma. And you've completely shut me off from Aunt Hetty, Uncle Gavin and the boys. I miss them. I miss feeling normal. It's not fucking fair."

I am shaking from head to toe, devastated that Summer has been holding all of this in, and completely appalled that I have made her feel like this. Perhaps I've been kidding myself that my intentions are good.

I look at my beautiful, broken daughter in the doorway, boiling over with a cocktail of repressed emotions. I have no idea how to fix this. No words are enough, but I have to say something. "I love you, Summer."

Summer's face softens, and her shoulders sag, releasing the tension that was holding her up. "I know, Mum. I love you, too. But we need more than that. You're not okay, and that means I'm not okay either."

The emotional intelligence and awareness that my daughter is displaying both astonishes and embarrasses me. Our roles have reversed. Shame engulfs me. We look at each other and nod resignedly, both teary-eyed and utterly exhausted.

"I'm going back to bed, Mum. Throwing up all night was horrendous, and then you added the cherry on top with your screaming." I wince, but I am relieved to see a hint of a half-smile cross her face.

"I hope you feel better, beautiful girl." She turns gently this time and I hear her breathing deeply as she climbs the stairs. I know how hard it was for her to let herself go like that. "I've got an appointment with a psychiatrist this morning," I blurt out after her.

"I know, Mum. It's on the calendar."

"Oh... er... okay."

"I know a lot more than you think I do."

I'm not sure what she means or what she thinks she knows. She made it abundantly clear she thought my confession about my hallucinations was a lie.

As horrendous as it was, I need to see what happened last

night as a turning point. I have to make my sessions with Dr McCabe count to fix this mess for my daughter.

Hearing that she feels isolated and alienated from her family was like a gut punch. Explaining to her why I've been keeping my distance from them all this time will be hard, but I want Summer to trust me again.

I shout one final thing up the stairs at her. "The family are coming over on Sunday. For some food."

I'll have to get Mum to invite Hetty and the boys along. I'd rather not call Hetty with how I'm feeling just now.

"That's great, Mum. Honestly, but I need some rest. I'll chat to you later."

8

TAMSIN

I quietly slide Summer's bedroom door open and sneak into her room. She is lying on her back with her mouth wide open and snoring loudly. Despite this, she still looks lovely – my not so little girl. I perch on the end of the bed, and she stirs slightly but doesn't wake. She needs to rest.

How could I have gotten this all so very wrong? I have a wonderful daughter. She deserves a life filled with happiness and beautiful things. I mustn't doom her to a life of worry and sadness. I need the family gathering this weekend to go well, and then I have to ensure that I don't make her feel alone and detached from her family again.

I apply much less make-up today and attempt to dress more casually. Summer's comments were undeniably cutting, but nothing she said about me was false. I've been following the same paint-by-numbers routine on my face for years, not letting even the slightest glimpse of my natural skin see the light of day.

I'm pleased with what I see. I look a little tired, but then I am tired. My eyes are puffy from crying and a disturbed night, just as they should be. I look like I've made an effort rather than hiding from the world. I've replaced my usual expensive-looking outfits with a simple white cotton shirt and navy-blue trousers. A plain silver chain around my neck completes the look, and I leave my earrings in the jewellery box. This is how I used to look when I was happy – before my brain started misfiring.

I see a steely determination in my eyes. I will not let mine and Summer's story end in disaster. Last night was the moment I needed to start to face all this head on. Seeing myself through Summer's eyes was heartbreaking, and I am under no illusion that this will be a quick fix.

All I need to do is keep walking in the right direction. My visit to Dr McCabe yesterday felt like a disaster, but at least the ice is broken now. Demolished rather. And I think that I can start to be honest with him and let him help me.

It's my fault I've ended up in this terrible state, and all the lies need to stop. I've lied about my feelings, I've lied about the shadows and shut away my poisonous thoughts inside my head, hoping that I could maintain them and continue with a normal life. I've been foolish. But it stops today.

———

I check in with Jackson, Dr McCabe's receptionist, without incident. Initially, I felt embarrassed, given my performance yesterday, but I'm not sure he even remembers me. I'm just one in a sea of faces to him. Completely unremarkable. Dr McCabe calls me before I even have the chance to take a seat. I'm relieved. It allows me less time to get anxious and overthink everything.

He's dressed the same as yesterday except for a slightly different shirt with thicker stripes. He smiles warmly at me as I enter his office and sit on the sofa. I resist grabbing for an emotional support cushion and instead cross my legs and rest my hands on my knees.

"Good morning, Tamsin. May I say you're looking much more comfortable today."

I look down at my clothes and try to hide the swell of pride that he noticed. "I thought it might be a good first step. You know, dressing a bit more like I used to. Not trying to look quite so well put together."

"I agree. Whilst you looked very… I'll use your words, 'put together' last time I saw you, today you look much more congruous, much more real."

I beam. "Thank you."

"It tells me something about your intentions towards your session today." I nod. "Let me just remind you about the 'showing your arse' rule."

I laugh when he puts his hand to his mouth conspiratorially and whispers, "Showing your arse."

"Pretence and omission are not needed here. This is a safe space, and you can say whatever you wish. There is no judgement from me." He opens his arms wide, palms up in a gesture that makes me feel instantly calm, and just as he said, safe. "So, how was the rest of your day yesterday?"

I wring my hands together and swallow several times. Am I going to do this? Am I going to bare my soul to this man?

I am desperate to say, "rather well, actually", but I push those words far away into the recesses of my brain and let out a deep breath.

"It was absolutely fucking horrendous, and the night was even worse. A pure, unadulterated disaster." His face lights up. Tears of relief and pride prick my eyes.

"Tell me all about it, Tamsin. Tell me everything." And I do. I tell him the whole sorry story from deciding to afternoon drink from a coffee mug to my pissed behaviour with Summer after her football game and the grand finale of me screaming hysterically at her in the bathroom during the night. I end my ridiculous tale with my conversation with Summer this morning and how I hope we've also opened the doors for a bit more honesty between us.

Dr McCabe listens intently as I speak. He doesn't interrupt once, and he doesn't make any notes or look away. When I finish the story, I reach for a sip of water to indicate that I'm done speaking for now.

"That's quite a time you've had. I must say that you're clearly very perceptive. You seem to understand yourself very well indeed."

I'm not sure what he's getting at. I nod. "Well, I overthink a lot."

He looks up, clearly trying to work something out, before scribbling something down in his notebook.

"Tamsin, I think there's lots to celebrate here, lots of positives. And plenty to help us get to the foundations of what might help you. Thank you so much for sharing all that with me."

I smile. "Well, it's what you asked me to do." My cheeks flush and I look away. I've done so much better today and I am pleased and proud of the things I've managed to tell him. But there are things that I have left out of the story. I had come here intending to tell him everything. But I just can't say the words. I'm not ready to tell him about the guests. I will. At least, I hope I will. But I need time.

"Can I ask you something?"

"Of course."

"I'm sorry to jump in immediately with a question, but there's just something that I can't make sense of."

My heart starts to race. Panic emerging. I nod and take another sip of water.

"Why did finding Summer in the bathroom scare you so much? Was it dark? Did you think she was an intruder or that she was hurt in some way? That's the bit that doesn't quite fit for me."

It's a very direct question and will require a lie. I am so desperate to be truthful that I find myself saying nothing and looking down at my knees. I suddenly feel very small and vulnerable.

"I can see I've hit a nerve, and it is not my intention to force you to go too far." I keep my head down but raise my eyes and look briefly into his kind eyes. "Please know that telling me you're not ready to share a certain aspect of an event is an absolutely acceptable and complete answer. I won't push the issue, and we can move on to something you're more comfortable with today."

I clear my throat. "Yes. There is a reason. And you're right. I'm not ready. I will be, I think, eventually."

"That's brilliant. Thank you, Tamsin." He makes a quick note and adjusts his position in the seat. "How about we discuss why you decided to drink wine in the afternoon. It's clearly something that you don't want…" His voice floats away as the blood in my ears starts pounding, and my thoughts start racing. I can't talk about that either without mentioning the woman in the garden. Sure, I could say it was down to loneliness or boredom or simply wanting to quieten my mind and pass out in the hours when I'm alone and have nothing to do or enjoy. All entirely true, but rather pointless with the omission of her presence. I lean forward and grip the top of my head in my hands, squeezing with my fingertips until it hurts.

I'm vaguely aware that he has stopped talking and I hear myself let out an exasperated moan, a primal expelling of all my feelings of frustration and anger. I sit up straight, my eyes still closed, and I start to speak. Croaky at first but then gathering strength and purpose.

"I had a drink because I couldn't think of anything better to do. There is a woman in my garden. She's not real, but she's there every afternoon." My heart slows, and I open my eyes and continue to speak. I've said it now so there's no point in holding back. "I screamed at Summer because I thought she was the little ghost girl that lives in my bathroom. And while we're at it, a phantom baby is crying at the bottom of my bed every morning when I wake up."

I stare at Dr McCabe, almost challenging him to question anything about what I have just told him.

"I lied when I told you that I no longer have hallucinations. I have them every day. I know they are not real. They are scary but weirdly comforting sometimes. I don't want to tell anyone in case they take Summer away. It's why my husband left me."

I'm gasping for breath when I finally stop talking. Dr McCabe leans forward and mimes taking a deep breath. I copy him and take several, feeling my heart rate begin to settle. He then motions for me to continue.

"I'm listening."

The words continue to fall from my brain and out of my mouth. "I'm so scared that Summer will somehow become like me. I have horrendous thoughts about it sometimes, and I've no idea what to do."

My body crumples with the enormity of what I've just said, and I start to cry. Tears fall soundlessly from my eyes before I lose the ability to hold back, and I begin to wail. I shake my head wildly, letting go of anything and everything. I whisper through my tears, "I am completely broken."

I feel the sofa shift as Dr McCabe sits down slowly beside me. He passes me a tissue, and I wipe my face.

"I'm here, Tamsin. Take your time. I'm here."

Dr McCabe sits quietly. I give my body time to quiet down and feel a silent determination begin to form in my veins. I have always wanted to protect Summer. That has and will never change. But the way I have been going about it is damaging her and damaging me, too. I need to try and find another way.

So I talk. I tell Dr McCabe about my sessions with Dr Pathirana. I explain that I can't remember why the guests appeared but that they arrived around the same time I started drinking harmfully and pulling away from my family. I honestly can't remember a significant event or something terrible that happened at that time. I think I just stopped being able to cope with life.

"It's weird, really. I always thought I'd managed to escape any kind of mental illness. I thought if it was going to happen, it would have already." Dr McCabe nods, and his face is full of warmth and understanding. For once, talking to someone about my life does not feel painful. "My dad was a horrible man. He was emotionally abusive and controlling. He wore my mum down gradually and then finally broke her. When he died, we were all relieved. There was not a hint of sadness from any of us. Mum flourished. People barely recognise her anymore. But I..." I stop and take a breath, feeling a surge of emotion I don't understand.

"Grief is very complicated, Tamsin. It's okay to feel relief at the death of someone who was such a negative presence in your life. But it's also normal to feel sadness or regret too. It's okay to feel anything at all."

I nod. "That's what I mean. Mum felt better almost immediately after he died. It was like she could move and breathe again. She became who she was when I was younger. Full of life and love. I feel like I've been forcing myself to be happy because I should be, but it's not as easy as that. I wish it was."

"And did you tell Dr Pathirana all of this?"

"Yes. I was really honest with her at the start. I told her all about my dad and how he treated my mum and especially my sister. He was horrible to her. My little sister, Hetty, is incredible. She has some difficulties with her movement and walking, and he used to be so obviously shamed by her when she was a little girl. It was really sad to watch."

"How does Hetty feel about that now?"

I let out an unintentionally inappropriate laugh. "She couldn't care less. She has a gorgeous family and is the most loving and positive person you could meet." I sigh and look down at my hands. "This is the problem... Mum is fine, Hetty is fine. I don't feel like I have the right to feel like this. They both had it harder than me. If I were them, I'd think I was weak and pathetic for not being able to pick myself up like they have. I've tried. I've tried so hard. I figured I would take the 'fake it till you make it approach', but… when the guests, my shadows appeared…"

I swallow hard. I hate how pitiful my words sound, but I know how important it is to let them out.

"Sometimes I feel that my guests are my punishment for being so weak."

I lower my head. The weight of these words is so great for me, but there is definite relief in sharing them.

"This is amazing, Tamsin." I look up, confused. "No, what I mean is. I can feel the importance and the truth in everything you are saying. We can absolutely work together with all of this. So, thank you." He looks at his watch briefly. "I'm getting a little conscious of time, and I think there is a crucial part to this story that I need to have some detail on to get a more rounded picture."

"Okay. What is it? I'll do my best."

He smiles again. "Could you tell me about your treatment after you told Dr Pathirana about the hallucinations and what made you decide to stop seeing her?"

I feel a sense of creeping trepidation. The ever-present threat of being separated from Summer hangs over me. If I had broken my leg, then I wouldn't fear losing my daughter, I know that I would get the support I need to heal. But this is different. People understand that bodies need to heal, but a broken mind is uncomfortable and dangerous.

"Well, when I told Dr Pathirana that I was having visions, she changed my treatment and started me on some strong medicines to help. She said I had developed psychosis. I think that's what she said, at least. I'm sure it's in my notes anyway. The drugs didn't work. They made me eat a lot, which seemed to make everyone else happy. I didn't drink as much either, but my guests continued every day. The same routine as always."

"Routine?"

I tell Dr McCabe in detail about my three guests. The baby on the bed, the girl in the bathroom, and the woman in the garden. I explain that they come at the same time every day.

"And they always look and behave the same?"

"Yes, they never deviate. I used to be scared they would, but they are always there. Same time, same place. The baby cries, but the other two don't speak to me."

I keep expecting him to look at me disparagingly but he doesn't. All I see is interest and concern. It's nice to see that reflected back at me, and it dampens down my own negative perceptions of myself. Maybe the only person who thinks about myself that way is me.

"Sorry, I interrupted, Tamsin. You were telling me about your medication." He motions for me to continue.

"Er, yes, the psychosis drugs. I tried a couple. I had to take them for a while each time, but they didn't do anything for me. Dr Pathirana said there was another even stronger option for me to try, but I decided not to. I wasn't feeling very good on them, so stronger ones didn't feel like a good idea."

"I think I know what medication that might be, but I'll check your notes to be sure. Is that why you decided to stop your sessions with her?"

"No, not at all. Dr Pathirana was always very supportive of my choices. She wouldn't ever have pressed me to take anything I didn't want to. She simply explained what she thought might help. I really liked that about her."

"Then what was it?"

"She said that in some rare cases, visions like this may be memories or flashbacks. She said she wanted to explore whether I might have PTSD or something similar. She started asking a lot of questions about my family, and I think I just got scared. I was worried she might think Summer was in danger. I found myself either dodging her questions or just making things up. Eventually, I lied and told her that the hallucinations had stopped, telling her I would start sessions again if they came back. I've never been in touch with her again since."

Dr McCabe starts to flick through my folder. "That fits with what you told me at our first session."

"Yes. I still take the anxiety tablets she prescribed. I have ones I take every morning and others that I take if I feel stressed. I think they help, but I mix them with lots of wine. I like the numbness that the wine gives me, and I barely get hangovers these days."

My words are coming out so easily now. It feels as though I am talking to a friend.

"This is nice. Talking to you is actually nice." I feel a bit silly for saying it, but the regret ebbs away when I see Dr McCabe's face light up.

"I am so glad you feel like that. I hope you don't take this the wrong way, but I am incredibly proud of you."

I beam at him. "Thank you." I feel proud of myself, too. We decide not to make any significant changes today and agree that I should continue seeing him twice a week, our next appointment being Monday.

I tell him how good it feels to have told the truth. There is no need to remember what lies I have told him, and I won't have to feel nervous about contradicting myself or tripping myself up at our next appointment.

"My family are coming this weekend. My mum kind of invited herself. Summer has been complaining about me distancing her from the rest of the family. I'm hoping she'll enjoy herself."

"Perhaps you might enjoy yourself too?"

Anxiety rises within me. "Perhaps."

9

SUMMER

I wasn't sure what to think when Mum told me we were having family over. I was so exhausted from all the throwing up and the madness that followed it that I barely considered it at the time.

Mum is clearly super stressed. She keeps walking around the kitchen, muttering to herself, picking things up and putting them down, and then seemingly forgetting where she's put them. She's cooking a salmon en croute, which she has made a million times. Still, she's acting like she's undertaking some kind of impossibly complicated task.

"You need any help?"

She doesn't answer. Just looks around frantically. "Eggs. Eggs. Where are the…"

I pick up the eggs from the kitchen table. She put them down there only a few seconds ago. "Here you go, Mum." I put my hand on her shoulder. "Mum, what's with all the stress? You're a great cook. Stop worrying!"

She gives an exasperated laugh and leans against the kitchen counter, wiping her brow with the back of her hand.

"Thanks, Summer. I'm getting myself wound up. We haven't

had everyone over in forever, I guess I'm just feeling out of practice."

I fill a glass with water, and Mum gratefully accepts it.

"Are you sure I can't help?"

"No, honestly. Despite appearances, I'm actually organised and right on track." She gestures at the cluttered kitchen countertops and I raise my eyebrows questioningly. "Organised chaos! Now, you go upstairs. I'll feel much better once this is in the oven. Then there's only potatoes to boil and a salad to pull out of the fridge when they arrive."

"If you're sure?"

"Very sure. Go on. Have some time before the rabble arrive." Mum laughs nervously and keeps glancing out of the kitchen window. She waves me away again. "Go on." A little more forcefully this time.

"Okay, okay."

"I'll shout you down when they're here." I reluctantly leave, and I notice Mum's knuckles are white and bloodless as she grips the kitchen counter and stares into the garden.

Grandma Arabella, Auntie Hetty, Uncle Gavin, Luca, and Kai arrive together. The cacophony of noise as they bundle themselves out of the car and make their way up our front path is music to my ears. I see Grandma's face through the glass.

"Open the door. Our hands are full!" I oblige, and Grandma hands me two bottles of extremely cold white wine. A wave of exotic perfume assaults me as she kisses me on the cheek and wipes away what I assume is lipstick. Her lips are a bright fuchsia with a hint of sparkle. "Get these in the fridge, beautiful girl."

I watch the family bundle their way through the hallway and into the living room. Gavin is carrying a floral cake tin, and

Grandma yells at him, "Fridge for that too, Gavin," before she flops down dramatically onto the sofa.

Uncle Gavin ushers the boys into the back garden. "You've been sat down all morning. Get some exercise before lunch." They grumble but do as he says.

Mum looks very stiff standing in the kitchen. I leave her with Hetty and Gavin and sit down next to Grandma. She beams and appraises me with her eyes.

"I've missed you, Summer. I've really missed you." She reaches out her hand and grasps mine tightly.

"I've missed you too, Grandma. I've wanted to see you, but... you know." I nod my head in the direction of the kitchen.

Grandma reaches out her other hand and traces the side of my cheek with her fingertips. I notice her fingernails are lurid green.

"I know, dear. But you mustn't blame your mother." She smiles softly, and sadness dulls her features briefly. "That's why we're all here. We're family. We help each other." I nod, slightly frustrated at the vagueness of Grandma's comments. "Anyway, let's get eating. I'm sure I'm not the only one who's starving. Far too late for lunch this."

Grandma links my arm and we join the others in the kitchen. Gavin is telling a story about his friend catching a big fish. I can see he's trying to ease some of the uncomfortable atmosphere between Mum and Auntie Hetty. Grandma takes control.

"Summer, go and teach the boys some football moves. Show them how it's really done."

Luca is nine, Kai is eight, and coordination is not their strong suit.

"Tamsin, what needs doing?"

"Potatoes have just gone on, Mum. Ten minutes and everything will be ready."

"Excellent. Hetty and Gavin, you are on table setting, and I'll crack open the Chablis." Grandma walks towards the fridge.

"How did you know I bought Chablis, Mum?"

Grandma opens the fridge and laughs raucously as she sees her two bottles of wine alongside two identical ones that Mum had bought.

"Great minds, Tamsin!" Grandma doesn't notice the pinch of irritation on Mum's face as she turns away from her and checks the potatoes. A knot of tension forms in my chest. Why can't Mum just relax? She avoids my gaze as I make my way out into the garden as instructed.

10

TAMSIN

It's lovely to have some noise in the house again. I'm being weird with Hetty, but I don't mean to. I'd like to apologise for ignoring her and distancing myself, but I don't want to start the afternoon on a negative note.

A pang of nervousness hits me as I realise that four bottles of wine are in the house. I bought two and no more so I wouldn't be tempted to overindulge. My willpower is still pretty poor, and I don't want to have more than a glass. Choosing oblivion when I feel nervous is too easy and will likely have disastrous consequences. Both Gavin and my Mum are a law unto themselves when it comes to unsolicited wine top-ups.

Lunch is actually lovely. I get lots of compliments about the food, and the conversation flows easily. We chat mostly about the kids and what's been happening at their respective schools. Everyone chimes in at some point with an anecdote or a story, and we laugh easily together. Summer is flushed with excitement, and I watch her face light up as she recounts tales of her football games and tennis tournaments. I'm once again struck by the pointlessness of my avoidant behaviour with my relatives. There are only good people here.

My dad was the negative force in the family, and he is gone. I don't need to be ashamed about the fact that my marriage broke down and my husband left me. I don't need to pretend that I have it all together. Excluding these people from my and Summer's lives is not only wrong but harmful.

We decide to have a break between the main course and dessert, and I usher everyone into the living room, insisting that I will tidy up. There are no complaints, and everyone takes a seat. I'm happily scrubbing pots in the sink when I feel a gentle tap on my shoulder and turn to see Hetty. Her cheeks are flushed, and I can see she has had more than a couple of glasses of wine.

"Need any help?"

I look at my sister. My gorgeous little sister. I fight the urge to tell her to leave me to it. My instinctual reaction is to move her away from me and my sadness.

"It's fine, Hetty. But why don't you keep me company." I smile, and she leans against the kitchen counter closest to me.

"How have you been? I'm so sorry, but I've been so wrapped up with the boys and their busy social lives. I should have tried harder. But time just passes, you know?"

"Not at all, Hetty. I've been horrible at keeping in touch. I've just been hiding away. Pathetic, really." I curse myself for my negative and self-absorbed response.

"Hiding from what?"

I know I can trust Hetty. We were so close before Alex left. When I didn't have things I needed to hide.

"I just feel a bit broken since Alex left. I'm getting some help now. Trying to be better. It's affecting Summer."

Hetty glances through to the living room.

"She looks like she's blooming to me." Hetty walks towards me and places her hand on my back, leaning her head into my shoulder. "You're not to blame, you know."

I turn and kiss her gently on the top of the head. My hands are wet and soapy, so a hug will have to wait.

"I am. There's a lot you don't know about how I behaved before Alex left. I was… I wasn't behaving normally. I scared him. I scared him away from his daughter."

Hetty steps back, her eyes flitting around nervously before settling on a spot on the floor. She hesitates weirdly before finally spitting out what she wants to say.

"I know. Alex told me."

Incredulity rises within me. "He did what?" My breathing quickens, and my whole body tenses. "Why didn't you tell me? It's nice to know you two were having a good old laugh about me."

Hetty is wide-eyed and nervous. "It wasn't like that."

My face twists, and my voice is a menacing whisper. "Sure it wasn't. Poor fucked up Tamsin. I can't believe you didn't tell me he discussed our marriage with you. That's just… wrong. Really fucking wrong."

I glance over my shoulder. Thankfully, nobody seems to have noticed the change of tone in our conversation.

"He only talked to me once. It was the day before he left."

I feel a burning rage flash through me.

"And you're only telling me now? Did you tell him to leave me? Is that what this is, a confession?" I'm struggling to maintain the volume of my voice.

"No. No!" Hetty pulls her shoulders back and looks me straight in the eye. Gone is her meekness. She is strong and insistent now. "Do you want to hear this or not? Because, believe it or not, I am trying to help you. And not for the first time, either. I have tried to talk to you many times, but you just won't listen!"

I give a childish shrug, dry my hands on the kitchen towel and fold my arms across my chest, my face a stony mask. "Go on then. I'm listening."

Hetty takes another step back.

"This isn't easy for me, Tamsin." My heart begins to race at the thought of what she might be about to say. She takes a deep breath and puffs out her cheeks. "He told me."

I fix her with a look of disdain. "You're going to have to do better than that. Told you what exactly?"

Hetty's shoulders drop, and she suddenly looks exhausted. "He told me about your... visions."

A mixture of shame and betrayal almost knocks me off my feet. I can't find any words, so I stand, silently simmering.

"It's okay, Tamsin. I understand."

Anger bubbles up to the surface again, and my words are laced with venom. "You understand? How could you possibly understand?"

"No. No, I'm not making myself clear. I told Alex I could help you, but he wouldn't let me speak to you. I had no idea that he was planning to leave you, that he was planning to disappear."

Hetty and I stare at each other for a moment. I can see the regret and sadness behind her eyes, but there is something about the last sentence she just said. A change in her delivery. A deception of some kind. She is quivering, and suddenly, I want to run away from her. I'm not strong enough for any of this yet.

"We never talk about what happened, Tamsin. We've let ourselves forget, and it's hurting you."

I feel cornered, dread tying my stomach in painful knots. I don't want to hear what she has to say.

"You know exactly who they are. The baby. The child. The woman. Come on, Tamsin. I know that you do. You can't just keep ignoring it. I've tried so many times to talk to you about it, but you just shut me down, and now you're avoiding me completely."

My world tilts. It's as though I can feel every brick of the carefully constructed wall I have placed around my memory falling down. I have never wanted to face this. No matter how hard my mind has been forcing me to. I can't bear to live day to day with that reality.

"Do you still see them?" I nod, still barely holding on to my crumbling thoughts. "If you don't face this it will never go away." I want to tell her to fuck off with her amateur psychology, but I know there is a profound truth in her words. "You were only a child, Tamsin. It was not your fault. In fact, it wasn't even Mum's fault. You can't punish yourself forever. And to be honest, I don't understand why we are all pretending it didn't happen. Can you imagine how that feels for me? I don't blame you, Tamsin. But I have had enough of the denial in this family. It's like a sickness, and it's clearly beginning to poison you."

Tears begin to fall silently down my face.

"It was my fault. It was. And I am so sorry, Hetty. So very sorry."

Hetty moves slowly towards me and envelops me in a fierce embrace. I weep into her shoulder, and I feel her hot tears join mine as they fall against my cheeks.

11

ARABELLA

BEFORE

I sit at the kitchen table, feeding a gurgling Hetty her bottle of milk. It's barely 8.30am, but we've already been up for a few hours, and fingers crossed, she will have a long nap after this bottle. I will definitely be joining her if she does.

Harold is crashing around upstairs. He pays absolutely no heed to whether Hetty might need peace and quiet. Although that is the least of his faults. When I became pregnant with Hetty, he announced with pleasure that he had secured a well-paying position closer to home so he could spend more time with me, Hetty, and Tamsin. And it was that specific moment that confirmed what I had already suspected for a long time. I didn't love him anymore. I didn't even like him anymore. Not only that, but our relationship was only surviving because he wasn't here most of the time. I could put up with him at the weekends. He was usually tired and didn't want to do much with us anyway.

Tamsin has started to avoid him recently, disappearing up to bed early on a Friday evening to avoid him. I have always felt an obligation to keep my family safe and secure, and something deeply antiquated entrenched within me believes that means staying with Harold.

I hear his heavy feet thump down the stairs, his breathing heavy and laboured. He is nothing like the man I married, neither on the inside nor the outside. He used to smile, he was thoughtful and kind, and he used to make me laugh every day. Now he looks at me like I'm something he's scraped off his shoe. He is grumpy, selfish, and mean. I look up as he enters the room. Sweat is blooming on the back of his rumpled shirt, and the buttons are holding on for dear life from the pressure of his swollen middle. His face is red and blotchy. The man who used to run several times a week can no longer walk downstairs without sweating like a pig.

Hetty is beginning to fall asleep in my arms, the bottle teat has fallen from her mouth, and her lips are pursed in the sweetest, most contented smile. My heart swells as I look at her. I can't believe how lucky I am to have two such beautiful girls.

Harold shows no interest in us, and Hetty startles as he fills the kettle noisily and slams it down onto the base. Hetty lets out a tiny whimper before sucking her lips gently together and drifting back off. I swallow down my irritation, reach out with my free arm, and poke him in the back, my fingers sinking into the excess flesh. He swings his body around faster than I have seen him move in a long time and glares at me with contempt. I press my finger to my lips and then gently stroke Hetty's wispy brown curls. Harold puffs out his cheeks and exhales before shaking his head.

"I am making coffee, Arabella. It would have been nice to have some waiting for me, seeing as I'm going out to work all day. But at the very least, I shouldn't be berated in my own home for turning on the fucking kettle."

He makes no effort to control the volume of his voice and crashes a mug from the cupboard down onto the counter with such force I'm surprised it doesn't break. I feel a red mist descend, blood whirls in my ears, and I am grateful that I have

Hetty in my arms, as she is the only thing that's keeping me from screaming and lashing out at him.

I have no idea what he would do if I did. I have never struck him, and he has never struck me. His torture is psychological in nature. Gradually wearing and beating me down until I'm sure that soon, there won't be much left. I used to build myself back up on weekdays when he was in London. The house was mine, and I filled it with friends, family, and joy. Tamsin loved those days, too. But we are both fading now. That's how he wants us.

I stand on shaking legs, my whole body trembling with rage, and storm out of the kitchen, holding a now wriggling Hetty close to my breast. Harold stands at the bottom of the stairs, watching me ascend, and laughs. A disgusting, obnoxious bray.

"That's right, love. Fuck off upstairs. I'm sick to death of the lot of you."

I pause briefly. Feeling as though I am about to lose control of my body before looking down at Hetty, composing myself, and continuing to my bedroom. I can still hear him goading me from the bottom of the stairs.

"There's not an ounce of respect from any of you. I work my fingers to the bone, and what do I get? Nothing. Nothing but grief." He starts muttering, and I can't make out any of the words until he finally shouts up, "Anything to say, Arabella? No, I thought not. You just stay here all day sitting on your lazy arse. You and those bloody girls." He says the word "girls" with such venom. How can he feel this way about our children?

I can hear him pacing around at the bottom of the stairs. It's evident he wants a reaction from me. Well, he's not going to get one. It's school holidays, and Tamsin is still in her room. She'd typically wake up in an hour or so, but I'd be surprised if she was sleeping through this.

"Things are going to change around here, Arabella. You mark my words. I have had it with flogging my guts out. No more. I am the man of this house."

Anger is fizzing in my veins, but I stay exactly where I am. I lay Hetty down gently on the bed, and watch her beautiful, peaceful face and her eyelids fluttering as she dreams peacefully. I hear a creak as Tamsin's door opens, and she peers out cautiously. I tiptoe to the door and beckon her over, holding my finger to my lips. Her eyes are filled with alarm, and I'm sure I can see her heart beating through her tiny chest.

"It's okay, baby." I pull her into me, and we sit beside Hetty on the bed. I whisper gently into her ear. "He'll tire himself out soon. Just a lot of bluff and bluster."

Tamsin seems to calm down a little but I can still feel her shaking in her thin nightdress. He shouts again, more menace and threat in his words this time.

"Get down these stairs, Arabella. Now!" Suddenly, I'm afraid for my girls. Just because he hasn't hurt them before, doesn't mean he couldn't. I don't think I've ever seen him behave so unreasonably. And over what? Asking him to boil the kettle quietly. Ridiculous. I hold Tamsin close.

"I'm going to go downstairs and sort this out. Stay here with your sister."

TAMSIN

BEFORE

I don't want Mum to go downstairs. She should stay here with me and Hetty. We should just pack up all our things and leave, I hate it here. It's not safe.

I look at my baby sister. She hasn't got a clue about anything that's going on and won't remember any of this. My heart is racing as I hear Mum go down the stairs. Dad's going crazy. She's walking straight into danger. I rest my hand on Hetty's soft tummy. She grips my finger and tries to bring it to her little mouth.

Mum needs to make him leave. We could go back to the way things were when he was working in London, and Hetty wouldn't have to grow up to see any of this fighting or learn how mean Daddy is.

The house has become scarily quiet. No doors have opened, and I don't think Dad would have calmed down so quickly. Goosebumps appear on my arms and slither up my back.

My stomach lurches, and I physically jump as there's a heavy thump. Furious screaming and shouting fills the house. I hear both of their voices. Both yelling. Both screaming. I clamp my hands over my ears, but it does little to drown out their horrible fighting. Hetty's face hasn't changed, but that doesn't mean much. She can't even smile yet. She only cries or sleeps.

The neighbours must be able to hear. I cross my fingers and squeeze my eyes tightly shut, praying that someone will call the police. They would come and take him away.

Hetty has started squirming more but doesn't seem upset. She is thrusting her tongue in and out in a way that almost makes me smile. I try to block out our warring parents as I stroke her cheek with my trembling fingers.

Something smashes. Maybe glass, or plates or something. Then there's another crash. It's like smash tennis, and I bet the living room's a mess. I can hear Mum's voice, so I know she's still okay. Although I'm terrified, I know I can't just sit here doing nothing. What if something bad happened to Mum, and I just listened to it all from up here, safe in the bedroom?

Slowly and gently, I tiptoe to the door. I don't want to attract his attention and make him come up and start on us. I listen at the top of the stairs, my heart still racing.

"Get out! Just get out. You don't want us anyway, so just leave!" Mum is screaming. I've never heard anything like it, and I think it's her who's grabbing things and smashing them on the floor.

Dad speaks. Only it doesn't sound like Dad, he sounds cold and wicked, almost as though he's laughing at Mum. "I am not going anywhere." His voice sends an icy chill up my spine. "This is my house, and I'm going to stay right here. And so are you."

He spits out the last sentence like a threat. The menace in his words makes me feel ill, and I press my hand to my mouth to prevent any sound from escaping that would reveal my whereabouts. I can't understand why he would want Mum to stay. It's obvious he doesn't like us. We'd all be so much happier. His voice becomes a quiet growl. Like an animal.

"You are my wife, and you're going to start behaving like it.

I've had it with playing second fiddle to those children. I want some respect from all of you. I demand it!"

Mum lets out a pained shriek, and for a second, I worry that he's hurt her. But then she stops, and I realise it was a battle cry of sorts.

"You don't deserve our respect. We are leaving! Now! You can't stop us."

Before I have a chance to move from the top of the stairs, Mum flies around the corner and begins clambering towards me. A split second later, Dad follows her, his face a mask of hatred. I don't think he even sees me. He's so fixated on Mum. He grabs at her ankle, and she tumbles violently, her face crashing into the stairs. She lets out a nauseating moan as the air is knocked from her lungs.

He drags her back down the stairs, her legs kicking out at him. She won't go down without a fight, but she has no chance, he is so much stronger. I want to scream, but my voice has been robbed, and I let out a barely audible, breathy shout. I'm desperate to go downstairs and save her, but my legs won't carry me that way. Instead, I find myself running towards the bathroom. Inside my head, I'm begging myself to go downstairs and help Mum, but I have lost all control over my actions. I sit on the bathroom floor, with my back against the bath and cry quietly.

I can't hear anything anymore except the pounding of blood in my ears and my own sobs. I hang my head and pull my knees up to my chest. Horrible visions of what he might be doing to Mum flash in front of my eyes. I need to go down there, run out of the door, and get some help. Grab the phone and call the police. Shout and yell at him to stop. Anything. Anything at all. Instead, I sit here and do absolutely nothing, completely frozen by fear.

The bathroom comes back into focus as though I'm emerging from a trance. I'm shivering, but I'm not cold – I think my body's sort of switched off. I don't know how long I've been sitting here. Mum and Dad sound as though they are downstairs talking. It's not friendly, but at least they're not screaming or attacking each other anymore. My vision is blurry, and I'm coated in sweat. I climb slowly to my feet. Black spots explode in front of my eyes, and I steady myself on the side of the bath until my body adjusts. I creep to the bathroom door on shaking legs and open it to listen.

Mum is crying now, and Dad's voice is softer. Should I go downstairs? Things seem to have calmed down a lot, but then I glance across at Mum's bedroom, and my whole world comes crashing down. An indescribable and all-consuming pain floods my entire body. How could I have forgotten Hetty?

Through the gap in the door, I can see her. She is lying face down on the bed, and she isn't moving. A thunderous scream emerges deep from within my chest. I feel as though I am going to burst open. I know I should go to her. I need to go to her, but instead, I stand rooted to the spot, screaming and slapping the side of my face with my palms.

The world seems to fall away. I vaguely feel Mum and Dad rush past me and into their bedroom.

Dad comes up close to my face. "Out of the way!"

I run back to the bathroom again. Falling, scrambling, breaking apart. Within minutes, I can hear an ambulance outside and even more footsteps and noise in the house. There are machines and voices I don't recognise. My head is spinning, and I no longer feel like I'm in my own body. I'm in some weird in-between place. A place where people who kill their sisters must live.

Just as suddenly as it started, all the noise stops, and I hear the front door slam. Somehow, I know that Mum has gone with Hetty in the ambulance. Am I alone in the house with Dad?

Have I killed my little sister?

My head is whirling with possibilities, and I can't handle the reality of any of them. I want to curl up into a ball and never face the world again. Dad calls for me. I swallow back a swell of nausea.

"Come downstairs, Thomasina. Now." He sounds extremely serious but not angry. I have to face him if only to find out how Hetty is. I stagger downstairs, legs quivering and almost stumbling before I reach the bottom. I wait outside the door, trying to push some air back into my lungs.

I can see Dad's legs. He is sitting on the sofa. Not moving. Just waiting.

"In here, Thomasina. I won't ask again." My whole body is shuddering. I feel like I'm outside of my body again. Dad and I are hardly ever alone, and a sudden wave of panic washes over me as I remember why we are here now. Hetty. Oh, Hetty. What have I done?

I walk into the room slowly and stand in front of him. My head bowed, and my hands twisting the ends of my sleeves. I don't think I've ever felt as scared and hopeless as I do now. It feels like my life is over. He points at the armchair across the room. His face is a deathly white mask.

"Sit."

I scurry quickly to the chair and sit, pulling my knees into my chest and hugging my legs close to my body. I think I might fall apart otherwise.

"I want you to listen, Thomasina. I want you to listen very carefully. Do you understand?" I nod my head but don't look up. "Hey!"

My head jerks up at his sudden, deafening outburst, and I nod frantically, tears falling down my cheeks.

"Okay. Good. Now, I'm going to tell you what just happened, and then we are never going to speak of it again." I feel like I might throw up at any moment, but I stay seated and listen. "Your mother found Hetty in her cot." I furrow my brow and open my mouth to speak. What is he talking about? That's not true at all. He holds out a hand and fixes me with a fierce glare. "I am going to tell you what happened, and you are going to listen. Nobody will ever ask you. You are only a child. But if they do, then you will repeat what I am going to tell you now."

My eyes are wide with amazement, and I notice that I'm shaking my head. He suddenly erupts with anger; his face is scarlet and spit flies from his mouth as he growls at me.

"Do you want your mother to go to jail? Because that is what will happen if you don't do exactly as I say."

My heart drops. Is he right? Will Mum be blamed for this? She didn't do anything wrong. I was the one who left Hetty by herself on the bed.

"No." My voice is croaky and weak.

"Your mum found Hetty in her cot. She put her down for a nap and found her face down and not moving when she went to wake her up." I want to shout and scream at him, but I sit utterly still, silently sobbing. "She picked her up, took her to our bedroom and tried to wake her up. She called for me, and I called an ambulance. That is it. That is what happened."

I play his story in my head like a movie. Imagining Mum finding Hetty, and how she must have panicked and shouted for Dad.

"There is nothing to be gained by telling anyone that Hetty was in the bedroom with you."

I feel happy as I realise Dad's trying to protect me. He doesn't want me to get in trouble. He's never done that before. A fresh tide of nausea rises inside me, and I hate myself for being so utterly selfish. My sister is dead, and it's all my fault. I should be punished. I deserve it. I wipe my red, swollen eyes on my sleeve and make myself look at Dad. It's very clear that arguing back will not be tolerated. How I feel and what I think we should do doesn't matter.

"Okay, Daddy. That is what happened." The words are bitter in my mouth, but there is nothing else to say. I have no power here. None. He nods his head and comes over to me, kneeling down and lowering his face to mine. I can't remember him ever showing anything but dislike towards me. I'm uneasy about him being so close, but also grateful that he does care about me.

"Outside of this house, nobody will ever know what happened here today. Things like this happen to babies every day." He tilts his head and looks deep into my eyes. I force a small smile. "But inside this house, we will always know this is your fault. You did this. You ruined everything, and me and your mother will never forgive you. Don't you ever forget it."

He pats me on the knee, stands up, and walks out of the room and up the stairs. I can barely breathe. I start to shake uncontrollably. I want to run out of the house and never come back, but I sit rooted to the spot, forcing breath in and out of my lungs.

I don't deserve to run away.

This will be my punishment.

This house and him.

Forever.

13

TAMSIN

I'm a bundle of nerves as I enter Dr McCabe's office. This morning has been a whirlwind. I'm about to do something that I never thought I would. Revealing what I did at my last appointment feels minuscule in comparison to what I am going to tell him today.

Since speaking with Hetty at the barbecue, I've been in a world of torment. I have always known what happened to her, but years of initially forced and then voluntary denial have left it feeling like a story or a nightmare rather than a memory. I can play back that day in my head perfectly, but I have refused to do so for decades. There are too many parts that I simply cannot deal with. So much sadness and regret. In many ways, I'd rather keep the guests than reveal the truth about their origin to a single soul. But I have to. For Summer.

My denial is like a cancer spreading through our tiny household, and I won't let it take her. I must fight it. I have to own what happened and my role in it. It hits me differently as an adult and especially as a parent. I'm more equipped to consider that I am not to blame, but I'm not sure I can ever extinguish the gnawing guilt I feel deep in my soul. Dr McCabe feels like someone who can help me finally come to terms with it all.

Dr McCabe can sense instantly that something is very wrong. He greets me kindly, as usual, and I sit down.

"Did the family gathering not go well?" Dr McCabe sits across from me and fixes me with deep concern.

"No. No, I mean, yes." I stop and take a deep breath before starting again. "It went fine. Summer had a lovely time, and there was no major incident. But me and my sister got into a conversation…" My voice falls away, and all the moisture disappears from my mouth.

"It's okay, just take your time."

The rhythm of my heart feels unusual, and my whole body is vibrating with the weight of the secret I have held inside my entire life. A secret so deep I have hidden it from my husband, and even myself.

"I have told you about Hetty before." I look up, and Dr McCabe nods in agreement. "Well, most people assume that her condition has been present since birth. That is often the case – that something happened during labour and, well… anyway, that doesn't matter. What I'm trying to say is that I did it."

Dr McCabe's eyebrows raise, and I force myself to continue before he can interject with a question. "She was a tiny baby, and my parents were having a horrific argument, so Mum left me to look after her on the bed in their bedroom. The fight got scary and violent, and I ran away into the bathroom to hide. It was horrible, and I was so afraid, but I left her, and she must have flipped over or something because when I came back, she was face down on the bed and wasn't breathing." I pause for breath, and Dr McCabe doesn't break my flow. "I thought I'd killed her, but the paramedics saved her, and she was fine. Well, not fine, but you know, she's wonderful and just the best sister anyone could have. I don't deserve her. I abandoned her."

I wrap my arms around my chest and start to cry. I can hear

Dr McCabe's deep, slow breathing. I know what I have just revealed is shocking.

"Thank you for sharing that with me. I can't imagine how hard this must be for you to talk about."

I sniff loudly and wipe my streaming eyes. "Well, it's not just that. I wasn't allowed to talk about it." Dr McCabe's eyebrows shoot up with intrigue. "Mum became a completely different person afterwards. She was withdrawn and nervous, and my father told me that I had to stick to a fake story where Hetty rolled over in her cot. I tried a couple of times to tell him that I wanted to tell the truth, but he kept threatening me that Mum would end up in jail because she shouldn't have left me with a newborn baby."

This unbearable truth of mine is bitter, and I want to get it out of my mouth as quickly as possible.

"He was so convincing but also terrifying. He would taunt me in secret and tell me that I should be grateful I wasn't a murderer and that it was all my fault. I believed him with absolute certainty, and then when he died, it just seemed like his version of reality was the one we were all living." My heart aches for the little girl I once was. The girl whose existence I have been denying all these years. No wonder I don't feel like a whole person. "Once Dad was gone, Mum became happy again, and I didn't want to spoil it. I just left things the way they were, and it was all fine. Until it wasn't…"

My throat is raw from forcing these words out through strangled sobs. My heart is throbbing and empty. I look up at Dr McCabe, and he puffs out a deep breath.

"I am sorry that you've had all that to deal with. And if I understand you correctly, you haven't told this information to anyone, ever?" He sounds choked with emotion.

I shake my head and whisper. "I haven't even let myself believe it. I've completely rejected that it ever happened anytime the memories tried to resurface. I've been living a complete lie." I hang my head in shame.

"Is there anything else I need to know before we start talking about this in more detail? Something you may have left out, intentionally or unintentionally." I furrow my brow and close my eyes.

"I don't think so. I mean, nothing major, at least. That's it all. I have thought about it a lot since Hetty and I spoke. I know she is the baby on the bed, and I am the girl in the bathroom. I guess I've always known. I think it's been my way of punishing myself, and I just drink wine to send it all away to the back of my mind again."

"That definitely fits with what you've told me about your hallucinations, and it also fits with Dr Pathirana's suggestion that what you've been seeing could be linked to trauma. But more importantly, now that you have been completely honest, I can help you."

"But I'm not sure I even deserve help." I know I sound pathetic and childlike saying that, but it's true.

"A big part of our time together will be getting you to the point where you know and understand that you do deserve to be happy." He reaches out to me with the box of tissues and I take one. "Now I know the full story, we can start you on a journey of healing. And you deserve to heal. What you have shared is shocking and traumatic, but I can tell you with one hundred per cent certainty that what happened to your sister is not your fault. You were a child, and you shouldn't have been put in that position, not to mention how you were treated afterwards." He stops, and I let his comforting words sink in. "There is much to unpick here, but I want to start by emphasising that point in particular. You are not to blame."

I wring my hands to try and expel some of the pent-up energy coursing through me. My emotions are all over the place. I don't know where to put myself, and I am dangerously close to becoming completely overwhelmed.

"Tamsin, look at me." I do as he asks, and I see that his eyes are glistening. He locks his eyes on mine with an intensity that quietens everything inside me for a moment. "I'll say it again, and I want you to listen. You are not to blame."

I nod my head slowly and lean back gently into the chair, letting his words wash over me, hoping they'll somehow implant into my brain.

Dr McCabe slowly takes me through the events of that day, stopping regularly to allow me to regain my composure. He continually emphasises how young I was, and that my father was wrong to suggest that I had any culpability in Hetty's injury. Deep in my heart, I know he is right, but he is the first person to ever say this to me. I always heard the exact opposite my entire childhood, and it's so difficult to unlearn how I feel about myself.

"I know that you see Hetty as the victim and you as the perpetrator, but that is simply not true. You were frightened, and the responsibility for the safety and care of a newborn baby lies with the parents, not their sibling. They were wrong to put you in that position."

"I get that, I do. But it's not like I asked them not to. I think they trusted me and thought Hetty would be safe with me."

"That doesn't matter. Your response of running away and hiding when you were terrified of the escalating fight between your parents is completely understandable. You did not leave Hetty on purpose. You did it as a response to what was going on around you."

I want to believe him, but I can't stop myself from arguing the contrary to every point he makes.

"I should have picked her up and taken her with me. Did I not care if she was going to be hurt? Why did I just want to save myself? I think that's almost the worst part. It's such a selfish thing to do."

Dr McCabe pauses for a moment. I know that he at least partially agrees with what I've just said. He takes a deep breath.

"I'm right, aren't I?"

Dr McCabe leans towards me and shakes his head. "No. No, you're not right to think that you did something wrong. I'm just thinking of the best way to explain this to you." He clasps his hands in front of him. "Okay, what I mean is, you are an adult now, with a fully formed set of emotions, including empathy." I nod. "I think that you are trying to judge your actions as a seven-year-old child by the standards you have for yourself as an adult."

I sit quietly and listen intently. I hadn't thought about it that way, and I'm interested to see what he says next.

"Children learn in lots of different ways, and they develop emotionally through modelling what they see, being able to discuss how they are feeling, and receiving praise when they show positive behaviour. From what you have told me, your parents, particularly your father, did not provide you with an environment where there was much opportunity for that."

He's right, but if anything, that makes me feel even worse.

"So what you are saying is that I was a bad and selfish child, but it's not my fault because my parents were shit?" I screw my face up. Dr McCabe raises his eyebrows and almost smiles. I feel my hackles rising.

"No, that's not what I am saying at all. I've said it before and I'll say it a hundred times if I need to. Your response to being in a violent, terrifying domestic situation at seven years old is completely understandable. You have nothing to feel guilty for at all. All the responsibility lies with your parents. I'm simply trying to add to this and show you that the effects on you as a child from your father's behaviour towards you cannot be understated. Parents should be loving and encouraging, set a good example and clear boundaries for their children. From what you have said, you didn't always have that."

I nod, my flurry of irritation gradually receding.

"I can see that you have grown into an adult who has a genuine love and care for your own daughter. I want you to think of that day from the perspective of a parent. How would you feel if Summer had been put in the same position as you? Would you blame her? Would you threaten her so she stayed quiet and buried a secret that would eat away at her?"

A look of horror crosses my face. The thought of me behaving towards Summer like that is absolutely hideous. How on earth could anyone do that to their child? I look at Dr McCabe, and a moment of understanding and sadness engulfs me. Fresh tears pulsate behind my eyes. I clear my throat and manage a whisper. "I get it."

"Good. Now I know what I've said is not easy to hear and will bring up a lot of complicated feelings regarding your relationship with your mother. But it's important you do see it and understand something terrible also happened to you that day. Something we can spend time working through together."

I smile weakly. He's right about Mum. I know that nearly all the horrible things in our house were because of my dad. But he's not here to answer for it anymore. I love Mum dearly, but she has some explaining to do. In order for Summer and me to be happy, I'm going to have to pop the toxic family bubble that we've all been living in.

The truth needs to come out.

14

TAMSIN

I hope Dr McCabe knows how much I appreciate him. Everything is so raw and intense during our sessions that I often forget to articulate to him just how much this is helping me. I worry all he sees from me are tears and frustration.

I left his office quietly today, feeling dazed and wrung out. I have to do this for Summer, but I am completely exhausted by it all. I hadn't realised that recovering from trauma would be so bloody traumatic in itself. My whole body is heavy, and I lumber into the house, letting my bag fall to the ground as soon as I enter and click the front door closed. The house smells musty, I didn't tidy up properly this morning, and there are the aromas of leftover food from last night and this morning. They mingle unpleasantly in the air.

I feel a slight sense of pride as I realise I don't want a drink of alcohol. Instead, I want to think and feel and work through things carefully in my head. I smile to myself at the small victory of not wanting to block out the world and hide away for the afternoon. I will make myself a cup of tea and something healthy and nutritious to eat. A small positive step to care for myself. I sit down on the bottom stair and check my watch. The woman in the garden should be outside right now. Surely, one short session of discussing the past with Dr McCabe will not eliminate the guests altogether.

I need to steel myself for both her presence and her absence. I suspect either will leave me confused. Although I feel like I'm on the right path, I'm by no means better, so why would she be gone? But perhaps all I need to do to make the guests disappear is acknowledge their reasons for haunting me. To accept that I need to face my past.

There is little point in preparing for both eventualities, so I stand up slowly, my knees cracking in protest as I do. I need to start doing some exercise. My body is ageing through a total lack of care and attention. As I enter the kitchen, I immediately see the woman at the bottom of the garden, facing away in her pink dressing gown. I don't feel disappointed. My memory of her is the least formed, and even if I push myself, I can't quite grasp her intentions for me.

I feel a sudden urge to go to her. Goosebumps break out and climb up my arms. This woman is a part of my soul, and I can feel her calling me, willing me to understand. She has something to tell me, something critical, and I think that today, I am ready to hear it.

Butterflies flutter in my stomach as I walk to the window to watch her more closely. She looks no different than any other day, but there is a new intense magnetism coming from her that I can't ignore. My shoes are where I left them by the front door, but the pull of her is so insistent. She won't wait for me; I have to go to her now. My eyes are glued to her. I can't look away.

I open the back door and stumble down the garden towards her. The wet grass is soaking through my socks. I don't care. She needs me to go to her. I stand behind her, shaking, with both cold and fear. Instinct orders me to go around and face her. She wants to see my face. She has something that I need to know.

I didn't discuss her in detail with Dr McCabe today. Describing the baby and the girl was enough, and I know I am right about them. But something about this woman is missing in my memories. My assumption has always been that she is my mother, that this is where she stood when she found out what had happened to Hetty. But I don't think she was dressed like this, and I don't remember her going to the garden that day. Surely, there wouldn't have been time during the panic to stand in the garden staring like this. Perhaps it is something she did subsequently when she started closing down and ebbing away into herself. But why would my mind be so focused on this particular image of her?

I tiptoe around her slowly and stop at a spot about two metres in front of her, looking at the grass as I do. I'll be able to see her clearly here, but she won't be able to touch me or hurt me. My heart is thumping wildly, but I force myself to stand directly before her. I raise my eyes slowly and wipe away the tears obscuring my vision to look directly at her.

The woman is indeed my mother.

Her eyes are closed, and I can see her chest heaving as she breathes in and out forcefully. Something takes over me, and I speak without planning to. The words come out of my mouth without effort, but the voice is not my own. It is a child's voice, a little girl's voice. A terrified little girl.

"Mummy, what should I do?" Mum doesn't open her eyes. "Mum!" My voice is my own again, piercing and demanding. Mum's eyes open slowly, empty and soulless, as though she has no emotions at all. I have never seen her eyes like that.

"You should leave him." Her voice is cold and uncaring. She closes her eyes again, resuming her heavy breathing, her face tilted towards the sky.

"What?" My mouth is dry, and my whole face is trembling. What on earth does she mean? Alex has already left me, and I would never have left him. I completely ruined everything. Why would she be saying this to me? Mum liked Alex, at least that's what she always told me.

"Mum, please, help me."

Mum opens her eyes slowly, and their callous vacancy almost knocks me backwards. "You should leave him." She repeats the same words again and closes her eyes.

I stand in front of her, confused and terrified. My feet are frozen, and I am trembling from head to toe. Inside my head begins an incessant chanting. The word "no" is repeated over and over. Naively, I hoped that facing her would give me some understanding, and that she would help me.

This cold-hearted woman is not my mother. This guest is me, torturing myself for how I treated Alex and leaving Summer without a father. The chanting in my head finds its way out of my mouth, and now I am shouting at her with escalating volume.

"No. No. No!"

She doesn't move or acknowledge me in any way. She merely stands there, eyes closed, as though I don't exist. I run past her towards the house, falling through the back door and cracking my knee on the hard floor. I wince, pull myself to my feet, and steady myself against the kitchen counter. My breathing is disordered, and my vision begins to cloud over.

I stagger to the sink and run my hands under the cold water, splashing it over my face to revive myself. Standing precariously, I force my eyes towards the window and take in the view from the garden. Mum is still there, but she is now on her knees weeping, having fallen into the familiar position she adopts before leaving each day. This is more akin to the woman I knew and loved. Someone who was always full of emotion and turmoil, doing her best to get through each day whilst dealing with horrific oppression from her husband.

I yank off my soaking socks and discard them on the kitchen floor before grabbing a blanket from the back of an armchair, wrapping myself up in it, and curling into a foetal position on the sofa. I am chilled to the bone. I close my eyes and replay what the woman said to me.

I always thought I was the major problem in my marriage and Alex was putting up with me until it became too much for him. But maybe that's not how Mum saw things. Have I also been wrong about how Summer saw my and her dad's relationship? I've avoided talking to her about it. She's old enough to have whatever relationship she wants with her father, and I have always told her I would be completely supportive of whatever she decides. But days just seem to pass, and it's probably been many months since his name was even mentioned in this house. There is already so much that Summer and I need to discuss, and now this feels like a priority, too.

My mind is swimming, and I pull my knees in tightly to my chest. This is going to be a hard road, but I am determined to make it through for me and my daughter.

15

SUMMER

Amma and I walk out of college together, knocking shoulders with the stampede of other teens.

I'm in no rush to leave. Things at home are okay, but not great. Mum has been a bit quieter and contemplative, and I think she has stopped guzzling the wine. We'll see how long that lasts. I feel guilty for thinking Mum was going to ruin the family reunion at our house because she didn't. Amazingly, it all went pretty well. There was a moment when I thought Mum and Auntie Hetty were going to have an argument, but they ended up hugging. Everything else was surprisingly normal. Getting to see and speak to all of my family was wonderful, and I felt really emotional when they all left. Not in a bad way. Just grateful and a little overwhelmed.

I zip up my thick black puffa jacket and pull up my hood as I feel tiny drops of rain start to fall. Amma turns to face me and pulls me to the side, away from the mass exodus of other students.

"I'm getting a lift. Want to come with me?" She smiles, and her eyes twinkle. I would love to go with her. The thought of sitting next to her in her car is almost irresistible. But I need to clear my head a bit before I get home. The walk, even in the rain, will do me good.

"I'm going to walk today."

Amma's face falls before she recovers and gives me a nonchalant, "Cool."

I don't think I imagined her disappointment, and I'm even more convinced when I see apparent embarrassment cross her face. My heart leaps at the thought that maybe, just maybe, she feels something deeper for me than friendship. I would love to tell Amma how I feel about her, but I can't risk putting any strain on our friendship or, more horrifyingly, losing her altogether. I need her and will always love her as a friend if that's all we can ever be.

We hug, and I hold her close a little longer than I usually do. She doesn't pull away. I hear her dad call her name in the distance, and she suddenly pulls away and turns around, waving her hand in the air to acknowledge him.

"Call me later, Sunny. Okay? I feel like we haven't talked properly in ages." I furrow my forehead. We talk every day. "I mean about your mum and stuff. I think we need a good heart to heart. I can see you've got a lot whizzing around that beautiful brain of yours."

I smile and roll my eyes. She is not wrong there.

"I will, and you're right. My head is a bit full, and I could do with letting some of it out. I'll warn you, though, it's not pretty in here." I tap my finger against my forehead. Amma smiles and puts her hand on my shoulder. I can barely feel it through the thick padding of my jacket, but my stomach still flips at her sudden touch. Amma's dad shouts again, and she starts to walk away, still facing me.

"I'd better go before he gets out of the car. There are no limits to his ability to embarrass me!"

I laugh and wave her away, watching her run towards the car. I pull my hood up tightly around my face and begin the walk home. It's obvious all Mum wants to do is protect me. But secrets and lies do not protect, they only hurt.

I think of Amma as I walk. Even with my worries about Mum and what she'll be like when I get home, I can't get Amma out of my head. I'm starting to see flashes from her, subtle signs that make me think she'd like to be more than friends. And even if she said no, I know she'd be kind about it and hopefully still want to be friends. But I'm not ready to handle the potential devastation and embarrassment I would feel.

Amma knows that I'm gay. I've never felt the need to hide it from her, or from Mum. As far as I know, Amma hasn't had a romantic relationship with anyone and doesn't really tell me about anyone she's interested in. There's too much uncertainty to act at the moment. When it comes to Amma, my heart is fragile. She means too much to me. I need to wait it out.

I'm at my front door before I know it. Although Mum's been showing some really positive signs of taking care of herself and reintegrating into the world, I still always worry about what I might find when I get home. She has good intentions, but it's still early days, and she's delicate. I open the front door quietly. The house is still and peaceful. No footsteps and none of the usual sounds of cooking from the kitchen that usually greet me after college. The uncertainty fills me with dread. Silence is unusual, and unusual is not good.

I walk quietly into the living room and see Mum curled up on the sofa under a blanket, sleeping. Her eyelids twitch intermittently, and her breath moves in and out soundlessly. I creep past her to the kitchen. There's no smell of alcohol in the air or evidence of any afternoon wine drinking. Her socks are dirty and strewn across the kitchen floor, but otherwise, everything appears exactly as it was when I left that morning.

I know she had an appointment with her mental health doctor today. Perhaps she's just worn out after it. Talking about my feelings always exhausts me. She looks so peaceful, but I know I need to wake her. There's no way to know how long she has been sleeping, and I want her to be able to rest well tonight.

I sit down lightly next to her, and an urge to stroke her hair comes over me, but I don't want to make her feel like a child. She stirs and looks up at me, her eyes squinting. She rubs them and sits up.

"Summer, I'm so sorry. I must have fallen asleep." She yawns, putting her hand over her mouth and turning away.

I lift the blanket and cover her back up. "It's okay, Mum. You must have needed it."

She gives herself a shake and rubs her face and neck as though trying to bring life back into them. "How was college?" She stifles another yawn.

"Tell you what, Mum, I'll make us both a cuppa, and then I'll tell you all about college, and you can tell me all about your day, too. You had the doctor today, right?"

She smiles warmly at me and reaches out to hold my hand. "That sounds lovely. Give me two minutes to splash some water on my face."

I leave her to straighten up and head to the kitchen to make the promised cups of tea. Mum climbs the stairs to the bathroom. When she returns, she looks considerably brighter, but her hair is still flattened on one side. I don't mention it. She sits, tugs the blanket back over her knees, and pulls the cup of tea into her chest.

"Thank you. This will wake me up. So, how was your day?"

In the spirit of moving away from small talk and diving straight into talking about things that matter again, I tell her exactly what's on my mind.

"It was good, and... I think I'm in love with Amma." I wait for her shocked response, but it doesn't come.

She gives a beaming smile. "Well, I know that! The question is, do you know how she feels about you?" I don't know what to say. "I know I might not always seem tuned in, but I do know you very well, Summer. I can see how you feel about Amma, and I suspect, if I can see it, then she can too."

My eyes widen and I feel my stomach lurch. "You think?"

Mum gives a small laugh. "I think. And for what it's worth, I also think she has feelings for you, too. Granted, I'm not exactly a success when it comes to relationships, but I think you two could be very happy."

I see her face fall at her admission, and I know she's remembering something about Dad. I'll get to the stuff about him later. I want to keep talking about Amma just now.

"I'm worried I might spoil our friendship, but I think if I don't at least try, then I'll massively regret it, you know?"

Mum is nodding knowingly. "I do know, and I still think you should tell her how you feel. Amma loves you. How she feels about having a romantic relationship with you won't change that."

I twiddle my fingers and my heart flutters. "I know. I just don't want to make Amma feel weird."

Mum smiles, reaches out her arm, and places it on my forearm. Her hands are lovely and warm from holding the cup of tea.

"If you don't try, you'll never know." She fixes me with eyes so full of love and compassion and rests back into the sofa.

"That's super profound, Mum." We both emit a chuckle. "I need to think about it and decide what to do. I think I'm going to speak to her, but I need to get my head around it all first. But... thank you. It means a lot that I can chat with you like this. You've never made me feel, like... weird or anything." I blush a little. I'm not articulating my thanks very well.

"No thanks needed. I'm here whenever you need me. Relationships are hard. I hope you will always talk to me about it." She stops there and I smile and wipe my eyes. There are lots of things about Mum that I forget to be grateful for.

"Anyway, it's your turn now. How was the doctor? So exhausting that you had to take a nap?"

Mum's face pales, and I regret my flippant attitude. I move closer, stealing some of her blanket and leaning towards her.

"I'm serious. I want to know. It's just us, Mum. We need to be there for each other."

Mum takes a big, deep breath, purses her lips, and exhales slowly. "It's a lot, Summer. Seriously, a lot."

"And that's okay. I'd rather hear 'a lot' than be worrying and making up things in my head about what's going on. Just tell me. No judgement. I promise." I raise both my hands, palms facing outwards, as a gesture to cement what I've just said.

"I think I need to tell you it all at once. One part doesn't make sense without the other."

"That works for me." I lean into her again and feel her small body trembling.

"Aunt Hetty wasn't born with cerebral palsy. She suffocated when she was only a few weeks old."

I try not to tense up. This is more serious than I was expecting.

"Your grandma left me alone with Hetty while she and your granddad were having a huge fight. The fight got a bit, well... a lot, out of hand, and I got scared. I ran away and hid, and Hetty..."

Tears start to fall from Mum's eyes. Her shoulders are hunched over, and she releases a small moan. I wrap my arms around her and hold her close. A big part of me is aghast, horrified even, but I know she needs comfort, not questions. There will be time for that later.

"They never let me tell anyone what happened. Your granddad told me I was to blame..."

She trails off again, and I feel anger well up inside me. How could she have been treated so horribly by her parents? I've always known that Granddad Harold was a bit of a shit, but

Grandma Arabella? I'm appalled that the woman I know could have behaved like this.

"But you were only a–"

Mum cuts me off before I can finish. "I know. I know. This is what I'm working through with Dr McCabe. It's hard for me to talk about, but I needed you to know. I think it will help you understand the next bit better."

I hope Mum feels able to keep going. This feels like the tip of the iceberg, and I sense there is so much more to say. Plus, I'm anxious and impossibly curious to know what the next part could be. Mum straightens her back and blurts out the last thing I was expecting her to say.

"I see ghosts."

I gasp, and despite myself, I almost laugh. Not this again.

"Not actual ghosts. I have visions, hallucinations, flashbacks, whatever you want to call them. They're of me, Mum, and Hetty from the past. I call them my 'guests'."

I remember Mum explaining why she freaked out at me in the bathroom and how dismissive I was. Is she serious?

"They're like a constant replaying of the day that Hetty was hurt, and Dr McCabe thinks they appear because I've been forced to forget it all and pretend. I think he might be right, and I'm scared, and..."

Mum sobs and wraps her arms around her knees, pulling them up to her chest tightly. Guilt engulfs me. She is deadly serious. And the last time she tried to open up to me, I yelled and ridiculed her.

"Oh, Mum." I find myself sobbing, too, and I pull her head in toward me, letting her weep onto my shoulder. I whisper into her ear, "I'm so sorry. I didn't believe... I had no idea. I can't imagine..."

Honestly, I truly can't imagine, and if I'm honest, the whole idea completely creeps me out. How has Mum managed to cope with all of this? How have I never known that she was suffering with such terrible secrets? The fact that she is seeing things – seeing people in our house – terrifies me to my core, but I can't tell her that. It's scary for me to hear her say these things, but, for her, it must be utterly petrifying.

We hold each other, and we cry. Mum lifts her tear-stained face to look at me.

"I'm so sorry that you have me for a mother. You don't deserve any of this."

More tears fall down her face, and a hot rage rushes through me at the injustice of it all. It's downright unfair that she should feel this way. She has done nothing wrong. I put my hands onto her cheeks and speak as clearly as I can.

"I am lucky to have you as my mother. You are brave, kind, and stronger than I could have ever imagined. I love you." We embrace again, and I feel some of the weight and tension in her shoulders dissipate.

"Thank you, beautiful girl. Thank you."

I can sense she is done sharing for now, and I don't blame her. She has been carrying a burden I knew nothing about; a burden so heavy I'm surprised she hasn't broken already. Telling me must have been so hard, and I meant every word about her bravery and strength. It's like meeting a completely new person.

We sit quietly and hold each other. Conversations about Dad will have to wait for a little while.

I don't think she could handle what I need to tell her.

16

TAMSIN

When I wake, I know immediately that the baby, baby Hetty, is not there. It's the absence of sound that hits me first. I panic and sit up too quickly, worrying that she will have flipped over like Hetty did in real life, and I'll be greeted with a lifeless, still body. But she's not there at all.

I climb out of bed cautiously and walk around the bed, even checking under it, but she has gone. I lower myself slowly and sit next to where she has been every morning for as long as I can remember, stroking the crumpled cotton of the duvet cover. Warmth spreads through me as I understand that all I need to do to set us free from this waking nightmare is acknowledge her and accept her. What happened is no longer hidden and festering in my brain. I have freed us both. There isn't a lot that I have been proud of recently, but I feel a welcome sense of pride in this moment. I bend down and gently plant a kiss on the surface of my covers, and I imagine the feel of Hetty's soft forehead beneath my lips.

"Thank you, Hetty. Thank you for helping me." A tear escapes, and I mark the moment with a few minutes of quiet contemplation.

The possibility of a shower alone feels like too much to hope for. I will understand if the girl – if I – am still sitting in the bathroom. But I hope I've done enough to prevent my mind from conjuring up her presence.

As I tiptoe towards the bathroom, my anxiety increases with every step, despite my gut feeling that the bathroom will be empty. The door creaks ominously as I push it open, and my eyes immediately lock on to the side of the bath. The place where I ran to hide. The place where I felt a terror so acute that I didn't remember my baby sister.

There is nobody there.

Entering the bathroom, I breathe a huge sigh of relief. This is the first step on my road to recovery, the encouragement I need to continue on my path of truth and honesty. I crouch down and sit in the very same spot that she inhabited. I pull my knees up to my chest, and instead of shaking and crying with fear as I did as a child, I close my eyes and smile. I take myself back to that moment many years ago and allow myself to be immersed in the memories.

I begin to tremble as familiar feelings of terror and confusion begin to flow through my body. I inhale and exhale slowly, welcoming the emotions and memories of my younger self. They are my memories, and I mustn't try to push them away.

Finally, I make a promise. I vow to the little girl who once inhabited this very space that I will forgive us both for what happened. This will not taint our future.

"It was not your fault, Tamsin."

Immediately, my mind attacks me with the counter arguments and the horrible things my father said to me. I let them in and this time, I fight back. I defend us as I should have done many years ago.

"You are wrong. This was your doing, not mine, and I am not to blame. You let me and Hetty down." Guilt still creeps in despite my insistence, and I know it will take a long time for me to stop feeling this way. "The guilt belongs to you, Dad." Pausing, I realise I am not being wholly honest. "And I'm sorry, Mum, but my guilt belongs with you too. I can't hold it for you anymore."

Placing responsibility on Mum is hard for me. She was also a victim of my father's cruelty, and I don't want her to be unhappy. But I need to talk all of this out with her, and I resolve to call her this morning once Summer has left for college.

Summer is in a rush this morning, but we make time to hug and exchange a few words. I'd hate it if we returned to being distant from each other.

"Thank you for last night, Summer." I pull her close to me and squeeze her tightly.

She emits a strangled noise and laughs. "Wow, that was a serious hug!"

"Well, I am serious. Thank you. From the bottom of my heart."

She cuddles into my chest. "It's okay. I'm glad we talked. I mean, it was a lot, don't get me wrong. But I feel better. Don't you?" She pulls away and looks up at me expectantly.

"I do, sweetheart. I feel a lot more like me again. We need to always keep talking like this."

Summer glances at her phone. "I've really got to go, Mum. Love you."

I call after her as she races around the living room, haphazardly grabbing everything she needs for the day. "Love you, too. Say hi to Amma for me."

She turns and plants her hands on her cheeks in mock horror akin to Edvard Munch's *The Scream*. We both laugh and wave our goodbyes. Hopefully, her day goes well. I know that rejection from Amma would be devastating for her.

Cup of tea in hand, I make my way to the sofa. It's a little early to phone Mum, so I wait impatiently for half an hour with the phone in my hand. A symbol of my intention.

I dial Mum's number and wait for the cursory five rings. She answers, and I'm equal parts relieved and overwhelmed at the thought of actually having this conversation.

"Hello." She sounds bright and cheery as usual, and although I know this conversation will undoubtedly cause her pain, her happiness can't be at the expense of my own anymore.

"Hi, Mum." I try to sound light and breezy.

"Oh hello, dear. What a lovely surprise!"

She's right. I guess this is a surprise. We only saw each other at the weekend. I wouldn't normally be in touch for a while.

"Everything okay? How are you and Summer? Gosh, it was absolutely lovely to see her. What a fantastic young lady she's becoming–"

"Mum," I interject. She'll keep talking forever if I don't butt in, and I don't want to lose my nerve and end up in a conversation about her latest social activities.

Mum is quiet, and I hear her breath quicken, her voice considerably quieter now. "What's happened?"

I swallow and steady my nerves. "Nothing's happened, Mum. Everyone's fine."

"Then what…"

"I need to talk to you about something. Something important." I swallow again. My throat is dry and my tongue feels too big for my mouth.

"You can talk to me about anything. I hope you know that."

I scoff internally and then shake away the negativity. I have to approach this the right way if I want it to help me.

"It's about Hetty." Mum is silent, so I continue. "I want to talk about what happened to Hetty when she was a baby. What *actually* happened."

Mum's voice is high-pitched and dismissive. "What do you mean? I'm not sure that–"

"Mum!" I interrupt her forcefully, and she stops talking straight away. I can't let her derail me. It has to be now. "I know what happened that day. I remember it as if it were yesterday. I can't live in this lie. It's making me… well, it's making me unwell… mentally, I mean."

Admitting any concerns about my mental health is always hard for me with Mum. She's fantastic in so many ways. When Alex left, she was so supportive and understood that I was sad and upset. But she was present in a very practical way. I know she's always there, but emotionally, I only feel comfortable discussing positive things – the celebrations and the good news in my life.

She sounds upset. I can hear sniffing, and her usual confidence has vanished.

"If it's already making you sad, I can't see how going over old ground again is going to help."

Getting angry with her will not be helpful, but I can feel the years of oppression rising to the surface. Being unreasonable will give her an easy excuse to hang up the phone and avoid me. I weigh all of this up in less than a second and decide to let it all out anyway.

"Again? What do you mean again? We have never once talked about what really happened. You have never once told me the truth. Not once! I have carried this horrible memory with me every day. Dad was a fucking monster towards me, constantly telling me it was my fault. My fault! A fucking child."

I can hear Mum trying to break in and speak, but I don't listen and keep going, momentum and rage building. The lid is off Pandora's box now, and I'll be damned if she is going to force me to put it back on.

"Dad may have been the worst, and if he was here, he'd be hearing this too. But you! You, with your fake cheeriness and ludicrous bright clothes and lipstick, as though dressing like a clown will somehow make you happy and lovely. It's all a complete fucking lie. You should have protected me. I am your child, and you let this happen to me."

I'm going off track now, being spiteful and spitting out things

I'm not sure I agree with entirely. My heart is hammering, and the heady rush of finally releasing all of this poison is invigorating. Mum has stopped trying to interrupt.

"You left me with Hetty. You should have been taking care of her. You left your children scared and alone. I was terrified. You should have taken us away. You knew what he was like. What if Hetty had died? You wouldn't be wearing all those stupid fucking clothes in jail, would you? Would you?"

My throat is raw, and my voice breaks painfully as I begin to weep. I throw the phone away from me in disgust, livid with myself for letting things escalate so quickly and not giving Mum any time to talk. I lost control, and I'm not proud of it, but at least it's out there now.

This truth of ours is ugly, twisted, and agonising, and I simply couldn't control how it left my body. I reach for the phone and wipe my swollen eyes. It's no surprise that Mum is no longer on the line. A deep sadness encompasses me as I hold the phone close to my chest and try to steady my runaway breathing.

The phone buzzes against me, jolting me. Unsurprisingly, it's a text from Mum.

> I am coming over now. We can talk. Not shout. I will tell you everything. I'm sorry. Mum.

The tone is very different to her usual messages, and I'm impressed that she wants to speak to me in person. I'm not sure I'd like to face me just now. In hindsight, I shouldn't have tried to have this conversation on the phone. It was a weak thing to do, and I ended up screaming my frustrations out into the ether and forgetting the impact my words would have on Mum. I need to see her face, look at her, and remember that she is a flawed human being who, I know for a fact, loves me dearly.

I text back.

> Okay. Thank you.

I consider adding an apology, but I think she deserves that in person. I make my way to the bathroom to freshen up and wait for her to arrive.

No more anger. No more hate.

Only healing.

17

TAMSIN

Mum's familiar footsteps crunch up the garden path, and I open the door before she needs to knock. I have tried to stop crying, but the tears keep reappearing. My face is swollen and painful, and I have a thunderous headache.

Guilt slaps me in the face when I see her pale, make-up-free complexion. Insulting her appearance was completely out of order, and I feel utterly ashamed for it. It's obvious she's been crying, too, and she wipes her eyes with a macerated tissue.

"Can I come in?"

Sadness crashes over me at how meek her voice is. I haven't heard her speak like that since Dad was alive, and I'm devastated I have brought that out in her again. I pull her into the hallway and throw my arms around her, sobbing violently into her shoulder. We stand there holding each other, and she strokes my hair gently. I don't want to let her go. I want her to tuck me into bed and keep stroking my hair, but we need to talk. I slowly pull away from her embrace and hold her cold, shaking hand. We walk hand in hand to the living room and sit next to each other on the sofa.

The atmosphere is so tense I can barely breathe. Mum's chest is rising and falling rapidly. She doesn't take her eyes off me. I whisper and try to hold back the tears.

"I am so sorry. I shouldn't have said a lot of what I did. It all just came tumbling out, and I was angry, and well, I'm sorry. I really am." Mum reaches out with her other hand and clasps both of mine in hers.

"Shhh." She is smiling lovingly at me. Her eyes are watery. "There is no need to apologise, sweetheart. I'm the one who should be apologising." She lets go of me and covers her face with her hands, emitting a long, mournful moan. Her shoulders shake, and I'm overwhelmed by how vulnerable she looks.

It's hard to find the right thing to say. She does owe me an apology and, more than that, an explanation. Instead of speaking, I place my arm around her shoulder and give her time to compose herself. After a few minutes, the silence starts to feel uncomfortable. If she doesn't say anything soon, then I'm going to have to. She must sense a shift in my mood as she sits up and holds my hands in hers again before breathing out a long sigh through pursed lips.

"I know I don't deserve any sympathy, but this is going to be very hard for me to talk about, so, although you have every right to, if you could not shout at me, I think I'll be able to tell you what you need to hear." Her eyes are pleading.

"I won't shout. I just want to know, Mum. I need to know. It's killing me. I don't think I can cope anymore."

Mum's face drops, and she winces as though suddenly pained.

"I can see that you know this already, but yes, the story we told everyone about Hetty rolling over in her cot was a lie." Resentment bubbles, but I push it away and stay perfectly still. "I've thought about it every day since, and I need you to believe me when I say I had absolutely no idea that this was hurting you so much. I didn't even think you remembered. If I'd have known…"

She drifts off, and I have to stop myself interjecting. I won't be taking any blame for hiding how I felt. It's what they told me to do. No, it's what they made me do.

"I hate myself for not taking you and Hetty away from your father before that day. None of this had to happen, and it was because of my weakness that it did. I will never forgive myself for it."

Hearing how much she hates herself is hard for me to listen to.

"It wasn't all your fault, Mum. It wouldn't have happened at all if Dad hadn't been so horrible." Mum holds her hand up gently, and I stop speaking.

"That may be true. But I could have stopped it at any stage. I could have left him beforehand. I could have grabbed you and Hetty and left the house when that argument started. I could have told the truth when the ambulance arrived. But I did none of those things."

I can see how much this hurts her, but what she is saying is true, and we need to share this pain, not hide it.

"I have been living with my head in the sand for so long. Fooling myself that because you and Hetty were thriving, I owed it to you to move on and be happy. Your father was such a dark cloud in my life, and when he was gone, I felt so much happier. You and Hetty both had children and families, and I didn't want to rock the boat or affect your bond as sisters. Carrying this darkness with me every day is soul-destroying, and you're right, the clothes and the silly earrings are all for show. They help me create a version of me that I'd like to be for you and Hetty. I have put you both through enough. I didn't want you to have to think about me at all. I just wanted you to be happy."

I am stunned to hear how similarly Mum and I have been feeling all these years. We've both been suffering in silence, thinking it was the best thing for our children.

"I think I understand, Mum. That sounds a lot like what I've been doing with Summer. But since Alex left, I've been failing. In fact, even before he left, when we stopped being quite so happy, it all started coming back to the surface."

Mum squeezes my hand. "Tell me. I'll understand if you say it's too late for me to listen, but I want to try. I don't expect you to forgive me for what I have done, but I want to be here for you."

I squeeze her hand back. "I started getting flashbacks of that day." I think that's probably a better term to use than hallucinations, and perhaps now I understand what's been happening, a more accurate one, too. "I would get flashbacks of Hetty on the bed, of me in the bathroom, and of you, too. They were relentless and happened every day. I started drinking too much wine to try and cope. But in reality, drinking only made it so much worse." I see Mum flinch as I mention alcohol, and I'm not sure why. "I've been seeing a psychiatrist, and he is really helping me. The flashbacks seem to have disappeared. This is the first day I haven't had them in such a long time. Dr McCabe has helped me see that I need to confront all of this to be well. That my body has started to reject the lies."

Mum is quietly listening. Focused on my every word.

"I haven't been drinking either. It's early days, but I think it's going to work as long as I know and accept the truth."

Mum reaches out and strokes my face. She looks genuinely heartbroken by my admissions.

"I had no idea you were suffering. I knew you were upset about Alex leaving, and I'm so sorry that what happened has affected you so terribly. You don't deserve any of this. I should never have left you with Hetty." A strangled sob escapes from Mum's mouth. "The consequences of that day fall completely with me and your father. You are one hundred per cent not to blame, and I'm so sorry that you ever felt like you were. I was so selfish and caught up in my own miserable life. There is no excuse." Mum is babbling now, overcome by emotion. I grasp her hand tightly.

"I can't imagine what it must have been like for you living

with Dad. When he wasn't there, when he was working away in London, I loved our life. Even after what happened with Hetty, we were all so much happier when he wasn't around."

We sit in silence for a few moments, and I remember Mum's bright, happy face from when we were younger. I know she did what she could to keep us happy and protect us from Dad. I know I haven't told her that enough.

"You did your best, Mum. You were stuck in an impossible situation, and I know I haven't said this enough, but I think you were amazing." Tears prick at Mum's eyes, and I feel mine welling up, too. "I mean it. You loved and protected us the very best you could." Mum opens her mouth to speak, but I want to get this out. "What happened with Hetty was tragic, and after all the guilt I've suffered over the years, I can only imagine how you feel." Mum hangs her head, sad and wounded. "But we owe it to Hetty and ourselves to live a good life now. To look to the future. Dad is gone. Hetty is happy, and I don't want to speak for her, but I am sure she loves you dearly and appreciates everything you did for us."

Mum raises her eyes to the ceiling and lets out an almost exasperated puff of air. What was that? Certainly, it's a weird response to what I've just said. I raise my eyebrows at her, and she turns to face me.

"Sorry, I didn't mean that to come out like that."

"Well, it did come out like that, so what did you mean by it?"

Mum wipes her eyes and gathers herself. "It's nothing really, just that sometimes I think Hetty puts on an act too."

I'm shocked by this. I thought it was apparent to everyone that Hetty is one of the most genuine people you could meet. I have never thought she was putting on an act. If anything, she's more honest than I can cope with most of the time. As though Mum has been reading my thoughts, she continues. "No, I didn't mean with you or with her own family, just something under the surface directed at me, but it's probably just my own paranoia.

Ignore me, I'm being silly." She waves her hand as though to flick the words away.

I watch Mum carefully. I've seen her lie before and I know she's lying to me now. Trying to push this under the carpet. I don't call her out, but I don't change the subject either. There's something here that feels important, something that I will have to tease out of her.

"Does Hetty know what happened?" I feel a sudden flash of annoyance at the thought that maybe I've been the only one of us living this damaging lie all these years. "She said something to me at the weekend. Telling me that it wasn't my fault and that it pissed her off that we didn't talk about it. It totally took me off guard and was the thing that forced it all back to the front of my brain. Does she know?"

Mum squints and twists her mouth. She's irritating me now. I sit back slightly and fold my arms, letting her know I won't be fobbed off this time. Mum straightens, and I can see she has sensed the change in tone.

"Sort of. Well…" She stops talking and focuses on a spot on the wall.

"Just answer. If it's the truth, you don't need to stop and think. Don't make things up, otherwise what on earth are we doing here? Tell me. Does Hetty know or not?" My voice is louder now, and my breathing has quickened significantly.

"Okay. Okay, sorry. Look, I am telling you the truth. I'm just trying to find the right words."

"The right words are the truth, Mum. Just get on with it."

Her face becomes stony, but I'm not backing down. I mean everything I've said to her about her protecting us as children, but we are both adults now, and I want complete honesty from her.

"Hetty and I had a conversation a bit like this a few years back."

I can feel a pulse pounding in my temples, and I immediately want to cut in and demand to know why I wasn't included. Why I've been left out. It takes all of my self-control to sit still and keep my mouth shut.

"It wasn't as... intense as this. Hetty asked me about something she thought she'd overheard as a child and didn't know if it was a real memory or not."

I'm impatient and rattled now. I also have a weird nervous energy rising inside me that I can't explain. A dark apprehension. "What did she say?"

"She said she'd heard me and your father having an argument, and I'd said something about blaming myself for what happened to Hetty, then Harold said something like, 'Not this again. Stick to the story', and then something else about too much time having passed and... well, I think that's it really."

My mouth is dry, and my chest is tight. "What did you say to her?"

"Not a lot, just that when it happened, me and your father were having a big row downstairs and that I blamed myself for not checking on her sooner, or maybe I could have heard something if we weren't yelling so loudly."

Mum is being far too blasé about this, and my chest is getting tighter. "And me? Did she ask about me?"

"She didn't. But I thought she might, so I mentioned that you were in the bathroom, probably trying to stay out of my and your dad's way. I told her you came out when you heard all the commotion and ambulance noises and that you were very scared."

"So you lied to her?" My voice is a hoarse whisper.

"Actually, Tamsin, I don't think I did." I'm surprised by Mum's indignant and overly confident response. "Look, I know what happened has been very traumatic for you and I am sorrier than I can say about how it has affected you. But do remember that Hetty's life was changed that day."

I'm winded by her words, knowing she is right. It's too easy for me to get caught up in my own part in all of this, and I need to remember to be grateful.

"Almost everything I told Hetty was true. There's no good in telling her about you. Yes, technically, it is a lie, but I stand by it. It is not an act of selfishness. It is an act of love. For both of my daughters. I think if you take a step back and consider what hurt the truth would cause, then you will agree with me."

I don't know what to say. I both agree and disagree with her. This is all so utterly exhausting. Mum reaches out tentatively and places her hand on mine.

"Hetty was very understanding. As you said yourself, she knew exactly what your father was like. She told me that she doesn't blame me for what happened, and she even said how sorry she was you had to see all that and wanted to make sure you didn't feel guilty either."

"She did?"

"Yes, and I told her you were very upset about being in the bathroom and worried about whether you could have done something. She was very insistent that it was just a terrible accident."

"Why didn't you tell me?"

"Because I had no idea that you even remembered. Clearly, I was wrong, but I promise that the decisions I have made were to try and cause the least harm. The lesser of two evils. None of my decisions have been perfect, but then I've always had imperfect choices to pick from."

Mum looks precisely how I feel. Wrung out. Her shoulders hunched, a tear-streaked face, and an overwhelming air of sadness emanating from her. She opens her arms, and I move closer. We hug tightly, and a silent understanding passes between us. We are done talking for today. I feel a flood of relief. I can't give any more right now. I give Mum one final squeeze before releasing her and shifting back across the sofa.

"I'll make us some fresh tea."

"I'd love a tea. I'll just go and sort myself out in the bathroom while you put the kettle on."

She leaves the room, and once again, I notice that just recently, she's looking older. Hopefully, we can try to end our morning together on a much better note. Now everything is out in the open, we can talk without this hideous cloud hanging over us.

My hair feels dry and frizzy as I run my fingers through it before stretching out my arms towards the ceiling. My joints screech.

Something catches the corner of my eye, and I freeze. A cold sweat starts to break out on my neck as I slowly turn my head towards the kitchen. I rub my eyes and walk tentatively towards the window. Her form becomes clearer the closer I get. A scream begins to rise up in my throat, but I push it back down, planting my palms on the sink and staring directly at her. My admissions have ridden me of two of my three shadows. Yet the woman in the garden remains. I can feel her reaching out to me, tugging at a memory that is just out of reach, on the periphery of my consciousness. What do I need to do to make you disappear?

I scrutinise her. Willing myself to understand what she wants. Her answer to my plea appears abruptly in my head. A simple sentence that drops seamlessly into my thoughts.

"You need to remember."

I beg her silently. I *have* remembered. Can she not see what I have been through? First with Dr McCabe and then with Mum. I speak aloud this time, hoping she'll reveal her secrets and set me free. "Why are you still here?"

I spin around suddenly as I hear Mum's footsteps entering the kitchen.

"What did you say, dear?"

I fumble for words. "Nothing, just trying to… uh… remember something."

Mum walks purposefully towards me. I turn my back to the

window, trying to shield Mum from the visitor in the garden. Will she be able to see her? Mum looks distractedly around the kitchen before grabbing the kettle and walking to the sink. She gives no sign that she can see the willowy figure. I glance at the garden and back to Mum, knowing that I must be behaving strangely.

"What have you been doing? You haven't even put the kettle on, never mind made tea." Mum pats my back and smiles. "Don't worry, sweetheart. You sit down, and I'll sort it."

Mum switches the kettle on and stops, looking directly through the kitchen window. My heart lurches, and time seems to stop as I wait for her reaction. She points into the garden, and I hold my breath before Mum turns towards me. I examine every inch of her face, my eyes dancing wildly.

"I've got an excellent gardener who can trim that tree for you. It's blocking the sun."

I exhale harshly and try to regulate my breathing. Mum continues to make tea. Either she hasn't noticed my erratic behaviour, or she's being kind and not pointing it out.

"Thanks, Mum. That would be..." My mouth is too dry to finish the sentence.

Mum pushes me gently towards the table. "Sit down, would you? You're obviously parched. I'll bring this over with some biscuits in a minute."

I walk zombie-like to the table and almost fall onto the chair. I can see Mum pottering around in my peripheral vision, but I stare straight ahead and focus on the wall.

The words fall into my mind again. So clear and precise.

And this time, they feel like an instruction.

"You need to remember."

18

SUMMER

Amma's waiting for me at college the next day. I can sense her annoyance as soon as I see her. I'd promised I'd call her last night, but after everything with Mum, I just couldn't face it. I feel awful for ignoring her texts, and I hope she understands.

She's leaning against the wall, with her arms folded and her legs crossed at the ankles. Despite her irked expression, my heart flutters as I approach her. She is so incredibly beautiful it hurts.

"Well, hello, stranger."

I'm not surprised by Amma's sarcastic comment. If I were her, I'd be annoyed, too. We never ignore each other. I hold out my arms as though in surrender. "I am so sorry."

She raises one eyebrow. "I mean, Sunny, someone better be dead or dying. Otherwise, I am seriously pissed with you."

My face drains of colour, and I see Amma instantly regret what she's just said. She rushes towards me and grabs my shoulders.

"Oh shit. I'm sorry. That was a stupid thing to say. Has... I mean, are you okay?"

I pull Amma into a hug.

"No, nothing like that. You just freaked me out a bit. Everyone is fine. It's just..." Amma fixes me with a severe, concerned look. "Look, my mum told me some really serious stuff last night. I couldn't call you. I wanted to."

Amma squeezes my hand and looks deep into my eyes, urging me to share with her.

"It was a super heavy conversation, and I really want to talk to you about it. Can we walk together after college?"

"Of course, we can. Can I get even a hint?"

I laugh at Amma's cheekiness. "I mean, this isn't the kind of thing where a hint is even possible. It's pretty deep and a bit sad, really. For my mum, I mean. There are so many things I didn't know, and it explains a lot about why she's been really weird recently."

We turn and walk into college together.

"In that case, I will wait with bated breath until the end of the day. But no running off, okay?"

I roll my eyes playfully. "No running off, I promise."

"Okay. I better run. Come find me at break. Not about this serious stuff. I just want to see your lovely face." She flashes me a wide, bright smile, and my heart swells.

"No problem. I'll see you later."

The tips of my cheeks flush as she waves and jogs away.

My concentration is appalling, and I barely scrape through each lesson without my inattention being noticed. I don't think I've taken in a single word, and I have no idea if I have any homework. I've been back and forth all day about what to tell Amma. I think I need someone to talk to about it, and I trust her implicitly. She wouldn't tell anyone. We're best friends. She would never betray me. But I love my mum more than anyone in the world, and I know she would be completely crushed if she thought Amma knew what had been going on.

Amma is already waiting for me when I leave the building. I've purposely dawdled from my last class, trying to make sure that most people have already left. I don't want anyone to be able to hear us. My heart is thudding in anticipation of what I am about to reveal. I share almost everything with Amma, but never anything this serious, and I'm scared it will freak her out. What if it means she doesn't want to be around me anymore? Amma throws her arms around me, and I hug her back weakly.

"Sorry, I was late out of class."

"No, you weren't. But I don't care. You're here now."

My eyes fill with tears, and I swallow with difficulty. Amma links my arm and encourages me to walk with her. We amble slowly and in unison.

"Okay, I can see how scared you are. So I'm going to say this once, and then all I'm going to do is listen until you're done." She pauses for dramatic effect. "I love you, Sunny."

My heart stops, and I am completely taken aback until Amma continues, and I realise she's not declaring the kind of love I initially thought.

"You're my best friend, and you can tell me absolutely anything. I mean it." She squeezes my bicep and then releases her arm from mine. We walk side by side, our shoulders occasionally brushing.

"Right, here goes, then. My mum is a lot more unwell than I thought. Yes, she's been drinking a bit too much, and yes, she's been really down since Dad left us. But it's worse than that." My mouth feels so dry, but I force myself to continue. "She's been seeing things."

I feel Amma stiffen beside me, and I swiftly turn my head towards her. Her face is blank before she forces it into a sympathetic smile.

"Keep going. I didn't mean to be weird. It's just not what I expected you to say. Honestly, keep talking." She faces forward and takes a step.

I fall in sync with her and take a deep breath. "She's been seeing people, like hallucinations or something. She's seeing a psychiatrist and getting help. I'm actually really proud of her."

My voice cracks, and I suppress a sob. Amma squeezes my hand and rubs her thumb softly across my fingers.

The whole story begins to tumble out. I tell Amma what happened to Aunt Hetty and how Grandma Arabella and Granddad Harold made my mum keep everything a secret. I can hear Amma's breathing quicken as I speak. I tell her about Mum's visions and how she's trying to talk through it all with her doctor in the hope she'll come to terms with it all and they'll disappear.

Amma simply listens. Just as she promised she would.

"Anyway, that's about it. Sorry to dump it all on you, but I kind of needed to say it out loud, and I haven't got anyone else who I trust or who isn't involved in some way. I just..."

Amma stops walking, and I stop, too, anxiety clawing at my insides. When I turn to look at her, I see her eyes are filled with tears, too. Guilt overwhelms me.

"I am so sorry. I shouldn't have made you listen to all this horrible shit. It's not fair for me to put it all on you. Just forget I told you. Honestly, I'm fine. Mum and I can sort it out. It sounds scary, but honestly, it's not a big deal."

Amma hugs me fiercely, and I melt into her arms. She whispers into my ear, "Shut up, would you? You should have told me sooner." She pulls away and wipes her eyes. "And it is a big deal. A very big deal. Don't you ever hold things like this in. It's not good for you. Always tell me. I'm always here."

I can see the sincerity on her face, and she almost seems mad at me for not telling her before now.

"Thank you." It's all I can manage to say before my voice deserts me.

"Anytime."

We start to walk again. I feel a sense of freedom at having this out in the open and enormous relief at her reaction.

"I think it's pretty cool that your mum told you. She must trust you loads. My parents totally treat me like a kid, and they'd never open up like that."

I feel another stab of remorse for betraying Mum by speaking to Amma.

"Well, your parents have each other. It's just me and Mum now. We kind of have to share with each other. Plus, things had started to get beyond weird. She had to tell me something."

I go on to tell Amma about the night with the throwing up and Mum screaming like a banshee at me. I manage to tell the story with a hint of humour, relieved to discover that I've actually gotten over the horror of the events of that night. Amma's jaw literally drops at the story.

"Are you serious?"

I laugh. "Believe me, I wish I wasn't. It was horrendous."

"Wow, I don't know what I would have done. But at least you're both okay, and it got you talking."

"Yeah. We just need to keep talking. And that brings me to the next thing."

"Er, there's more?"

I puff out my lips and roll my eyes. "No, thankfully not. What I mean is, I need to tell Mum what happened with Dad."

Amma's eyes widen. "Do you think that's a good idea? She's obviously got a ton to deal with just now. Do you think she can handle it?"

My stomach is in knots even thinking about it. "Honestly… I don't know. But look at what Mum told me. I can't hide this from her forever. I think I just need to tell her."

"I guess so. She might be really mad at you for hiding it from her."

Amma's right. Mum and I are in such a good place at the moment. The last thing I want is for our relationship to go backwards.

"I know, and she's probably right to be mad. I should have told her at the time, but I didn't know how to. She thinks Dad leaving us is all her fault and that I'm pining for him or something. I think it might help if she knows he wasn't the man she thought he was."

"Sheesh, rather you than me."

"Right? Mum has been so messed up because her family have been lying to her. It's going to be awful telling her that I've been lying, too. But I'm just going to have to do it. And now that we're in this huge sharing situation, I reckon I should do it sooner rather than later."

Amma grimaces. "Quick and painful!"

I decide it's best to speak to Mum tomorrow and make sure I'm feeling less drained before I tell her about my last ever conversation with Dad.

I've always believed that some lies are kind, but mostly, I've discovered they only fester and start to leach out and poison everyone. It's time for a fresh start for our little family of two.

I only hope she'll forgive me.

19

TAMSIN

I'm looking forward to seeing Dr McCabe this morning. An opportunity to release the tirade of things that I need to expel and get his thoughts on. Much has happened in a short space of time. My honest conversation with Summer, speaking with Mum about Hetty, and the disappearance of two of my guests.

Hopefully he'll be able to help me understand the persistence of the woman in the garden. Her continued presence is telling me something and memories keep trying to come through, but they are poorly formed, and they fall away from me before I can begin to piece them together. I've been living a strange partial existence with so many key pieces missing, partially asleep and only now beginning to wake up. I am desperate to open my mind to the past but, despite my best efforts, my mind continues to shut me out. The woman in the garden holds the key. I am certain.

———

"Good morning, Tamsin. Please don't take this the wrong way but you look exhausted."

I crash down onto the chair. "No offence taken. I am completely exhausted. Things have been very full on."

"Then I guess we'd better get started. Start wherever you think is best."

I tell Dr McCabe everything that has happened since I last saw him. It all rages out of me like a tsunami, and on several occasions I have to remind myself to breathe. He jots down notes occasionally, but mostly focuses closely on me. I am used to this now. I no longer feel any need to hold back anything from him, nor does he need to provide me with any encouragement to talk. When I am done, I glug down almost the entire glass of water in front of me.

"Well that explains why you are so exhausted. That is a lot to have happened since we last spoke."

"True. I am worn out, but I want to keep going. I need to keep going. I feel like I'm on the precipice of something even bigger than what has already happened, and if I don't keep going forward, then I might run away and hide again. I don't want to do that. It will make everything I have done so far feel like it was for nothing."

Dr McCabe nods in understanding. "I appreciate that, but you mustn't push yourself too far. That could be detrimental, too. I think you're in danger of becoming overwhelmed by all these revelations, and if, as you believe, there is more to come, perhaps you need a little decompression time."

I know he is right, and perhaps I haven't explained all the positive things well enough.

"Yesterday evening was nice. Summer came home from college exhausted and we made a conscious decision to have a nice, quiet evening together. It was lovely. We didn't avoid talking about things, instead, we just decided not to. It took all the anxiety away, and I ended up sleeping really well. I think if we had talked rather than relaxed, I would be comatose today rather than just knackered." I manage a small laugh.

"That is so good to hear, and very sensible. There is a lot for you to work through together as a family, but you need to remember to take time together and just be in the moment. Actively prioritise it, and schedule it in if necessary."

I nod, imagining myself writing, "be in the moment" on the calendar.

"We've got about half an hour of our session left. There is no way we can talk in depth about everything you have just told me. My suggestion is that we explore the incident with the woman in the garden and try to tease out what that might mean. But I am very happy to be guided by you."

He leans back and crosses his legs, a flash of lurid green sock catching my eye as his trousers hitch up slightly.

He sees me looking. "I'm a fan of a jazzy sock." We both laugh. "So, what would you like to talk about?"

"The woman in the garden. Definitely. I think she's trying to tell me something." Dr McCabe nods and waits for me to elaborate. "I can understand why she would be telling me that I need to remember. I've been suppressing so many memories. But it's hard for me to accept that I've been living this almost zombie-like existence. My brain only partially working. Isn't that hideous?"

Dr McCabe furrows his brow. "You're being rather hard on yourself there. Yes, you've been living in denial of some things, but that doesn't mean you've been living some sort of partial existence."

I consider this. There have been so many full and wonderful experiences in my life. Summer easily occupying the top spot.

"What I can't comprehend is why she would say, 'you need to leave him'. Alex left me, and Mum never told me she thought I should leave him. I thought she had a decent relationship with Alex. Our marriage broke down because of the strain of what was happening to me. I naively confided in him I had started to see things, hoping he would help me, but I'd already pushed him too far and rather than help in any way, it broke us completely. Summer lost her father because of me."

Dr McCabe leans forward. "Do you mind if I come in there?"

"No, not at all."

"Lots of marriages break down for lots of different reasons, but that doesn't mean the people involved don't continue to be parents. Why isn't he in Summer's life anymore? She is old enough to maintain a relationship with her father separately from you. Unless there's something you've not told me yet?"

I don't enjoy being challenged like this, but everything he says is absolutely true.

"Well, there are a couple of things. First, he's not even in the country anymore. He got a job in New Zealand. I still can't believe he did that and abandoned Summer."

Familiar resentment blossoms inside me. I may be to blame for pushing him away but disappearing halfway across the world is on him.

"I've always assumed that's how she feels about it too. Anytime I bring it up she changes the subject. I used to ask her about flying out to see him but she always brushed it off, and eventually I stopped asking."

I sit and ponder that for a while. It's been a long time since I asked Summer how she feels about Alex and whether she'd like to see him.

"She doesn't even speak to him on the phone. Unless she doesn't tell me about it. Although, I get her phone bills, and I haven't seen anything that could be a call to Alex."

I sit quietly for a few moments more. Dr McCabe is right. Something doesn't quite fit.

"It sounds like you and Summer need to have a conversation."

We certainly do. Selfishly, I could do without dragging up everything about Alex again, there is only pain and regret, and those are the last things I need to be feeling at the moment.

"Yes," I say quietly. "Yes, I think you are right. I need to at least give Summer the opportunity to talk about it."

"Let's put a pin in that for now if you don't mind. I'd like to go back to why the woman might have said–" He looks down at his notepad to check the exact words, but I don't need any reminders and we both say in unison. "–you need to leave him."

Dr McCabe watches me curiously, waiting for me to try and explain these words, but I can't find anything to say. I've been going round in circles in my head about it and only becoming more confused. Eventually he breaks the silence.

"I think we've ascertained that the baby and the girl you were seeing were some sort of flashback, a memory of something that really happened. What do you think about the woman? Do you think she is a buried memory too?"

It hadn't actually occurred to me that she could be anything else.

"Uh… I think so. She is definitely my mother. Not my mother as she is now, but she looks like Mum did when she was younger."

Dr McCabe nods. "So, that day, the day when Hetty was…" I see him searching for an appropriate word. "…injured. You told me that Hetty was on the bed, and you were sitting in the bathroom. Do you think this means your mother was in the garden? Did you go out to the garden or speak to her?" My face creases with confusion. "I'm simply extrapolating. If this woman is your mother, on that same day, then I'm asking you to try and remember her being in the garden, then you might be able to understand why you're visualising her."

My head is swimming and I do my best to play back the events of that day. None of it makes any sense. Mum and Dad were arguing downstairs. I could hear them. There's always a slight chance Mum went into the garden while I was hiding in the bathroom, but even if she did, I wouldn't have seen her.

Abruptly, something occurs to me in a flash and I physically jolt at the realisation.

"No."

Dr McCabe leans towards me. "What, Tamsin? What is it? Let the memory come. Don't hold back."

My mind is jumbled, and I shake my head to try and focus on what I want to tell him. "The woman is wearing a dressing gown. I wasn't sure before but I am now. Mum wasn't. She was wearing clothes that day. I'm sure of it. I can remember."

"Keep going. Talk it out loud with me."

"Mum had a dressing gown just like that and when I've seen her face in the garden, it's definitely her." Dr McCabe nods along, and I continue to verbalise every thought the minute it comes into my head. "She's my mum when I was a child, but she's telling me to leave Alex. That makes no sense at all. How could she say that when Alex wasn't even known to us then?"

I'm missing something, something huge, but I just can't get to it. It's like a word being on the tip of your tongue, but no matter how hard you try, it just won't form in your head. I rest my head in my hands and squeeze. Willing it to work, and to stop hiding things from me.

Dr McCabe interrupts politely. "Would you mind if I say something?"

I don't look up. "No, please, do. I'm at a complete loss."

"Okay, what I'm hearing is that you are sure the woman in the garden is an image of your mother when you were a child, and that she is telling you two things – 'you need to remember' and 'you need to leave him'. Is that all correct so far?"

I manage a nod.

"You're also telling me that in the vision your mother is wearing a dressing gown but you are sure she was dressed differently on the day Hetty was rushed to hospital. Yes?" I nod again. "Plus, after confronting the events of that day, you are no longer seeing visions of you or Hetty, but your mum is still in the garden."

I take in his every word, baulking at the ridiculousness of my life. I look up slowly, meeting his gaze. "What are you saying?"

"Nothing revelatory, I'm simply repeating back what you have said to me, but I do have a thought."

I am so confused, and my nerves are frayed beyond belief. I rub the back of my neck.

"What? I'm glad you have a thought. I'm drowning in nonsense in here." I point to my temple.

Dr McCabe's face softens, there is genuine sympathy in his expression. "I know you've already had a difficult conversation with your mum this week, but I think you're going to need to have another." Even the suggestion of this fills me with dread and exhaustion. Why does this all have to be so hard? "It depends on how open you're prepared to be with her, and my advice would be to be as open as you possibly can. Ask her what she thinks this means. Ask her if there was ever a time where she said those things to you, a time where she was as you describe her in the garden."

I know he's right. It was the conversation with Hetty at Sunday lunch that was the catalyst for me remembering what happened to her. I've tried so hard, but I think I need Mum's help to unlock my memories. Dr McCabe and I chat for a while about the best way to approach the conversation, and I leave our session feeling a little less apprehensive.

On the drive home, I make a promise to myself to call Mum as soon as I get home. I won't make the same mistake as last time, there will be no yelling down the phone. I'll simply call and ask if she can come round, or if I can go to visit her. Nerves roil in my stomach, and I feel once again as though I am standing on the edge of an abyss.

Something enormous, something life changing is about to happen.

I try to convince myself that it's only anxiety and apprehension eating away at me.

But somehow, deep inside, I know I am wrong.

20

TAMSIN

Mum sounds a bit under the weather when she answers the phone. Her voice is croaky and lacking any of her usual exuberance.

"You okay, Mum? You sound awful."

Mum gives a little cough and sniffs. "Nasty cold, dear. Nothing a tea and honey won't fix." I feel unreasonably annoyed at this unexpected hurdle in my plan. Surely, it's unfair to ask Mum to have a serious talk when she's feeling unwell. She obviously needs to rest. "Anyway, don't worry about that. How are you?"

"Um, I'm fine. I've... well, I've just come back from my psychiatrist appointment, and I wanted to come and chat with you about something. But... I can wait until you're better. It's nothing serious, just something–"

"Come on over then."

I'm glad Mum interrupted. I was babbling and probably in danger of blurting something out over the phone again.

"No, no, you need to rest. It can wait."

"Tamsin, just come over, will you? I can hear something in

your voice. And honestly, I'm fine. It's only a bloody cold. Get in the car and come over."

"If you're sure?"

"I'm more than sure. As long as you don't mind me looking a little snotty and dishevelled. It would be lovely to see you."

I can hear sincerity in her voice. Although she's kept a major secret from me, I still believe Mum is almost always genuine and has no hidden agendas. We say goodbye, and I jump in the car before I can change my mind.

Mum wasn't exaggerating. She opens the door, wrapped in a blanket. A wad of tissues crumpled in her hand. Her nose is swollen and bright red. She looks exactly like the people you see in adverts for cold medicine. I step inside and close the door quickly.

"You need to keep the heat in. Gosh, Mum, you look dreadful. Are you sure you're okay?"

"I'm fine. It'll pass in a day or two." Her pronunciation is blunted by her heavily stuffed-up nose. She smells of eucalyptus and the general aroma of illness. She gestures to the sofa and sits in the armchair across the other side of the room. "I don't want you catching this and taking it home to Summer. Keep your distance."

I do as she says, crossing and uncrossing my legs nervously.

"So, how was your appointment?" Mum wipes her nose and looks at me through hooded, watery eyes.

I'm getting used to being more open about how I'm feeling with both Summer and Mum. It's nice to see that the shame I felt has dissipated and was, in fact, completely unnecessary.

"It was good. It's helping. I feel... better. Not completely, but definitely much better."

Mum nods pensively. "What did you want to talk to me

about? I'm glad you called. We do need to keep talking." Mum smiles. She is trying to be patient, but the undercurrent of anxiety is unmistakable.

"I have a memory. At least I think it's a memory, but I can't work it out, and I think you might be able to help."

Mum's already pale face drains even further, and she can't hide the apprehension in her voice this time. "I'll do my best."

"It's a flashback of you, and you're wearing a dressing gown, but you're standing in the garden. You look like you did when I was young. Maybe around the time that everything happened with Hetty. But I don't remember you being in the garden then. Were you?"

Mum looks shell-shocked. I've undoubtedly hit a nerve. She speaks very clearly and purposefully. "No. I was downstairs with your father."

I nod and keep my eyes on her, watching her every move. "That's what I thought, too."

Mum doesn't offer up anything further, but this conversation is far from over. "But did something like that happen? Maybe the day before or after? When you were in the garden and I came up to you?"

Mum's eyes are flitting around the room, and she blows her nose noisily in an obvious bid to distract me and delay the conversation. Finally, she answers me, "No. I don't remember anything like that." Her tone is clipped. An obvious ploy to disguise her deception. I'm not doing this with her again. I won't let her hide things from me.

"In the flashback, you say to me, 'You need to leave him.'" I watch as my words physically knock the breath out of my mother. She puts her hand to her heart and holds it there. "Don't even try to tell me there is nothing in this, Mum. I saw what those words just did to you."

Mum wipes her eyes with the mangled tissue and takes a raspy breath in and out.

"What I can't understand is why you would be telling me to leave Alex. I don't ever remember you telling me to do that. Did you? What don't I know?"

Mum's eyes are closed now, and she focuses on her breathing. The urge to shout at her is strong, but she looks awfully frail and vulnerable. I need to know what she's hiding. So, instead of leading with anger, I try desperation.

"Mum, please. I won't be mad. I promise. I just need to know. I can't get better otherwise." I mean every word that I say. I need to clear the fog that has been preventing me from seeing my life for what it really is. I can't heal until everything is out in the open. Mum looks up, and I plead silently with her, my eyes drilling into hers.

"Tamsin, I don't ever recall telling you that you should leave Alex. In fact, I'm certain that I didn't."

I nod, unsurprised. I've come to realise that the words "you need to leave him" are perhaps more of a message than a direct memory. But I am at a loss as to what this all means, and I hope Mum has more to reveal.

"However…" Mum's throat rattles as she tries to clear it. I can see that speaking is painful for her. "…that's not to say I didn't think it sometimes."

I'd been prepared for this. Although I have run every possible scenario through my head in the last few hours. From the sublime to the ridiculous.

"What do you mean? Alex wasn't a bad husband. It was my bat-shit behaviour that drove him away. I'd say he put up with more than most men would have."

Mum sighs. "I know that's how you feel, and I'm not denying that you must have become very… challenging to live with."

I can see Mum treading carefully with her words, but I wish she'd just spit it out. "But…" I gesture with my hands for her to keep going.

"But there are things I think you didn't see properly."

"You mean things people have kept from me." Resentment crackles inside me, but I do my best to maintain a civil tone.

"In some cases, maybe, but mostly, I'm sorry to say that I think you were rather blind to some of Alex's faults and behaviours. He wasn't as supportive as he should have been about a lot of things. And far too eager to throw in the towel."

Mum is being kind and gentle with her explanations, which I appreciate, but she is frustratingly vague.

"You blamed yourself far too much. Your marriage breakdown was not entirely your fault. I know that's what you believe, and I've tried hard to tell you that you can't take all the blame, but you don't want to listen."

She is right. I've ignored everything she ever said to that effect. I felt like I was being pandered to and didn't want to hear it.

"So what are you trying to tell me, Mum? Be honest. I need to hear it. What did Alex do that made you think I should leave him? Tell me, please."

Mum inhales noisily. "I can't."

Anger rises up inside me. "Of course you can! How can you say that?"

Mum holds a hand up to silence me, and I stop speaking immediately. The look on her face is serious. "I can't tell you."

I want to scream, but I sit and wait, knowing she is about to say something that could change everything.

"I can't. But Summer can."

All the blood drains from my face. What is Mum telling me? Has Summer been keeping secrets from me, too? I stand and quickly sit back down. Suddenly feeling faint.

"Summer?" I whisper.

"I promise, Tamsin, I will tell you everything I know, but you need to speak to Summer first. I'm so sorry to do this, but I can't tell you more than that. Summer needs to have the opportunity to speak to you before me."

My head is swimming with horrible thoughts of what my daughter might have been keeping from me. Summer has been so insistent about us being open and honest with each other. Maybe Mum has misinterpreted something Summer said, but I can see from Mum's grave and guilty expression that I am fooling myself. I stand slowly this time, barely able to focus on anything in the room. Mum tries to join me, but I put my hand on her arm.

"You rest."

She leans back without argument. "Will you call me later? I'm sorry, but I just don't think it's my place to say anything until you've had a chance to speak to Summer. But I'd like to know that you are both okay after you talk. Would you do that for me? Please."

I nod and gather my things. I have a gnawing craving for alcohol and nothingness, but I refuse to give in to that. I'm proud of my new-found sobriety, and I won't let alcohol back into my life. I need to be fit to have a serious conversation with my daughter as soon as she returns from college.

I have no idea what about, and I am terrified by the thought of what I might be about to learn.

21

ARABELLA

Tamsin leaves, and I pull the blanket up to my neck. I do feel very ill despite my reassurances to her. Guilt sweeps through my body. I know that I have broken Summer's trust in order to save my own skin. I have blatantly used my granddaughter to deflect further questions about Tamsin's flashback of me in the garden. But I had to say something, and in fairness, I answered the question she asked me, even if I swerved the pertinent point.

Alex was not the fantastic husband she thought he was, and Summer has been hiding things from Tamsin that need to be unearthed. But that's not the reason for my guilt.

Of course, I remember that day in the garden. It haunts me every waking moment. Tamsin has assumed the timing incorrectly, though, and I won't be offering up the truth unless I have to.

That day was not the day Hetty suffocated, or the subsequent days. It was years later, and a day that I can replay in my head second by second. A day that I had always hoped Tamsin would never remember.

22

SUMMER

BEFORE

The Day Alex Left

I'm weary as I walk up the path to our house. High school is hard and so different to primary school. Most of us in my year look exactly how old we are, thirteen or fourteen, but some kids in the older years look like fully grown adults. It's pretty intimidating. There's one guy who has a full, bushy beard.

It's not necessarily harder for me than anyone else in my year. I have great friends, am sporty, and I do pretty well in all my classes. It's just such a lot of work, and I come home every night exhausted.

Things would be much easier if I could come home and relax a bit more. Everything has gone completely sideways between Mum and Dad. They argue all the time, and it's making Mum really weird. Unless it's her being weird that is making them argue. I don't know, but it's definitely a mess.

Dad is super intolerant, too. It's like he can't be bothered with anyone unless they're behaving perfectly. He's only interested in us if we don't cause him any hassle at all. I feel awful saying this because he's my dad, but I don't really like him anymore. We used to play together loads when I was small, but we barely spend any time together now. He's not violent or really terrible or anything. Still, he's not a very nice person to be around, and he is so selfish. Like, if I told him I was super unhappy and really struggling, he wouldn't care, as long as I didn't show anyone or as long as it didn't impact him in any way. Technically, you could say he's been a good dad. He takes me to football practice and watches my games, he doesn't shout at me or anything, but he's just sort of… nothing. I don't know how to describe it better than that. I'm also pretty sure he'd prefer that I liked boys, not girls. He hasn't actually said it out loud, but I can see disappointment in his eyes.

As I trudge up the garden path to our front door, I wonder what greets me inside. Mum has been so agitated lately that it's as though she's afraid of her own shadow. I think she's a bit down too. She's changed a lot recently, and not for the better.

As I reach out to open it, the front door swings violently open, and I almost fall inside, my momentum and the weight of my school bag propelling me forward. Mum stares at me as though I am the last person she expects to see, despite school finishing at the same time every day. Her face is white, and her eyes are darting around as though looking for something. She clears her throat and runs her hands through her hair.

"I'm, uh, I'm just heading out." She gives me a manic smile that borders on creepy, and for a second, I can't quite believe what has happened to my mum. It's happened sort of gradually, and she hasn't really wanted to talk about it, whatever "it" might be. But the woman standing before me is a shell of the woman she used to be. She is frazzled and humming with anxiety.

"Okay, I'll come with you," I say, trying to force some brightness into my voice and not let her know she's scaring me just now.

Mum slows down briefly and seems to click back to reality

for a moment. "No, it's okay, love. I can see you're tired from school."

"It's fine. Yeah, I'm tired, but... anyway, where are you going?"

"Just popping to the shop for some bits. I forgot a few things we need. I won't be long. Thirty minutes, forty-five minutes tops. You go in and get settled, and then we can all have tea together when I get back. That sound good?"

In honesty, it does. I don't want to go straight back out again, especially not to the supermarket. But there's something niggling at me. I don't want to leave Mum alone, and a big part of me doesn't believe her anyway. Nobody acts like this on a routine trip to the shops. Mum doesn't give me time to answer before she jumps into the car and screeches out of the drive, barely checking for traffic as she takes off down the road. At least she does drive in the direction of the supermarket.

Maybe she just needs some space. Dad's presence can feel so oppressive. I hear Dad's footsteps approaching the door and I step in to meet him.

"Hi, Dad. What's up with Mum? She looked pretty upset."

Dad scoffs and rolls his eyes. "It would be easier to tell you what isn't wrong with her." I'm horrified but not surprised by his lack of empathy. He puts both his hands on my shoulders. "This has been going on for far too long. It's not fair of your Mum to be putting us both through all this." I furrow my brow at him. I can't work out how his brain works. "Oh, come on, Summer. Are you seriously saying you think she's a good mother? A good wife?"

He laughs mockingly, and I pull away sharply, letting his arms drop to his sides. I put as much strength into my answer as I can muster.

"Yes! Yes, of course, she is. I love Mum, don't you?" I cross my arms, and my eyes start to fill with tears.

"Look, that's neither here nor there. She's unstable, and we can't be around her anymore. There are things that you wouldn't understand."

I'm furious now. How dare he? Mum might be a bit anxious and wound up sometimes, but she's anything but unstable. Most of the time she's amazing, but she has bad days, just like the rest of us. I can't believe what I'm hearing.

"She is not unstable!"

"Summer, I know you don't get it, and that's fine. You're only a kid."

I've never felt more patronised. Dad has become like a complete stranger to me. He has no idea who I am or what I'm capable of understanding.

"I do get it!" The fact that I'm shouting and holding back sobs is not adding weight to my argument, but I can't believe how callous he sounds. "I am fourteen years old, and I understand plenty. You would know that if you actually paid attention to me once in a while."

Dad looks at me as though I am a toddler throwing a tantrum. "Stop trying to make this about you. I give you plenty of attention. What more do you need? Why do you and your mother have to be so damn needy?"

I wish I could see through his stupid face and into his brain. How can he possibly believe what he's saying? I hate the way everyone seems to think that Dad is the best thing ever. He is so good at putting on an act. With Mum, what you see is what you get. Surely that's better?

"Your mother will be gone for an hour, I reckon, and I don't want us to be here when she gets back."

My blood runs cold.

"What?" I whisper.

"I've had it, Summer. I've put up with more than most. I'm not spending any more time here being miserable and surrounded by her madness. Like I said, it's not fair. We deserve better. Now, go and grab some stuff, and we'll go to my sister's house. We'll work out what to do after that. I've got lots of options."

Options? Is that what we are to him, an option? I am

flabbergasted by his utter lack of care and love for Mum. No wonder she's sad and anxious if this is how he treats her. I feel as though I'm crumbling inside, but I force myself to stand firm.

"I'm not going anywhere. This is my home."

Dad puffs out a breath and looks at me like I am completely stupid. "Have you not heard what I've said? She's dangerous, and we're better off out of here. Leave her to it. That way, nobody else gets hurt." He stops suddenly and adopts the tone he uses when he thinks he's doling out the world's greatest life lessons. "Sometimes you just can't help people. You have to cut your losses and move on. Now, let's get on with it. Time is ticking on."

I am utterly floored by all of this. It feels so out of the blue. I must have missed something. I've always known Dad is a self-centred man with pretty poor emotional intelligence, but this is something else. This is wicked. I can't believe he is going to discard his wife of over fifteen years so casually. It's unbelievable.

Tears are falling freely down my face now, and I can feel myself shaking with a cocktail of fear, rage, and disbelief. I pray that Mum walks back through the door any second. She needs to see this. She needs to be the one to leave him. She doesn't deserve to be abandoned like this. I know it will break her.

"Can't you just wait and speak to Mum? Surely, she deserves an explanation. You can't just run away like this."

He starts to walk up the stairs, and I follow him.

"I can, and I will. You don't see it, but I have tried. I've tried everything, and it's only getting worse. I've had enough." He points towards my room. "Get some of your things. We can come back for the rest later."

I look into my room and feel completely helpless. I walk in and sit on my bed, feeling empty and totally lost as to what to do next. I can hear Dad opening and shutting cupboards and drawers, mixed with bursts of unintelligible muttering from their bedroom. All of my thoughts are clouded by a thick fog. I'm shook from attempting to untangle them by his sudden appearance in my doorway, with a pile of bags surrounding his feet.

"What are you doing? Come on."

I don't move. Tears fall noiselessly down my cheeks. "No," I croak and plead with him silently not to leave like this.

He walks over to me and tries to lift me up by one arm. I pull away, and he grabs me harder, digging his fingers into the flesh of my arm. It hurts, but I refuse to make a noise. I struggle against him and eventually wrestle free, leaning away from him and stroking my throbbing arm. He rolls his eyes at me. I don't think I care about him actually leaving, but doing it this way is so cruel and unnecessary.

"I'm not going with you."

Dad shrugs his shoulders and walks away from me as though I've just declined the offer of a cup of tea rather than refusing to leave our home with him.

"Well, don't say I didn't offer. I was willing to take you with me, and if you won't come, that's your own fault, not mine. I won't have people saying I left without you."

I watch as he collects his bags. As always, he only cares about how this looks and how it reflects on him. I'm sitting in front of him, destroyed and weeping, and it's like he can't even see me. I'm his only child, and he doesn't care one way or another whether I go with him or not. It's a devastating blow and not one that I think he is capable of comprehending.

I look down at my hands. Without noticing, I've picked up Jenny Bunny, my teddy rabbit that I've slept with for as long as I can remember, and I'm absent-mindedly stroking her ears. There is a horrible silence now. I'm not going to fill it. I have nothing to say, and I know I can't do anything to change his mind.

"Right, I'd better be off. I've left a note for your mother and..." He stops momentarily, but I don't look up. I won't make this easy for him. I want to stay silent and just let him leave, but his lack of ambivalence about walking out without me is too much. I hear myself shout.

"A note! You're leaving her a note!"

His eyes widen in surprise. I've never shouted at him like this. His lips curl, and he takes several swaggering steps towards me.

"Yes, Summer. I'm leaving her a note." He leans down and lifts my chin forcibly with his thumb and forefinger. "Is there anything you'd like to say about that?" His menacing face is uncomfortably close to mine, and I can feel his warm breath on my face. He is goading me. I shrink backwards and cuddle Jenny Bunny tighter. "Yeah, I thought not." I watch him smirk with a disgusting sense of satisfaction.

I've heard people describe "seeing red", and I'd never known exactly what they meant. But I do now. A red mist descends before my eyes, and my self-control disappears. I scream the words at him, spittle flying from my mouth, "You're a fucking coward and I hate you."

I want to throw things at him, bite him, stamp on him, but my head is suddenly thrown back by a sharp crack to my cheek. My eyes are blurry, and my brain feels as though it's rattling around inside my skull.

He's slapped me. My dad has slapped me in the face.

My hand flies up to my cheek, and I try to focus my eyes on him. He is standing over me now, and I see him reach both of his hands out towards my neck. My mouth falls open, and I am struggling to find any air in my lungs. He's going to strangle me. I know I need to move. Now. Right this second. I have to kick out or run past him to safety, or I'm going to die right here. But I can't. I'm completely pinned to the spot with terror and utter disbelief that he could do this to me. I close my eyes and wait for the inevitable. But nothing comes.

I open one eye tentatively and look him in the eye. There is still anger in his face but I can also see fear and disbelief. He looks down at his hands and whispers softly, "I'm sorry,

149

Summer." His face is white now and I watch as he stumbles out of my room. I hear him walk uncharacteristically softly down the stairs before gently opening and closing the front door. I lie down and pull Jenny Bunny into my chest, hugging her fiercely.

Once the numbness wears off, I cry. I pour out all the anger, sadness, and horror I feel at what just happened. I have no idea what to do next. Mum is going to come through the door any minute and find Dad gone and me lying on the bed. I can't think. My brain is a swirling mess of fear and guilt. I can't tell her what he just did – she'd call the police, and I don't want that. With Dad gone, they might think she's not fit to look after me. But I'm fourteen now and can mostly look after myself. Will Mum blame me for Dad leaving? My thoughts are coming too thick and fast, falling over and into each other chaotically.

There was nothing I could do to stop him, but I'm terrified that Mum won't see it that way. Should I have screamed and begged him rather than getting angry and lashing out? Would it have made a difference? I don't think so, but maybe it would have delayed him long enough for Mum to get home, and then they could have talked and worked something out. Instead, I screamed and pushed him so far that he hit me and – well, I don't want to think about what he was going to do next. It's too horrific to even contemplate. But what if I was mistaken? Perhaps he was only reaching out his hands to apologise. Oh God, I don't know. I really don't know. This is all such a fucking mess.

I lie still, willing myself to think of something I can say to her, but nothing comes. There is nothing I can say that won't break her heart. What Dad said is completely untrue. Mum is not dangerous or unstable. But she is struggling, and she definitely is anxious sometimes. This will smash her into a thousand pieces.

A car pulls onto the drive, and I pray with everything I have that it's Dad's car, not Mum's. Even though I never want to see him again, I still want him to come back and tell her to her face.

But my prayers are fruitless. I know the sound of Mum's car

engine. As she gets out of it, the sounds of her feet follow, softer and swifter than Dad's. Everything starts to go too fast, and panic flows through me. I close my eyes tight and roll over, turning my back away from the door and this new, horrible world that Dad has left us in.

My breathing is deep and thick, and it occurs to me that I sound as though I'm asleep. I can't pretend to be asleep, that would be cruel. I couldn't possibly pretend that I didn't see Dad leave or that I simply didn't know he had gone. I need to tell her what he did to me. I need to be strong and be honest with Mum. Help her understand that Dad isn't kind or nice at all and that we're better off without him. Yes, if Mum and I hold this devastation together from the beginning, if I tell her that we are in this together and Dad is selfish, cruel, and violent, then I know we will get through this much easier.

Mum enters the front door, the swish of shopping bags following her. I hear her walk around downstairs. She shouts my name and then my dad's. The silence hurts. She runs up the stairs, and I try to make myself sit up and run to her, to throw my arms around her and assure her that everything will be okay. But instead, I lie there. I hear Mum stop in my doorway. She gives a small laugh and comes over to the bed. All I need to do is sit up, or speak, or turn around, or anything at all. But I don't move. I keep my eyes closed and breathe in and out, feigning sleep, paralysed by cowardice.

Mum covers me over with a blanket and sneaks out of the room. I hear her tiptoe downstairs, the familiar creak of the floorboards groaning as she makes her way through the downstairs rooms. Suddenly, the footsteps stop, and I hear a kitchen chair scrape across the floor. Dad must have left his note on the table.

There is silence for a while. I am barely breathing. And then I hear Mum break. One loud strangled wail, followed by smaller, pitiful, heart-wrenching cries. I don't dare move, and I've already proven to myself that I simply can't move even if I want to. Tears squeeze out through my clenched eyelids, and I choke back the sobs that wrack my whole body.

I've never felt more alone or ashamed. It's all my fault. I let my mum find out this terrible news in this awful way. But I've missed my chance now. I wish I could go back in time, but I can't. I'll have to keep up this pretence. One thing is for sure, I never want to see or speak to Dad again. What he did is unforgivable. I stroke my painful cheek, a horrible reminder that I know I'll need to hide from Mum.

I need to pull myself together. Everything that just happened in this room has to stay in this room. It's just me and Mum now, and I only hope this doesn't break her completely. Otherwise I'll never forgive myself.

23

TAMSIN

I wait impatiently on the sofa for Summer to return. I have to remain cool and calm. Summer won't open up to me if I start berating her as soon as she walks in the door. We've been so good at talking recently, and I'm shocked and disappointed to learn that she has been keeping something from me. My mind has been through a hundred possibilities, most of them utterly ludicrous, but it must be something big, or Summer wouldn't have lied to me.

Alex left shortly after Summer started her third year of high school, and I can remember the day as if it were yesterday. Alex and I were having another argument. We'd been arguing about the same thing for weeks. My "weird moods" as he unkindly termed them. The guests had been visiting for a few months, but I didn't tell Alex about them right away, and now, I wish I hadn't told him at all.

Alex was a decent husband and father in lots of ways, but he was also extremely cold. He was like that about everything, and at first, I was really attracted to it. He was uncomplicated and unemotional. He rarely got angry, and he was never upset. I liked the predictability, but it came at a price. Over the years, his stability developed into an uncaring nature. If I ever tried to tell him about something that was worrying me, he was dead behind the eyes. He was completely uninterested, as though my feelings were none of his business. He wanted an easy life. A life that he wanted.

He wasn't interested in compromise, and I'm not even totally sure that he loved me. But he was always there, and he didn't hurt us. He just didn't help us. It felt like a trade-off worth making at the time. But deep inside, I always knew if something terrible happened or if we went through something tragic as a family, he wouldn't endure it.

We were a disposable family to him. Who we were wasn't important to him. We simply suited his needs at that time. And that is why he left. He didn't want a wife with a mental illness, even if it was temporary. He wasn't interested in supporting me through it. He was highly scornful of mental illness of any kind, and I'm not sure he had it in him to understand it. He didn't run that deep.

I blame myself. These weren't things I learned later on. There was no fraudulent behaviour at the start of our relationship. Alex was exactly who he was – take it or leave it, and I took it willingly. I will never regret a single moment because otherwise, I wouldn't have Summer, and she is worth the world.

When Summer came home from school that day, I'd been trying, unsuccessfully for the dozenth time, to get Alex to listen to me about the guests. I'm not sure why I kept trying, an act of desperation perhaps. I suppose I wanted him to tell me I needed some help, to go and see someone about it. To confirm to me that these things happened sometimes and I'd get better. This was what I thought, but I didn't trust my judgement. I needed Alex to validate me. I needed my husband. Every time I broached the subject, he dismissed me. Sometimes jokingly and often cruelly. He would tell me I was being silly, or looking for attention, or maybe just tired. He didn't want to hear about it, and he told me very clearly how he felt.

Until that day, he hadn't seemed concerned about it at all. It was merely an annoyance, like a fly buzzing around you occasionally needed to swat away. But that afternoon, everything changed. He treated me as though I was a threat to my family and told me I was a risk to society.

I remember his words precisely, "a dangerous lunatic".

Those were some of the last words my husband ever said to me. I know he was wrong, but the shame of it ate me up, and I promised myself from the moment he left that I would get on with my life and be normal. Denial has been a dangerous drug. It has allowed me to live a relatively normal life while slowly eating away at my soul.

Summer comes through the door, and I try to fix my face into a welcoming smile. She spots the facade immediately, and I let it drop.

"Hi." Summer's voice is quiet and filled with apprehension.

"Hi." I pat the sofa next to me, and Summer comes over without hesitation. I sense her trepidation is not simply because of the look on my face. "What's wrong? Did something happen today?"

Summer is fidgeting, and seeing her look so uncomfortable hurts me.

"No, I'm fine. I just... I need to talk to you." I soften and squeeze Summer's leg gently.

"I'm listening."

Summer takes a deep breath, and I brace myself.

"I'm so sorry. It's about Dad, and I've been meaning to tell you for the longest time, but there was never a right time, and then there was all of the rest of the stuff that's happened, and... I don't know, I'm just sorry."

Summer is talking ridiculously fast yet somehow not saying anything at all. I look at her, and my heart fills with affection.

There's nothing she can tell me that will make me love her any less, nothing that I won't support her with, and I tell her exactly that. She seems to relax a little and then starts speaking. I have a feeling I am about to learn what I need to about Alex without even asking.

"The day that Dad left..." Summer scrunches her face as though she has eaten something sour as she says his name, and dread lurches in my stomach. "...I wasn't asleep. I saw him leave. I talked to him." Her words are dripping with pain, and she hangs her head in shame.

I rub her back, knowing she has more to divulge.

"He wanted me to go with him, but I wouldn't. He was so cold and awful about it, and I could see he didn't care whether I went or not." She pauses, composing herself. "I couldn't stop him. Then I got angry." Tears fall onto her legs, and I wipe them away gently. "I yelled at him, and then–"

Summer stops suddenly, closes her eyes and takes a deep breath. Her lips flutter as she exhales. I can't bear to see my daughter in pain, and I take her hand, rubbing her fingers softly with my thumb.

"Then he slapped me."

I freeze. I feel the blood leave my face, and my stomach roils violently. I try to repeat the words in my head, but they don't make sense. Summer is looking at me expectantly, and I want to comfort her, but I feel as though I'm somewhere else.

"I'm so sorry, Mum." Summer starts to cry and the shock dissipates, my innate instincts as a mother finally kicking in. I hold her face in my shaking hands.

"Look at me, Summer." She stares at me with watery, bewildered eyes. "You have absolutely nothing, I repeat nothing, to be sorry for." I fix my eyes on hers, unblinking. I need her to know this. Guilt and shame will eat away at her if she lets it, and I will not allow that to happen. She nods. "What your father did was horrific, appalling, abhorrent. And I am so sorry you felt you had to hide it from me." I want to scream obscenities and call Alex every name under the sun. But I will not let this conversation be about him or me and how I feel about what I've just heard. This is about Summer. She is all I care about.

"It's not just that. I pretended to be asleep because I didn't know what to say. I am so sorry that I let you find out from a letter. I've always hated myself for it."

I shuffle closer to her and hold her tightly in my arms.

"Oh, love. How I found out is of absolutely no importance." Summer looks up at me with dreary, damp eyes. I smile and stroke her cheek. "Your dad left because he wanted to. I promise you. And now I know what he did to you…" I look at Summer's beautiful, devastated face, and my words trail off.

"Mum, I don't think I want to talk about it." I can't hide the concern that crosses my face. I, more than most, know the devastating effects of holding things inside. "No, I mean, I will talk about it, but I don't want to right now. Is that okay?"

"Of course, it's okay. I am always here. I hope you know that." We hug fiercely and tightly. I never want to let her go. I've always tried to show Summer that I am fully supportive of any relationship she wants to have with her father. But that was before I knew what he was capable of. I never dreamed he would be violent. He never was with me. How could he do that to his own daughter? What a pathetic excuse of a man he is.

Summer speaks softly as though thinking out loud. "If I'm honest, the slap wasn't the worst thing." My heart falls at what I might be about to hear next. Summer must sense something in me as she clarifies quickly. "I mean, he was never interested in me or anything I did. He made me feel like I bored him or that I was inconvenient or something. That stuff definitely hurt more than one slap. I guess I'm trying to say that I'm not sorry he's gone, and I don't want to see or speak to him. I don't think I've ever really said that. I've just sort of avoided it."

Summer and I sit together, curled into each other. Quiet on

the outside and our minds whirring on the inside. Her revelation is devastating, and if I ever speak to Alex again, he will hear precisely what I think of him. But now I know Summer's wishes, I will make sure he never gets to see or speak to her again. He doesn't deserve her, and I'm furious that he has gotten away with his violent, disgusting behaviour.

I stroke Summer's hair, and we remain in contemplative silence. The thought of my daughter living with guilt and buried secrets of her own is heartbreaking, and I hope she's feeling some sense of relief after telling me the truth.

None of today's events bring me any closer to discovering the intentions of the woman in the garden. I have to continue my journey of healing and discovery if I want Summer and I to be happy. I need to know the purpose of her visits.

I have to find a way to make her tell me what she wants.

24
TAMSIN

There is a lightness in the air the following morning. Summer and I eat a quick breakfast together before she leaves for college. It's clear that a weight has been lifted off her shoulders. I'm desperate to know more about what happened with Alex, but I have to respect Summer's wishes and follow her lead. She looks happy and I won't burst her bubble with my thirst for answers. Her eyes sparkle, and she looks healthy and full of optimism.

We eat together every morning now. A typical family breakfast of tea and toast. Gone are the days of waking up early to dodge ghosts and throw back enough tablets to make me feel human. I simply get up and have breakfast with my girl. It is such a simple thing, but it means the world to me.

Summer kisses me goodbye. I try unsuccessfully to convince her to take a coat. It's raining out there, but apparently, teenagers are impervious to the weather. I laugh, roll my eyes, and wave her off into the wet, blustery day.

I am seeing Dr McCabe today and am keen to hear his thoughts about what my mum and Summer told me about Alex. I'm considering reducing my sessions with him. I know I'm not ready to stop seeing him yet, but I get the feeling things are decreasing in intensity for me. It would be pointless to attend sessions and have nothing new to say.

I grab my things from my room and straighten my hair in the bathroom mirror. Abstaining from alcohol and eating proper food has done wonders for my skin. I haven't been happy with my reflection for a very long time, and it's wonderful to be content with what I see looking back at me. I run down the stairs to grab my keys from the kitchen table. If I don't get a move on, I'm going to be late, especially if there's traffic. People seem incapable of driving properly in the rain, and the roads are always slower than usual.

As I walk into the living room, the most horrible, stomach-churning sight unfolds before me. Fear leaves me paralysed. My mind searches desperately for answers, but I can't think clearly through the blood pounding in my head.

There is a body lying on my kitchen floor.

A body.

Every inch of my being is screaming with shock and disbelief. A shriek erupts from my throat, and I fall backwards, putting my hand out to break my fall. My wrist jars against the wall, sharp pains jolt up my arm as I narrowly avoid crashing to the floor. My heart gallops, and I scramble to my feet, knowing that I have to at least try and help whoever this is.

I can hear deep moaning, definitely the sounds of a man. His body is partially blocked by the table, and I can't see more than a bit of his torso and thighs through the gaps in the table legs. I need to get myself together and go to him. I'm always complaining to Summer about leaving the doors unlocked, yet I've been merrily wandering around upstairs while this man has been lying on my kitchen floor.

I pause for a split second. Should I call the police? What if he has taken refuge here after committing a crime? He could be a murderer, waiting to leap up off the ground and strangle me as soon as I approach. But what if he's just come in for help after being injured somehow, and I'm wasting the precious last minutes of his life by ruminating on the best course of action?

I turn and grab a heavy plant pot from the windowsill for protection and prepare myself to approach him. But when I turn around, he is no longer there. The kitchen floor is empty, with absolutely no sign of his presence mere seconds ago. I emit an involuntary yelp and scan the room wildly, looking for where he might have gone. He's not here with me in the living room. There's nowhere to hide.

Tentatively, I take small steps towards the kitchen, brandishing the Chinese Evergreen plant, the most ridiculous weapon ever known to man. I fully expect him to be waiting around the corner for me, brandishing a knife. The house is silent. Not a single sound other than my panicked breathing and careful footsteps. I'm convinced the back door didn't open, so he must be here somewhere. I consider calling out and telling him I'm going to call the police. But a tiny part of me is still worried there's a poor man propped up against my kitchen cabinet, letting out his final dying breath, and I'm standing here being an idiot holding a houseplant.

Cautiously, I take a small step into the kitchen, but only to the point where I can see the entire room. I exhale loudly. There is nobody here.

My body suddenly slips into gear, and I put the plant on the kitchen worktop before proceeding to check every corner of the kitchen and living room. The back door is locked, and my keys are on the table where I left them. There is no way he could have got past me to the front door. I spend the next ten minutes scouring the entire house, opening every cupboard and drawer, checking under the beds and behind every door. He's not here. The only reasonable explanation is that he somehow made it out of the front door when I grabbed the plant. I mean, I was terrified. Maybe I just didn't notice.

Should I call the police anyway? Just to be safe. But what

exactly would I tell them? A man was lying on my kitchen floor briefly. I don't know where he went, and I think he might have been injured. No, I didn't see his face. They would think I was going mad and accuse me of seeing things.

And then I stop, a thought too hideous to bear hitting me like a sledgehammer. Could this man be a new guest? Was he even there at all?

The possibility that my mind is attacking me again makes me want to weep. I run upstairs and check the bed and the bathroom. No guests. But that doesn't mean anything. It's too late in the morning for the baby or the girl to be here.

I collapse onto my bed, buzzing with anxiety but somewhat relieved that there doesn't appear to be a physical threat in my house. Can I handle another ghostly apparition in my life? What will I dub this one? Perhaps the man on the floor or the kitchen man?

I grab my phone. My appointment with Dr McCabe is due to start any minute. Shit. I have no chance of making it there now. I scroll to Dr McCabe's office number in my phone and hit dial.

"Good morning, Dr McCabe's office."

I compose myself. "Good morning, I have an appointment just now. It's Tamsin Cavendish."

I hear some clicking of computer keys, and Jackson's voice follows. "Yes. Are you calling to cancel?"

"No!" That came out far too loud and urgent.

"Okaaay." Jackson stretches out the word and I cringe at my inability to behave appropriately.

"Sorry, I've..." I really should have come up with something before calling. Coming up with things off the cuff is not my forte. "I've had some car trouble." I'm impressed with myself. That excuse sounds both reasonable and plausible. "I was wondering whether Dr McCabe could do our appointment on the phone today?"

"Um, he doesn't normally do that." Jackson is clearly unhappy at having to step outside of the usual procedure.

"Can you ask him?"

"Er, I guess. Can you hold?" He puts me on hold before I can respond, and the opening beats of "Opus Number One" hit my ears. Jackson returns quickly.

"Dr McCabe says that's fine. He'll call you in a few minutes. Phone number ending 9754?"

I'm not immediately sure, so I recite my whole phone number in my head before responding. "Yes, that's me."

"Okay then, he'll call you shortly."

"Perfect, thanks."

"Bye." He's gone before I have the chance to say goodbye.

I make my way to my bedroom and get comfortable on the bed, leaving the door open so I can hear any unexpected noises that might emerge from the kitchen. As promised, my phone rings a few minutes later.

"Hi, Tamsin, it's Fergus here."

Dr McCabe knows more about me than most people, but I don't think I could ever call him by his first name. "Hi, Dr McCabe. I'm so sorry about not making it."

"Hmm, car trouble, I hear?" He asks it as a question and with a tone that suggests he knows I am lying.

"Well, no, not exactly. But I didn't want to tell Jackson that."

"Gotcha. So, it's just us now. I'm alone in my office. Talking on the phone can be tricky for this type of consultation but do try to treat it the same way. And my socks are orange today with red Scotty dogs on, in case you needed a visual."

I laugh, and so does he. Ice broken perfectly as always.

"So, where do you want to start? With whatever has happened this morning, or maybe you have managed to speak to your mother? Up to you."

I lie back on my bed and stare at the ceiling. My whole body feels antsy now that the adrenaline has left me.

"Up until about twenty minutes ago, I would have said that I wanted to talk about my mother, but I don't think I'll be able to focus until I tell you what happened this morning."

"Okay, let's do that then. Are you okay?"

I don't hesitate. "I'm pretty sure I saw another guest this morning. A completely new one. A man, and he was on the kitchen floor."

I start to describe my discovery this morning step by step, but Dr McCabe stops me, and I'm glad of the opportunity to take a few deep breaths and slow my thoughts down.

"Can I just quickly ask you something?"

"Of course."

"Are you definitely, one hundred per cent sure, there is nobody in your house?"

One hundred per cent might be a little high, but I don't want Dr McCabe to be worried.

"Yes, I've checked everywhere. He just disappeared exactly like the other guests do. He didn't go out the door, and I've checked every inch of the house. Also, now I've had a bit of time to think about it, I know he wasn't real."

"How do you mean?"

I'm not sure how to describe it other than I just know somehow, but I try.

"The guests don't look any different than normal people. They're not like spooky or anything, but there's something that I can't quite put my finger on that tells me they're not really there." I try and find some more helpful words. "The best way I can describe it is that they somehow don't seem to take up any space. I know that doesn't make sense, but then none of this does really."

"Not at all, that's really helpful. And I now feel reassured that you're not alone in your house with some random man who decided to lie on your kitchen floor."

I'm touched by his concern and, as always, truly grateful for his complete lack of judgement. He has a gift.

"Well, I think you're right. We should probably talk about this man first, but let's make sure we leave time to discuss what happened with your mum, too."

"Yes, I agree."

"Did you recognise him?"

I explain to Dr McCabe that my view was obstructed, that I was panicking and probably not at my most observant.

"Does he make any sense to you as a memory? Something that happened to your husband, perhaps?"

A sudden, unpleasant flashback springs into my mind and disappears just as abruptly as it arrived, leaving no trace.

"Er... no, I don't think so."

"You don't sound very sure."

It's hard to be sure of anything when there is so much I haven't recalled until recently. So I answer in the only way I can, with what I can remember.

"I don't have any memory of Alex lying and moaning on the kitchen floor."

"Moaning?"

"He was kind of moaning like he was hurt. That's why I was so conflicted. He didn't feel like a threat or anything. He seemed like he needed help."

There is silence on the line.

"Hello?" I say, starting to feel uncomfortable.

"Sorry, this is another reason why phone sessions can be tricky. I'm just thinking. You'd see that if we were in the same room."

I manage a small mumble of agreement. I don't really like this phone thing either, but it's better than nothing.

"So, currently, you don't know who the man is. Speaking to family members triggered your memory thus far. Maybe that's something you could try?"

I consider this for a brief moment. "No, I don't think I can. It would totally freak Summer out, and I certainly don't want to contact Alex after what I've heard this week."

I update Dr McCabe on my conversations with Mum, and Summer's secret.

"I hate that this happened to her. I think Summer was carrying a lot of guilt and anguish about it, so from that perspective, I'm glad it's out in the open."

"Of course. That's a horrible thing to have happened and a painful secret for her to keep, but I hope you know that you clearly have a strong and healthy relationship with Summer. Not a lot of people have that."

I blush, even though I'm on the phone. "I do, and thank you. I've started to feel rather proud of us. It's a nice feeling." I prop a pillow up under my head. My body is beginning to calm down, thankfully.

"It sounds like you don't have a clear understanding about the woman in the garden either. Could she be connected to this new guest in any way?" I'm struggling to think of any possible connection. "Her words, 'you should leave him', could they be relevant?"

I'm confident they are, and I wonder if Mum told me everything the last time we spoke. Did something happen between Mum and Alex?

"At our last session, you were very insistent that you were the cause of Alex's leaving, and you pushed him away with your behaviour. But, after hearing what your mum and Summer had to say, it's clear they don't share that view." I'm not sure what he is trying to tell me. "I think there's a lot more for you to explore here. Perhaps these guests aren't as straightforward, not simply direct memories." I pick at the thumbnail on my free hand. I don't understand why this all has to be so complicated. "I hope you're not disheartened by this. You're doing so well. I'm astonished at the changes you've made in such a short time."

I squeeze my eyes shut and try to focus on the positives. My life has changed dramatically, and all for the better. This is just a bump in the road.

"You've only seen this man in the kitchen once, and he may or may not come back. We are not yet certain that he is indeed a recurring guest." He's right. Maybe it was just a one-off. Something I created at that moment for some unknown reason. "Before I spoke to you, Tamsin, I was going to suggest reducing our sessions. It seemed like the right step."

I smile. "I was thinking the exact same thing, but I'm not anymore."

"No, me neither. For a start, I think it's important to meet face to face, so let's stick with how things are for now. Is that okay?"

"Yes, that works for me."

"Great. I think you need to see what happens tomorrow, perhaps have another conversation with your mother, and see if you can move forward with what your remaining guests mean. However, I will say that they don't seem to be having such a negative effect on your well-being as the two that have now disappeared. That may or may not be relevant."

I nod before remembering I'm on the phone. "Yes, I agree with all of that."

"I've avoided discussing a lot of the technical aspects of what you've been experiencing, but I think it might help if you'll indulge me in a brief explanation?"

I'm intrigued to hear what he has to say. "Okay, sure."

Dr McCabe clears his throat, and I sit up, knowing I need to concentrate on what he's about to tell me.

"I think we are dealing with both your conscious and unconscious mind. I believe that you have repressed memories due to your traumatic experiences as a child. Your brain has stored these memories away from you as a form of self-protection. Memory is a very tricky concept, and it is hard to prove any of this to be true. But my assessment is that for you to remember, you need to feel supported. Something your family and I can help with. You also need to want to remember, and even if you do, I can't guarantee the full memory will be reached. What I think you are experiencing are memory fragments, and once you can recall the whole memory, these fragments disappear."

I inhale sharply. I've never heard anything that sounded so plausible yet completely unbelievable at the same time. "Wow."

"I guess the take-home message is that I can see you are doing everything you can, and we may recover more memories over time, but we need to relinquish an element of control. Be calm and curious, have conversations with your family, but try not to obsess over it. Does that make sense?" Dr McCabe has a beautiful way of explaining things. He can effortlessly make extremely complicated things feel understandable.

"Yes, actually, it does."

"Anything you want to ask before we go?"

I can't think of anything. "No, nothing."

"Then I'll see you at our next appointment, Tamsin. Take care."

"See you soon. Bye."

"Bye."

We both hang up, and I fling myself backwards onto the bed and lie in a starfish position, contemplating my next move. I close my eyes and breathe in and out, slowly and purposefully, searching for a sense of peace and calm.

If Dr McCabe is right, and I don't ultimately have control over my memory, I have to try and approach all of this differently. I've been on a sleuthing mission, trying to uncover the deep, dark secrets of my past that my family have been hiding from me, but if that's not how it works, I have to stop.

Mum is undoubtedly holding back, but I can't force her to tell me something she won't. I'm happier than I have been in a long time, and my relationship with Summer has never been better.

Sitting back up, I decide that a proclamation of sorts is in order. I speak out loud, addressing both my conscious and unconscious mind.

"I'm going to stop digging for lost memories. I accept things exactly as they are. I welcome any memory that decides to reveal itself, but I won't force it. I'm going to live my life to the full."

The room feels eerily quiet when I stop speaking, and I feel mildly ridiculous but pleased with the assertions I have made. My stomach is grumbling, so I make my way downstairs to the kitchen.

As I walk into the living room, I freeze. Incapacitated and chilled to the bone, utterly desperate to run back upstairs to the safety of my room.

I see him. The man is back.

He is standing in the kitchen, a look of pure horror and pain on his face. His hand is pressed against his chest, and I can see something is sticking out of his clenched fist.

My eyes are glued to him, and my legs frozen to the spot as he falls. His head collides with the kitchen worktop before bouncing off the tiled floor. He lies flat on his back, his form obscured by the table.

He is moaning now. It's the same moan I heard earlier, so deep and agonising. I walk slowly towards him, remembering Dr McCabe's words and my speech upstairs to myself. I steady my nerves and force myself to keep going. If I want to remember, I have to go to him. He holds the answers that I need.

Standing directly over his supine body, I examine his strained features. He croaks out a single word with difficulty.

"Help."

I have answered him before I even consider the words I want to say. They flow from me so naturally as though already predetermined.

"You should have stayed away."

25

SUMMER

Things at home are so much better. We're going through a lot, and it's undoubtedly exhausting. But there's a sense of purpose to it all, and we're recovering and becoming stronger together.

The conversation with Mum went so much better than I expected. Yes, she was horrified, and I could see she was furious and wanted to know every last detail. I will definitely tell her, but I didn't want her to focus on the hitting bit, and there's no way I'll ever tell her what I thought he might have been about to do. I didn't even tell Amma that. And over the years I've lost my conviction about it. I was scared and dazed. I'm not sure I knew what I was seeing. The thing I needed Mum to hear was that I don't want or need my dad. She is more than enough as a parent. How could he possibly think I would leave Mum to go with him? He was utterly delusional.

Anytime Dad has tried to get in touch, I've been civil and nothing else. I can't even remember the last time that happened, and he's never visited. Not once. His emigration to New Zealand was accompanied by promises to Mum that he'd be back to visit at least once a year. I'm not surprised and rather glad he's broken that promise. He's on the other side of the world now, probably starting a new family. Good luck to him. I'm perfectly happy to be left behind, and I have more than enough people who I love, and who love me, right here.

There's one final piece of my life that still feels artificial. Being true to yourself is hard. But I have learned that it's also worth it. It removes the grumbling anxiety that lives under your skin like a chronic illness. Doing it at the time is terrifying, but it's only temporary. So, in the interest of the new honest, authentic version of me that I want to be, I've decided to tell Amma how I feel about her.

I've run through things in my head many times, with various outcomes, and I honestly can't say how it will go. The worst-case scenario is that I lose her completely, that she can't handle being friends with me anymore, knowing how I feel about her. Perhaps I'm being naive, but I can't see that happening. Amma is too kind, and our friendship is too strong for that to happen, but I need to be prepared, nonetheless.

On our way into college this morning, I casually asked Amma if she fancied going to our usual coffee shop later. She agreed without a second thought, even promising to buy me one of my favourite lemon and poppy seed muffins.

The day drags, my anticipation slowing time down to a crawl. When college is finally over, I'm annoyed to see the weather's horrendous, so I wait in the busy corridor for Amma, my eyes fixed on the floor. The howling wind and torrential rain mean we can barely speak as we walk. Someone should tell the weather it's supposed to be spring.

Thankfully, the coffee shop is only a couple of minutes away, and we burst through the door, thrust forward by the violent wind. The comforting aroma of roasted coffee beans hits me, and we rush and grab a seat by the steamed-up window. We look at each other and burst out laughing. We're both a complete mess. Hair soaked and plastered to our shiny, weather-beaten faces. Amma stands up and takes off her coat. "I'll just go and sort myself out," she says before hanging her coat up and walking towards the toilets.

I pull out my phone and use the front facing camera to examine the damage to my appearance. It's not as bad as I thought, and after running my fingers through my hair and wiping a finger under each eye, I look pretty much the same as I always do.

The waiter comes over and after making small talk about the weather, I order two lattes and two muffins. Lemon and poppy seed for me, blueberry for Amma. Amma comes back to the table just as the waiter's leaving. She looks immaculate, and her skin is radiant.

"I've ordered." My voice catches annoyingly as I realise just how nervous I am.

I know that recent events with my family have been monumental and stressful. Still, for me, this is the life-altering moment that matters most in my heart.

"Cool, thanks." Amma is bright and breezy, and I don't think she has noticed my unease. "So, what's new, Sunny? What's the update on your mum and everything?"

We both pause and lean back in our chairs as the waiter returns to our table and places two steaming cups and two enormous muffins in front of us.

Amma beams. "Yum, thanks."

I manage a forced smile, desperate for the waiter to leave.

It's now or never. I adore the coffee here, and the cakes are to die for, but if I try to take even one bite, I'm sure I'll projectile vomit all over Amma's beautiful face. Amma swirls some sugar into her coffee, and I watch her stirring, hypnotised by the tracks the spoon leaves in the frothy milk. Amma interrupts my weird staring.

"So? Tell me." She gives the top of the muffin a big sniff, and I laugh when I see a crumb remaining on her nose. She is everything.

"I need to tell you something." There, I've said it. There is no going back now.

Amma feigns an exhausted look. "Oh my goodness, what on earth has happened now?" She takes a big bite from her muffin, and I don't take my eyes off hers.

"It's not about Mum, or my family, or anything. It's something else. It's actually about… you."

Amma looks shocked, but then a dark, serious look comes over her face before she swallows her muffin and wipes the crumbs from her mouth.

"Okay, do I need to be worried? I mean, your face is telling me I should be."

"No, it's nothing bad. At least I don't think so. It's just something a bit scary for me, something I've wanted to say for a while now."

I see a slight dawning of realisation in Amma's eyes, and the look of apprehension from a moment ago softens.

"You can tell me anything, Sunny. That's what we do, remember." She smiles and the anxiety peaks in my chest, before I decide to just come out and say it.

"I like you." The words are nowhere near enough. Amma nods and lets me know with her eyes that what I've said is not enough for her either. I need to say what I really mean. I gather myself and try again. This is my moment, and I have to own it. "What I'm trying to say is I like you not just as a friend, and I was wondering how you felt about me?"

My face instantly lights up with embarrassment. I could have said that in a hundred different and more meaningful ways, but it's out there now, raw and truthful. I watch Amma's face closely, and no words are needed to tell me I'm not going to lose her friendship. I can feel acceptance and reassurance flowing from her, and it soothes me.

"That was hard for you, right?"

I puff out my cheeks before breathing out forcefully. "Just a bit." We both sit in silence for a moment. It's not uncomfortable, but the air is burning with anticipation. "I don't really know what else to say. I just felt like I needed to tell you. It got to the point where I felt like I was lying to you, and that's not something I ever want to do."

Amma looks nervous now, straightening her plate and coffee cup in no particular way.

"But that's it. All I wanted was to be honest with you, and I don't ever want to lose your friendship. I don't expect anything at all, but I needed to say it out loud."

Amma nods, and for a moment, I'm terrified she's going to cry. Upsetting Amma would break my heart and the absolute last thing I would ever want to do. She eventually speaks, her voice small and tentative.

"Would it be okay if I said I didn't know?" I'm not exactly sure what she means, and it must be written all over my face as she suddenly clarifies without being asked. "Not us as friends. That's a no-brainer. We're the best of friends, and I hope we always are. But something more... I don't know."

My heart sinks, and I try not to let it show on my face. I force a smile and try to be relieved that Amma still wants us to be best friends, but I can't help feeling devastated and rejected. A big part of me was hoping she felt the same.

"I'm sorry, Sunny, this is a bit embarrassing."

I'm not sure I've ever seen Amma so coy and flustered, and I try to put her at ease. "Well, certainly no more embarrassing than declaring undying love for your best friend and being rejected!" Amma looks wounded. That did not go to plan. "No, don't be upset. I'm just messing, trying to lighten the mood. Get back to normal."

The tension is palpable, and I hate it.

"Sunny, what I'm trying to say is I think I'm a bit behind you with stuff like that. You're more... mature, I guess. I definitely have feelings for you, but I'm not ready for that sort of thing yet."

I should have thought of that, and she's right, she doesn't speak about having romantic feelings towards anyone. "I guess what I'm trying to say is... maybe... wait for me if that's an okay thing to say?"

A swell of protective love and warmth towards my beautiful friend rises in my chest, and I reach out and take her trembling hand in mine.

"Of course!" I squeeze her hand tightly and smile at her, tears pricking my eyes.

"Thank you."

"No, thank you. I don't know why I was ever so worried about telling you and sorry for not realising what you meant then. Of course, and even if you don't start to have feelings like that, just promise me that we'll always be friends. That's what matters the most."

"Oh, one hundred per cent. Friends forever and all that."

We stare into each other's eyes for a moment and share a silent promise. And then, without any unease or difficulty at all, we slip back into our easy, wonderful friendship. A true testament to just how strong our bond really is. We eat our muffins, drink our now lukewarm but still delicious coffee and talk about college, football, and our families.

It is natural and beautiful, and I will always be eternally grateful for what we have, no matter what the future holds for us.

26

TAMSIN

I know.

I know everything.

I remember everything.

And now I know why I hid it from myself. The only people in the world who know this terrible secret are me and Mum. Summer can never find out. Some things can be forgiven, but not things like this. Summer would never look at me the same way. She'd hate me and her grandma.

This is a memory that I was right to keep hidden, and I need to put it back where it belongs, far away from anyone else. I don't care if it poisons me with terrifying visions and flashbacks for the rest of my life. The past can't be changed, and my family do not deserve the consequences of this coming out. It would ruin everything. What I said upstairs, my declaration and oath to myself, still stands. I accept things exactly as they are, and I am going to live my life to the full.

The rest of my day is as expected. I have a shower and eat some lunch. The woman in the garden makes her usual visit and I ignore her. She can stay if she wishes. She has nothing left to tell me. At least nothing that I want to hear.

The rain is torrential, but she's not cold and isn't getting wet, just as she can't appreciate any of the beautiful summer days or the view from the garden. She only sees what she wants to see.

I busy myself with housework and start prepping dinner for this evening. Everything has a slight haze to it today, a dreamlike quality. It's weird, but I don't hate it. It won't stop me carrying on with my life if this becomes my new normal.

Summer is a little later than usual from college, and I suspect she has been waiting for a lift or hiding out from the dreadful weather somewhere. The door opens and a whoosh of air follows her through the door. I go to her and help her with her drenched bags. Her lips are shivering and I have to hold back on my consistently ignored lecture about coats.

"Good day?"

Summer is pulling off her sopping boots and socks and making a series of puddles on the hallway floor.

"Yeah, good, actually."

The smell of wet teenager is far too close to the scent of wet dog, so I'm relieved when she tells me she's going straight into the shower.

"I'll chat once I'm warm and dry, I've got some nice news, but I'm desperate for a hot shower first."

"That's great. And for once, I don't have news of any kind, so go and grab yourself a shower, and I'll put the kettle on."

"Cheers, Mum."

Summer runs up the stairs and straight into the bathroom. It's barely seconds before I hear the shower running. She has the capacity to stay in the shower for an inordinate amount of time. It's likely I won't see her for at least half an hour.

I settle down on the sofa and decide to call Mum. Draw a line under everything once and for all.

She sounds a little better than the last time I spoke to her, but her voice still has a definite croak to it. We make small talk for a little while, about how she's feeling and the horrid weather we are having, and then I come out with it.

"I remember what happened, Mum."

Mum doesn't say anything right away, and I'm relieved that this will be the last conversation of this kind we will ever need to have.

"I understand why you told me to leave him, and I know what happened afterwards. I remember it all."

I hear a sharp intake of breath from Mum, and I leave space for her to respond. I avoid any direct confessions. If this were to ever come out, I can't have anything on a phone call that could be used as evidence. Plus, whilst I can hear the shower running, I can't risk Summer hearing me, so ambiguity is the safest option.

Eventually, Mum speaks. "And what are you planning to do about it?"

I can hear her nervousness, the dryness of her mouth making unpleasant smacking noises between her words. Mum has spent her entire life trying to protect me from everything. My ability to bury and repress my memories and feelings has allowed us both to live in this weird lie of a life. I forced Mum to face the reality of what happened with Hetty, but I won't accept the same now. This is different. Being responsible for a death is oh-so different, and I won't leave Summer standing in the debris of a family battered and torn down by tragedy and death.

"I am not planning to do anything."

Even though we're not together, I feel the tension between us. Mum answers almost immediately and is very clear and confident with her statement.

"And I think that is best."

She doesn't offer anything further, and from my perspective, there is nothing left to say except, "I don't want us to talk about it again. Ever."

"And again, I think that is also best."

Our exchange is purely transactional. We are making a deal

and agreeing the terms. We have both been through enough and we will stand together and hold this between us forever.

"I love you, Mum."

"I love you too, sweetheart. More than I could ever say."

I hear her sniff politely, and I imagine her crying. I let my tears fall, too. Even through the telephone, this is one of the most intimate moments I have ever experienced. Beautiful and hideous in equal measure.

"Can I ask you one little question, Tamsin?"

"Yes, go ahead."

"I'm not saying I don't believe you, so please don't feel that way, but did you genuinely forget what happened? It just seems so unbelievable, mostly because those thoughts barely leave my mind for a second. They are the first things that hit me in the morning and my last thought before going to sleep at night. They are like a constant companion."

It saddens me that Mum is affected like this, but it's not surprising and perhaps an expected penance. I take a moment and try to remember how Dr McCabe explained it to me.

"It's not that I forgot. My doctor called it repressed memories, and how he described it made a lot of sense to me. I've been letting the memories through but not in a straight line, and they've been coming back to me as flashbacks, which has been really scary." Mum makes the odd noise of understanding and encouragement as I do my best to explain something I don't quite grasp fully myself. "I've got another appointment with him tomorrow. I missed today's because... well, never mind that, but I'm going to keep seeing him for a while until things feel more settled and then, hopefully, everything will be okay."

"I hope you know you are doing so well, Tamsin. Honestly, I'm amazed and so proud of what you are trying to do for Summer. We need to leave the past in the past where it belongs."

Mum's words are exactly what I needed to hear, and I'm

grateful we're on the same page. I hear the bathroom door open, and Summer dashes across the landing to her bedroom.

"Mum, I better go. I called you quickly while Summer was in the shower."

"Yes, yes, go and be with your daughter. Give her a huge hug from me."

I smile and wish I could reach through the phone and hug her. "I will, bye, Mum."

"Bye."

I hang up and rub my forehead, smoothing out the tension. I make my way to the kitchen and busy myself with emptying the dishwasher as though the phone call with Mum never happened. If I must, I will step over a moaning, dying body on my kitchen floor every day for the rest of my life. I will do whatever it takes to protect my daughter and her future. He can haunt me relentlessly, and I will not break. My love for my daughter is stronger than anything my mind can throw at me.

When Summer enters the kitchen, I take a moment to stop and marvel at her. Her hair is wet, and she is rubbing it with the pale blue towel draped across her shoulder. She has skipped changing clothes and opted to go straight for her fleecy pyjamas.

"So, good news? Do tell."

Summer sits at the kitchen table and drapes the towel over the back of the chair next to her. I put a steaming cup of hot chocolate down in front of her, and she cradles it in her hands.

"I didn't say good news, I said nice news, there's a difference."

"Is there? Nice definitely sounds good." I'm really excited to hear what has made Summer happy today.

"I told Amma how I feel about her. We went for coffee after college, and I just told her."

Summer's smile and sparkly eyes tell me that it went well without her needing to say a word. I stand next to Summer and run my fingers through her freshly washed and combed hair, it gives off a wonderfully refreshing citrus aroma.

"Does that mean you're a couple now?"

"Actually, no. But we are still friends. No change there, which is the most important thing, I think."

I nod, confused. I agree that protecting their friendship is important, but I'm surprised that Summer determined this to be nice news.

"You can't say anything to anyone about this, Mum. I want Amma to trust me."

I sit, sensing the seriousness in Summer's tone. I've learned to recognise the moments that are of critical importance to her, and I treat them as such, even if they don't feel that way to me.

"I won't breathe a word to anyone. I promise."

Summer looks reassured. "Amma told me that she doesn't have feelings like that about anyone yet, which, to be honest, is something I've thought before. She's never mentioned anyone that she fancies."

I nod along, relieved at the fact my daughter hasn't had her heart broken but also astonished at the level of understanding these two girls have for each other. They could certainly teach a lot of grown adults a thing or two about kindness and compassion.

"And then what happened?"

Summer shrugs and takes a big gulp of hot chocolate, followed by appreciative noises. "Nothing, really. We're just going to see what happens. I'd never want to push Amma if she's not ready. Plus, now I know that even if she doesn't like me that way in the future, she still always wants to be my best friend. I can't think of anything nicer."

Summer grins, and my heart fills with joy at the incredible young person she is becoming. We chat briefly about the usual college stuff – assignments, money for various things, which teacher is currently annoying her. And it is all absolutely lovely. I am more certain than ever that I have made the right decision. Summer deserves this life, not the one she will get if the truth comes out, and I'll do everything I can to ensure things stay exactly as they are.

"I suppose you saying you had nothing to tell me means you've also had a good day?"

"I most certainly have! I don't want to be too presumptuous, but I think things will be on the way up from here on in. There are no more secrets left to jump out on me. There are no more horrible memories lurking in the recesses of my brain. I feel awake and alive and actually just bloody good for once."

Summer looks delighted, and I grin right back at her.

"That's amazing, Mum!"

"Isn't it just?"

She raises her mug as though about to make a toast and clinks her hot chocolate against my cup of tea. "To us!" she announces.

I repeat her words and mean them with every single atom in my body. "To us."

27

HETTY

BEFORE

Most people hate Monday mornings, but they are one of my favourite times of the week. It's my day off work, Gavin is in the office all day, and the kids are at school. I have six hours of uninterrupted me time, and it is absolute bliss.

Don't get me wrong, I love them very much, but the constant noise and commotion that a big family brings can be exhausting. For the next two hours, at least, I will be under a blanket, making my way through a pot of tea and diving into a novel I've been wanting to read for ages. I settle myself down on the sofa and get comfortable.

My movements may seem awkward to other people, but it's never caused me any major problems. I'm genuinely happy with my life, exactly as it is. A lot of people have it much worse than I do, and I'm grateful for everything I have. Look at Tamsin, she has arguably much better physical health than me, but mentally, she struggles a lot. She never seems happy, always fighting an internal battle of some description, constantly fighting demons. I'd find that exhausting.

I'm startled and then annoyed when there is a sudden loud knock at the door. I contemplate ignoring it. Even if somebody was rude enough to peer in the front window, they wouldn't be able to see me here on the sofa. But the knocking comes again, much more urgent this time. I'm sure it's just a pissed off delivery driver eager to crack on with his route, but there's always that small chance that something is wrong.

I throw the blanket off me, hoping I'll be back under it any minute and shout to let the impatient visitor know I'm on my way.

"Coming!" I see a dark shape through the frosted glass. It's not Gavin, but from the size and shape, I think it's a man. A nervousness creeps over me, and I have an awful premonition that my tea will go cold and my book won't be opened this morning. Something is wrong. I can feel it in my bones.

Opening the door cautiously, I'm relieved to see that it's just Alex, but when I look at his eyes, the feeling of relief dissipates immediately. He seems frantic but also furious, and I can't work out why he would come and see me. We aren't close at all.

"Can I come in?" He looks behind him as though he thinks he might be being followed. It unnerves me, but I reluctantly let him in. He looks dishevelled, his hair is messy, and he is unshaven. Alex is usually a man who takes pride in his appearance, verging on vain even.

He walks into the living room without being asked or even removing his shoes. It irks me, but I let it go in the interest of finding out quickly why he is here. He sits in Gavin's armchair, and I perch on the sofa I just vacated.

"What's up, Alex?"

He rubs his stubbly chin and exhales forcibly. "It's Tamsin. Honestly, I have no idea where to even start."

Panic sets in. "Has something happened to her?"

He snorts unattractively. "No, nothing like that. She's just..." He makes a gesture as though his head is exploding.

Anger is starting to bubble up within me. I'm not sure why he thinks he can come here and talk disparagingly about my sister to me. Doesn't he know that my loyalty lies with her?

"I'm not really sure why you've come here." I try to maintain an aura of calm despite the turmoil of emotions I'm experiencing. He huffs and puffs a bit more before leaning back in his chair and crossing his legs. I look at the bottom of his dirty shoes. Alex has always been far too self-assured, and as far as I can see, he has never had any genuine care or consideration for anyone. I have never said anything directly to this effect to Tamsin. I've gently poked her a couple of times to see if she was unhappy, but she was never forthcoming. Nobody ever really knows someone else's relationship. So I left it alone and figured that my view from the outside must be inaccurate, and who was I to object to his behaviour if she seemed happy?

"It's not exactly something I can discuss with my friends or my own family. It's… well, a bit embarrassing, really, and I don't want them thinking I'm married to someone who's losing the plot."

Losing the plot? I have no idea what he's talking about. I know that Tamsin is a bit on edge occasionally, and her anxiety can feel a bit oppressive and draining sometimes. But "losing the plot" is undoubtedly an exaggeration and not one I will let him get away with.

"How can you say that about your own wife? She has been nothing but good to you and she's an amazing mum to Summer. You've got some nerve coming here and speaking about her like that."

My breathing is quickening, and I feel flustered. I hate confrontation of any kind, and I certainly don't want to be having an argument alone with a man I don't know that well or even entirely trust.

"She's seeing things."

"What on earth do you mean?"

"Exactly what I just said. Tamsin is seeing things. Ghosts or something, people that aren't there, in the house. She's not who she used to be, Hetty, and quite frankly, I don't want me and my daughter around her anymore. What if that rubs off on Summer? I don't want both of them carrying on like that. It's bad enough dealing with Tamsin."

I fight an urge to stand up and slap his smug face. I'm very close to a couple of friends who've experienced serious mental illness, and his portrayal of it is absolutely disgusting. Futilely, I attempt to appeal to his better nature.

"It sounds like she needs some help, Alex, and by that, I mean both professional help and support from her family."

He looks at me like I'm completely stupid. "That's all very well and good, in theory. But in reality, I've got me and Summer to think about. This kind of thing isn't normal, and I'm not going to stick around to see anyone get hurt."

I'm flabbergasted by his complete and utter lack of care, but even after this short exchange, I can already see that I can't convince him otherwise.

"Is Tamsin in the house now?"

"Yeah, Summer has gone to school. She walks herself now. I'm not doing another morning like that. You don't know what it's like. How would you feel waking up to Gavin carrying on about ghostly figures in the bedroom and the bathroom? It's creepy. I'm telling you, she's lost it."

I take a deep breath and try to settle my temper. Me arguing back or shouting will not help Tamsin in any way.

"I'm sure it is difficult, and now you've explained, I'm glad you came here to talk it through. In answer to your question, if it was Gavin, then I would do everything I could to help him. I'd stand by him because he is my husband, and I love him. It's as simple as that."

Alex rolls his eyes. I'd love to throttle him.

"That's easy for you to say." Alex stands up suddenly and I'm acutely aware of the height and power difference between us, with me still sitting down, and I move to remedy it.

"No, don't struggle up."

Struggle? I get to my feet and can't hide the distaste in my words.

"It's no struggle. I can stand perfectly well, thank you."

I stare at him, and he doesn't even have the decency to look sorry or embarrassed.

"I'm going. I wanted to tell you, that's all. So somebody knows about it once we're gone."

My heart sinks.

"What do you mean, 'once we're gone'?"

"I mean, Summer and I aren't staying in that house one minute longer. As soon as she's back from school, we're going, so you or your mother need to expect a call sometime this evening."

I can't control myself any longer. This man is a disgrace and utterly oblivious to just how wrong his way of thinking is.

"Don't you fucking dare!" He looks taken aback and amused at my outburst, which only adds fuel to my already raging fire. "You are not, I repeat, not taking Summer away from Tamsin." I stand my ground, shaking like a leaf but determined to do whatever I can to stop his cruel intentions. "If you want to leave, then fine, go! And good bloody riddance, I say. You're a selfish prick and Tamsin will be better off without you."

Alex looks bemused, as though what I'm saying is entirely unintelligible. He has spent far too long coasting through life, taking from everyone around him and giving back only crumbs. He is a leech, and he has done a very clever job of painting himself as a good man. It's only when you take the time to look closer that you see he's got no depth.

Alex barely reacts and walks towards the front door.

"Piss off, Hetty. You've got no right lecturing me. Your husband is a joke, and your kids are feral."

The desire to whack him is so strong that my hand begins to

tingle. I manage to hold myself back yet again, and instead, I walk right up to him and scream directly into his face. No words, just an outpouring of hate and disgust for this soulless disgrace of a man. He wipes imaginary spittle from his face and laughs mockingly. I stop for a moment and look at him, really look at him, breathing in and out slowly, calming my rattled nerves.

He is not worth my upset or a single second of my time. Although I know that his leaving would hurt Tamsin and Summer dearly, I think in the long run they'd be happier without him. My voice has become a growl, and I bare my teeth at him.

"Get out of my house and out of my sister's life. If you even try to take Summer, then I will come for you."

He throws his head back and laughs exaggeratedly. I don't react or look away, and just for a moment, I see a flicker of unease in his eyes. It gives me strength.

"Don't underestimate me, Alex. I will come for you. That is not a threat. It is a promise."

He looks less sure of himself now but paints a fake defiance on his face. He throws up his hands. "Fine. Summer is almost grown up now and doesn't talk to me anyway. No great loss."

Even after everything he has already said, this is the comment that chills me the most. He is completely happy to leave without his daughter. He couldn't care less. I feel physically sick, but I nod at him and open the door, feeling like we have reached an understanding of sorts.

I slam the door hard as soon as he steps outside and lock it quickly behind him. I make my way slowly back to the sofa, wishing I could go back in time to the moment when I thought this was going to be a relaxing morning.

Guilt swirls around me, and I reach for my phone, considering a variety of options for my next move. Should I call Tamsin and warn her? Should I call Gavin? What if Alex comes back here? I don't want to be alone with him ever again.

Perhaps I should call Mum for advice. I have my suspicions

that she can see behind Alex's mask. I sit with my phone for a while, contemplating and coming up with no real answers.

Hours pass, I make fresh tea and I try to read, staring at the same page and rereading the same sentences over and over again. Time makes my decision for me. I can't decide what to do so I do nothing.

Hopefully Alex will go home, pack up his things and go. Then we can all support Tamsin and Summer to get through this and help Tamsin with whatever she is struggling with mentally.

I'm almost certain that he won't try and take Summer with him. He doesn't have the first idea of how to be a proper parent. In fact, how do you even take a fourteen-year-old girl? She has her own mind. It would be different if she were a toddler.

I sit in the bubble that is my living room and think, coming to absolutely no conclusions whatsoever as the afternoon seeps away from me.

28

TAMSIN

I slept well last night. Moving on is the only way forward. I can live with what I've done, and if memories choose to visit me, then so be it. It was the denial and the fear of the unknown that was affecting me. Everything is going to be okay.

It's wonderful to see Summer happy. I'm so proud of her and Amma. The care and empathy they have for each other is beautiful. It is so reassuring that if they ever do decide to enter into a relationship, it will be built on a solid foundation of mutual love and respect. And if they don't, then their friendship won't be lost.

Summer and I have a calm and peaceful breakfast together. Nothing but small talk. No major revelations or secrets to divulge. It is wonderful.

I am seeing Dr McCabe again this morning. He'll be expecting something significant after our impromptu telephone session, but I'm hopeful I'll be able to make my way through the questions uneventfully.

The sun has finally made an appearance today, a bright blue sky full of promise. I drive to Dr McCabe's office with the radio on, singing along to songs that I can't quite believe are on Radio

2. I've most certainly lost touch with new music, but I'm blissfully happy staying stuck in the nineties.

After parking the car, I relish the sun on my face as I walk towards the building. I'm used to coming here now, and I'm no longer flustered and unsure of myself. I check in with Jackson and converse with him briefly and easily. I have changed enormously in such a short space of time, and whilst confronting my past has undoubtedly made the biggest difference, ditching the alcohol has allowed me to behave in a way I can be proud of in public. I'm no longer plagued by the dreaded post-alcohol anxiety, and the thought of drinking now completely turns me off. Why would I want to sacrifice feeling like this for a few hours of oblivion?

Dr McCabe greets me with a big smile. There's a smell of eucalyptus in the room that is quite overpowering, and I wrinkle my nose.

"Is it really that strong?" He laughs and picks up something that looks like a portable white speaker, takes it to the bathroom attached to his office, and leaves it there. "It's a diffuser. My sinuses have been giving me bother. I can't even smell it anymore. Sorry, it will calm down, I hope. Let me know if you want me to open a window."

"It's fine, honestly." My eyes are watering, and I'm not sure he believes me.

"So, the last time we spoke was on the phone. How has everything been? I must say you look very well. Rested and peaceful." His voice is a little hoarse, and I suspect that if it wasn't for our appointment, he would be tucked up in bed right now.

"This wasn't what I expected to say after what happened when we last spoke, but things are actually amazing. Better than they've been in such a long time."

He raises his eyebrows. "I wasn't expecting that, but I can see from your face that you are genuinely happy. Tell me, I want to hear all about it."

My eyes flood with tears of happiness. "There's a few things. Firstly, Summer and I are in such a good place." I tell him what happened between Summer and Amma and how proud I am of her. "I can see that she is so pleased and relieved with how it went. She seems so purely happy. Plus, now that she's told me about what happened when her dad left, there's none of that making her feel anxious and guilty either."

"That's wonderful to hear, and I can see it's had a huge knock-on effect for you too. Your little family is thriving. I'm sure that feels fantastic for both of you."

I reach out and grab a tissue from the box on the table and dab my eyes.

"I hope those are tears of joy?"

I laugh. "Most definitely."

"What about the man you saw in the kitchen? Have you managed to talk to your family, or have you seen him again?"

This question was inevitable, and I've been debating how to handle it. The easiest way would be to lie and say that I never saw him again and couldn't work out who he was. Leave it as an unsolved mystery. But Dr McCabe has an incredible ability to see right through me when I am lying, and I don't want to taint my successes by making him think I am being dishonest. So I have decided not to lie to him, but also not tell him the truth.

"Yes, I saw him again. He was there when we finished our phone call."

"Okay, and could you see who he was this time. Did you recognise him?"

"Yes, when I came downstairs, he was standing in the middle of the kitchen floor, and I could see him very clearly."

I stop, blood thrumming in my veins, waiting for him to ask the obvious question.

"Who is he?" Dr McCabe looks very serious and has his pen poised for the big reveal.

"I don't want to tell you." My heart is thudding horribly as I answer and I have no idea why. These are my sessions, and Dr McCabe has been clear that I only have to reveal what I want to when I want to. But the nerves still wrestle inside me.

"Okay. Can you tell me why you don't want to tell me? You've been very open thus far. Is there a reason?"

I'm starting to panic now. "You said during our first appointment that as long as I am honest about not wanting to reveal something, then that is fine. Is that not the case?"

I'm trying to sound calm and grounded, but my voice is wavering. Dr McCabe puts his pen and book down.

"One hundred per cent. I will not push you to tell me something you don't want to. Please don't feel bad or nervous about it. If you're saying this is a deal breaker for you, then we will work with it." He smiles, and I smile back, beginning to feel a little calmer. "But, back to my last question, are you happy to say *why* you don't wish to tell me?"

I lean back in my chair and cross my arms, thinking of the best way to explain myself.

"I know who the man is, and what memory he represents. I remember all of it very clearly, and it's not something I want to talk about, that's all. It's not a past event that I need to unpick or understand better. I've worked it out on my own. Does that make sense?"

"Sure it does, and thank you for being willing to explain it. It's really helpful." I uncross my arms and sit forward again in anticipation of his next question. "Can I ask another thing? And again, no pressure to answer if you're not completely comfortable." I nod uneasily. "Was this another repressed memory, do you think? When we were on the phone, you seemed very confused about this man, and now you're quite happy and tell me that you have no concerns at all." I furrow my brow, irked by his challenge. "Please don't take offence – I'm simply wondering if this was a repressed memory or something else, something more like a secret you've been keeping."

Despite his request, I am offended, but I shouldn't be surprised that he is questioning my story's viability. Even to me it sounds suspicious. I try my best to help him understand my point of view.

"I've been living in an alcohol-befuddled haze for a long time. I'm lucid now and able to see things much clearer and recall past events more quickly. Not only that, but I've been in a perpetual state of denial with a head full of these repressed memories." I take a much-needed deep breath. "I feel like I have woken up, and at the start I needed help to wade through all these things that I couldn't understand. But I understand this completely, and I don't think it will help me to talk about it."

Hopefully, that is enough for him because I don't know what else I have to say. Dr McCabe clasps his hands together and nods silently for a while. I watch him and don't fill the gap. He likes to take a moment to process things sometimes, and I'm happy to sit here until he decides to speak.

"Very well. Actually, I think you explained that very well, and all I will say is that if you ever change your mind and want to tell me, then please do. There will never be anything other than a willingness to listen from me."

I nod and give him a half smile. There is little point in saying I will never tell him. It will only invite more discussion that I don't want.

"I feel happy, Dr McCabe. I really do. Honestly, that's not something I thought I'd ever say again. I'm excited about the future, and for the first time in forever, I feel like I am really living and not just existing. So, thank you."

Dr McCabe puts his hand out towards me.

"This is your achievement, not mine. I'm just the sounding board. But I am so delighted to hear you say you are happy. That's all anyone ever really wants, I think."

Emotions swell within me again, and I swallow down the lump in my throat.

"Absolutely."

We finish by running through the questionnaire that we did together at our first session. This time, I don't have to lie, and it is comforting to see how far I have come since I first stepped foot in here.

Dr McCabe and I say our goodbyes, and we agree to reduce our sessions to once weekly. He seems just as happy with this arrangement as I am, and unless he is hiding it exceptionally well, I don't detect any hint of disappointment at my holding back today.

He really is a wonderful man and so very suited to his job. I was worried about this conversation with him and once I tie up a couple of loose ends, I know that I can completely put it behind me.

Some things should stay in the past.

There is nothing to be gained from digging up dead bodies.

29

TAMSIN

As I drive home, I replay my conversation with Dr McCabe and consider one important thing I need to do before I can draw a line under all of this. I pull up onto our driveway, get out of the car and drop my handbag on the doormat as soon as I enter the house.

A "no time like the present" attitude has served me well with the decisions I've made recently, so there's no reason to change that now. Rushing upstairs, I rifle through my sock drawer, searching but not finding what I'm looking for. I start to empty the balls of socks, dropping them haphazardly onto the floor until I spy the small scrap of paper I hid years ago.

When Alex emigrated, he called and left me a voicemail with two numbers I could use to contact him. A new mobile number and the number of his house in New Zealand. I wrote them down and hid them in here with no intention of ever using them, until today.

Perching on the corner of the bed, I dial the mobile. It doesn't ring or go to voicemail. There is only a low humming sound as though I've dialled a number that doesn't exist. I double-check it on my screen and it exactly matches the one on the paper.

There's no way to check if I wrote it down wrong. That voicemail is long gone.

Carefully, I type in the digits of the landline number, including the code for New Zealand and hit dial. After a few quiet seconds, the phone begins to ring. Several rings later, a voice answers, sleepy and uncertain. Suddenly it hits me that it must be the middle of the night in New Zealand and I almost end the call, but surely that would be even worse.

Words abandon me and I hear the voice again, more awake this time and with a sense of urgency.

"Hello."

It's a woman's voice, which throws me for a moment. I can't hang up now. You can't call someone in the middle of the night and hang up. If that happened to me, I'd be awake all night worrying something was wrong.

Clearing my throat, I speak quietly, mindful of the sleepy state of the woman on the other end of the phone.

"Hello, could I speak to Alex, please?"

"Alex?" She says his name as a question.

"Yes, Alex Cavendish. I'm so sorry about the time. I forgot. I mean, I'm in the UK."

I hear the rustle of bed sheets and a low groan.

"He doesn't live here anymore." The woman's accent certainly sounds like that of a New Zealander. She yawns before adding, "Sorry."

I jump in quickly before she hangs up. "Wait. Sorry again. But do you have a number for Alex?"

She breathes heavily, exasperated by me delaying her getting back to sleep. "No, I don't. I own this house. He was renting here, but that was ages ago. He went back home."

"Home?"

"Yeah, back to the UK. He didn't like it here. Look, sorry, but it's like 1am here, and I have work in the morning."

I'm trying to digest what she has just said to me.

197

"Of course. I'm so sorry."

"Bye." She hangs up before I have a chance to say another word. I pace around the living room, trying to decide what to do.

I could do nothing. After all, if I hadn't made that phone call, I'd be going about my day as usual. But my head is swimming, and I need to talk to someone I can trust. I dial Mum's number, the five rings taking an excruciating amount of time.

"Hello."

"Hi, Mum. Just me, are you free for a chat?"

Mum is lighter and breezier than I would have expected, given our most recent conversation.

"Are you free to come over? Your sister is here. We're having pastries and tea."

Ah, that's why she's so cheerful, she has an audience. I'd rather Mum was by herself for this, but if Hetty is there already, I might be able to get Mum alone once she leaves.

"Sounds good, I'll be there shortly. Want me to bring anything?"

"No, we've got plenty here."

We say our goodbyes, and I grab a packet of shortbread biscuits from the kitchen cupboard. I don't like the idea of turning up empty-handed.

When I arrive, I try the front door and walk straight in. "You should lock this, Mum," I say, announcing my arrival.

Mum and Hetty are curled up on the sofa together, a smattering of pastry crumbs dusting their clothes. The box on the table has one solitary pastry remaining.

Hetty pipes up. "We accidentally ate five, but we left you the apple one. That's your favourite, right?"

Mum and Hetty burst into fits of giggles and I drop the shortbread biscuits onto the table and take the remaining seat on the sofa. I love it when they are silly together. We sit and chat about nothing in particular. I eat the apple pastry, which is indeed my favourite, and we sip tea.

Hetty seems like she's settled in for the afternoon, so when she announces she needs the toilet, I know this is my best chance to speak to Mum alone. When Hetty leaves the room, I lean into Mum and whisper.

"I called Alex's number in New Zealand."

Mum looks shocked. "What! Why?"

"Shhhh." I point at the door to indicate I don't want Hetty to overhear.

Mum puts her finger to her lips and repeats herself in a low voice, "Why?"

"That's not important. It's just something I needed to do. The important part is that a woman answered. She was pretty annoyed because I didn't factor in the time difference, and she was asleep." Why am I adding in this unnecessary detail when Hetty could be back any minute? "She said that he'd moved back to the UK."

Mum looks thoughtful. "Okay, why are you bothered?"

I'm surprised at her response. "What do you mean, why am I bothered?"

"Sorry, that came out wrong. I guess I was expecting you to say something else, I was a bit worried that you were coming here to tell me about some planned mad confession or something. That's really not something I think–"

Mum cuts her sentence short as Hetty walks back into the room.

"Well, this looks very serious." She eyes us with mock suspicion.

I laugh, but it sounds tinny and unnatural. "No, it's nothing. Just telling Mum about Summer and her best friend, maybe soon-to-be girlfriend."

"Ooh exciting. Young love, eh? Nothing like it." Hetty doesn't sit down and instead starts tidying away the empty pastry box and scraping crumbs into her cupped hand.

"Leave that, love. I'll sort it once you and your sister have gone. Sit down."

Hetty takes the box to the kitchen and returns a few seconds later. "I'll have to love you and leave you, I'm afraid. I've got something to pick up at the post office before the rabble gets back from school."

I feel a pang of guilt that our poorly disguised whispering may be the reason for her departure, but I'm pleased that Mum and I will get to finish our talk. I jump up and give Hetty a hug. It might be my imagination, but I'm sure I feel her stiffen. Mum stands up and does the same.

"Let's try and do another weekend get-together. Maybe at my house this time? Gavin can cook."

Mum and I both nod, and I follow Hetty to the door before waving her off and locking it. Mum and I venture back to the sofa. Checking my watch, I discover I don't have long either so I need to get to the point.

"Did you know that Alex planned to come back to the UK to live?"

"No idea. Why would I know if you didn't? What are you worried about?"

I have no idea if I'm honest. The woman on the phone said that he'd been gone for ages. Surely, if there was going to be a problem, I would have heard something by now. I rest my head on Mum's shoulder and feel suddenly drained.

"Oh, I don't know. I probably shouldn't have called." There is little point in continuing this conversation. In all likelihood, I'm worrying about nothing. I'm possessive about my new-found happiness and my blossoming relationship with Summer, but I don't care.

I will protect it in any way that I have to.

30
HETTY

I may appear naive and happy-go-lucky, but that doesn't mean I'm stupid. Tamsin wears her thoughts and emotions all over her face. Obviously, she didn't come round for a friendly catch-up with Mum. She had something to say, and, evidently, something she wasn't happy to disclose in front of me.

There's nothing wrong with that specifically, but curiosity got the better of me, and my fake trip to the toilet proved me right. What I can't work out is why Tamsin has suddenly tried to contact Alex when the general consensus from everyone, including her, is that we're all better off without him. Is Tamsin going to try to track him down now that she thinks he's back in the UK? How can she think that would be good for her or Summer?

From their quick conversation, it's evident that Mum and Tamsin know something I don't. Something they don't plan to tell me. That's nothing new. Our family has always had secrets.

31

TAMSIN

Chatting with Mum provided little reassurance, but there isn't much I can do. Technically, nothing has changed. I simply have more information. But I still wish I hadn't made that call to New Zealand. Sometimes, ignorance is bliss.

Summer should be home shortly. She has nothing on after college today, and I'm going to suggest a mum and daughter night. Takeaway and a movie. I need to focus on the good things in my life, and Summer is at the very top of that list. That thought is cemented when I see Summer come through the door with a massive smile on her face.

"Good day?"

"Yeah, good, thanks. Just a normal day, really." She smiles again.

I understand completely. Normal is brilliant. Normal is easy and exactly what we both need.

"Why don't you grab a shower and get changed, and then we can treat ourselves. Order pizza and watch a movie?"

"Ooh, yes, please. You read my mind, I'm in the mood for being a total slob tonight."

I laugh. "Perfect. Go and get yourself sorted, and then you can pick the movie while I order."

Summer puts her hand to her chest and puts on a ridiculous, shocked face. "What? I can pick?"

I roll my eyes. "What are you trying to say? I let you pick all the time."

"Er, no, you don't. You veto anything with the slightest hint of nudity or violence. I am seventeen, Mum. Movies rated fifteen are fine for me."

"Okay, okay. You pick, and I promise no vetoing. We can watch all the nudity or blood and guts that your heart desires."

Summer laughs and pumps her fist in the air. "Yes!"

She heads off to the shower and I busy myself in the kitchen.

Summer and I have the most amazing, relaxing evening. We eat until we are fit to burst, and Summer is goggle-eyed at the ninety minutes of non-stop violence and swearing that ensues.

"That was amazing!"

"Hmm, it was all right. But there wasn't really a story."

Summer punches me jokingly in the arm. "That's not really the point of it. I know it's not your type of thing, but thank you for letting me pick, and next time, I promise we can watch something you like. Something with ladies in bonnets and horses."

We both laugh, and I playfully shove her before dragging her back for a hug. Summer groans and gets to her feet.

"I've got a bit of French homework to finish off, so I'm going to do that and then have an early night if that's okay?"

"Of course. I'm going to have an early one, too. All that food and lazing around is very tiring."

Summer leans down and kisses me on the cheek. "Night."

"Did you ever speak to your dad again after he left?" I have no idea what made me say it, and I feel terrible when I see how shocked Summer looks at my unexpected question.

"Er, what?"

I lower my eyes sheepishly. "Sorry, it just popped into my

head. Guess it was on my mind. Don't worry, go on up and do your homework, I shouldn't have asked."

"No, it's fine. Just weird you blurting it out like that. And I think I've already told you that, no, I took a couple of calls, didn't really say much, and then he just stopped calling. Plus, I have a different mobile than when he left, and unless you've given him my new number, he doesn't have it." I nod along, my brows knitted together. "Is something wrong, Mum?"

I stand up and put my hands on Summer's shoulders. I'm worried I've ruined our evening with my stupid question.

"Absolutely nothing. It's just I like how things are now. Just me and you."

Summer hugs me. "Me too. I'm sure Dad is perfectly happy with his new life in New Zealand. We'll be a dim and distant memory to him now, and that suits me just fine." Summer gives me a squeeze, and we say goodnight before she goes upstairs.

I lower myself slowly onto the sofa and stare at the wall. In my peripheral vision, something stirs. A dark figure looming in the kitchen. Adrenaline crashes through me, and without a second thought, I turn away and leap off the sofa before scrambling up the stairs and into my bedroom, flinging the door closed. My heart is fluttering, and my breathing is shallow and ineffective. I crawl under the covers, curl up into a ball and shut out the world.

Trembling, I lie in a haze of fear. Everything feels like it is closing in on me. A fresh bolt of fear punches me in the gut as I hear him crash to the floor downstairs. His moans penetrate my thoughts. I see his mouth, pleading, begging for help. I scream and curl myself up tighter, pushing my palms against my ears so hard that my head pulsates and my hands shake. I cower helplessly, praying and pleading for it to be over. And then suddenly, it is silent.

He is dead.

Again.

3 2

TAMSIN

BEFORE

The Man on the Kitchen Floor

I fold up the freshly washed clothes and place them neatly into my drawers. It's unusually peaceful today, and I hum to myself to break the silence. I straighten the books on my bedside table and glance around the room. Everything looks neat and tidy. Perfect. I think I'll spend the next couple of hours reading. My idea of heaven. But first I need snacks, and maybe a hot chocolate.

Something catches my eye as I turn to leave my bedroom. I walk towards my window and wipe away the thin layer of condensation to get a better look at the garden. Closing my eyes, I give my head a shake. Mum is in the garden. My bedside clock confirms Hetty's childminder should have collected her over an hour ago, so I guess Mum is free for the morning, but this is still unusual behaviour for her.

She is standing with her back to me and is still wearing her dressing gown. I watch her curiously for a moment. Maybe she just wanted some fresh air? But there is something about the way she is standing, hugging herself tightly and staring defiantly away from the house. I suppress a shiver and run downstairs.

Dad is standing looking out of the kitchen window, his arms spread wide and his palms planted on the worktop on either side of the sink. His shoulders are heaving. I want to turn around and run back upstairs, but I somehow manage to maintain my position and let out a whispery croak.

"Dad?"

He whips his head around aggressively. His face is even more red than usual, and his eyes are filled with fury. He pants through his nose like a raging bull. I look past him to where I can see Mum standing in the garden and furrow my brow. I try to ask him why she is out there but my voice has abandoned me. Dad snarls, and I take a step back, stumbling slightly over nothing.

"Why am I not surprised?"

I'm confused. I haven't said or done anything. I have no idea what he is talking about.

"Everything is always my fault, isn't it? You only care about her." He points ferociously out of the window towards Mum, but he misjudges it and whacks his finger against the glass, wincing briefly before his expression returns to one of rage.

He turns and takes a menacing step towards me, his breathing terrifyingly loud.

"What... what..." Nothing I say will defuse the situation. They've clearly had another blazing row, and I've inserted myself into it at the worst possible time. I'm going to take the brunt of his anger, and I don't think I've ever seen him quite so furious.

Suddenly, an unusual look passes across his face, and the expression in his eyes shifts from fury to fear. He clasps his left hand to his chest and starts slapping his right hand on the kitchen counter behind him. I have no idea what he is doing. When his fingertips find our cordless house phone, I finally understand. I reach out my hand to take the phone from him, but he plants it tightly to his chest and stands up tall. I know he thinks I'm just a stupid child, but even I can see that him standing unsupported in the middle of the kitchen floor is not a wise move.

His face is almost purple now and etched with pain. My hand is still extended, but he shows no signs of handing it over. He emits a deep groan, and I reluctantly step towards him, shaking my outstretched hand.

"Give me the phone!"

His moans continue, increasing in volume and length. He finally squeezes two words out between painful gasps.

"Fuck you." He turns the phone towards himself and tries to stab at the buttons.

My heart is thumping madly against my ribcage. If he doesn't pass me the phone soon, I fear there will be more than one of us needing an ambulance. He looks like a man possessed. I look past his looming form to Mum in the garden. She hasn't moved an inch, utterly oblivious to the horror developing in our kitchen. I need to get to her. Even facing death, my father still loathes me.

I make a run for the door, but as I do, Dad lets out a horrific wheezing sound and his eyes lose focus. Everything happens in slow motion. I watch him fall. A monstrous tree being felled with no control over its path to the ground. A sickening crack reverberates around the room as his head collides with the kitchen counter, a brief interruption in his downfall.

His body is limp and languid as he slides gracelessly to the floor, the phone now inches away from his outstretched hand, his eyes searching desperately for answers.

I take a step towards him, my hands balled tightly into anxious fists, my blood a cocktail of adrenaline and fear.

He is still alive.

Confused, hurt, dying.

But not dead.

Yet.

I grab the phone and race out of the back door as fast as I can.

Mum hasn't moved, arms still folded, her hair and dressing gown fluttering in the wind. I stand at her side and thrust out the telephone. I'm breathing far too heavily to speak, and the thought that Dad might die because I can't get my words out is only making my attempts to breathe more futile.

Mum looks at me, her expression barely changing despite my emotional state. I swallow hard and jab her hip with the phone.

"It's Dad. He's having a heart attack. You need to call an ambulance." There. I did it. I told my mum. She's the adult, and it's her responsibility now. I whip my head back towards the house, hoping fruitlessly that Dad will somehow have picked himself up and be standing looking cross and disappointed at the window, but all I see are reflections of clouds and trees.

He is still on the floor. Dying.

Mum turns away from me and stares serenely down the garden. A small smile pricks the corners of her mouth.

"Mum!" I move myself to stand directly in front of her, but it's as though I am invisible. I yank at her dressing gown, and it loosens slightly. She doesn't move, and I'm crying helplessly now, desperate, wretched tears that rip at my insides.

I look at the house and then back at Mum. Balling my fists, I raise my head to the sky and scream until my throat feels raw. Nothing happens. Mum doesn't move, and the house is still. How can this be happening? I want to shake Mum, to claw at her skin and pound her with my fists until she does something. Anything. But I know deep down that she's not going to help me.

Out of options, I run back to the kitchen. Dad is on his side, reaching for where the phone was when I grabbed it. He flops onto his back. There is barely any life left in him now. His mouth is wet, his lips opening and closing like a dying fish. I should just call an ambulance myself. I should have done it minutes ago. What is wrong with me?

I run frantically back outside towards Mum. Desperately, I

throw myself down onto my knees in front of her, the phone falling onto the grass at her feet.

"He's dying, Mum. Please, help me. Please." I'm sobbing uncontrollably and feel as though I might pass out at any moment. Mum bends down slowly and picks up the phone. She looks at it curiously before hurling it aggressively down the garden. I watch, horrified, as it lodges in a tall, wiry bush, way out of my reach. I turn to Mum, my eyes wide and filled with utter disbelief. For the first time this morning, her eyes come into focus, and she fixes me with a look of pure determination. Nausea roils in my stomach, and I feel as though I'm not quite awake.

"Mum." The words scrape like broken glass against my strained throat. I kneel in front of her and plead for help one final time. "Mum, what should I do?"

Mum looks at me, her hair whipping around her thin face. There is not a trace of conflict or indecision in her reply.

"You should leave him."

I look at the ground and close my eyes. Surely, this has to be a nightmare. I'll wake up any minute, terrified but relieved to find myself lying in my bed. But my knees are cold, I can feel a cool draft on my neck, and my head is pounding.

These are not sensations that happen in dreams. I stay exactly where I am, at my mother's feet. Kneeling and following her orders to let my father die. My soul wrenches into a thousand pieces, and I feel something break deep within me, something that I will never be able to piece back together. I stay until my legs feel numb, and I'm shivering painfully. He is gone. I can feel it.

Eventually, I clamber to my feet. I have no idea how much time has passed. I expect my legs to give way, but they don't. Mum looks frozen, and all her exposed skin is covered in goosebumps. She looks at me, nods, and smiles.

"You should go up to your room. I'll be back inside in ten

minutes." Then she turns away and stares back into oblivion. I trudge slowly back towards the house.

The kitchen is quiet now. There is no movement. No breath. No life.

I step around Dad's body, refusing to look at his face. Somehow I climb the stairs and walk to stand by my bedroom window. Everything I'm able to do amazes me. I don't understand how I'm functioning. I'm like some kind of robot.

I watch Mum as she falls to her knees and raises her arms to her face, her shoulders shaking violently. The first show of emotion I have witnessed all morning. I close the curtains and climb into my bed.

Minutes later, I hear a siren that stops abruptly outside. I ignore it, pick up the book I was planning to read earlier, and turn to the first page, careful not to crack the spine. I turn on my side, my back facing the door, and start to read. There is a lot of commotion downstairs. I focus on the words in the book and keep reading.

A gentle tap on the door shakes me out of the story.

"Come in." My voice sounds robotic, and my throat is unusually sore. I crane my neck without moving my body and see Mum standing in the doorway.

"Tamsin, there's an ambulance here. It looks as though Dad has had a heart attack. I'm going to hospital with him."

It's like I'm an actor in a play, unable to deviate from the script.

"Okay, Mum." I'm numb, and I barely feel a thing when she tiptoes over and places a kiss on my forehead.

She whispers in my ear, "Everything is going to be okay. You just stay here. Mrs Ewan from across the road is going to come and sit with you."

I slowly turn my head away from her.

Thankfully she is called away by one of the many helpful strangers who have invaded our house. I hear everyone leave, and the front door slams before the ambulance starts up again. Squeezing my eyes closed, I imagine an entirely different kind of morning. One where I stayed in bed reading.

A calm and peaceful morning without any horror or death.

I reopen my eyes, take a deep breath, and start to read.

33

TAMSIN

The air is hot and stale under the covers. I fling them off me and take a deep breath. There are two choices. Remembering how Dad died is clearly not enough to make my visions of him or Mum leave me alone. This is pure self-torture, and I'm pissed off that I have no known way of controlling it. The way I see it, I either tell Mum that we have to get the whole thing out in the open, something I've already assured her I wouldn't do, or I somehow make my peace with it all.

Thinking back to my conversation with Dr McCabe when I told him about what happened to Hetty, he led me to understand I was not at fault. I was only a child, and the responsibility fell to my parents. If that is the case, then surely the same thing applies here. I was twelve years old that day and pleaded with Mum to help. She completely blanked me. Worse than that, she threw the phone out of my reach. The only possible way for us to save Dad.

Undeniably, Mum holds the most responsibility for what happened. But that isn't the only problem. I think I know why I'm being tormented, and perhaps there is a way that I can break free. I could easily have called for an ambulance. Without a doubt, I was old enough to know exactly what I needed to do. And I didn't do it. I made that choice.

Once Summer leaves for college tomorrow, I will confront my lingering guests. I need to prove to them and myself that they have nothing left to teach me. They are not welcome in my home.

My sleep is fitful and filled with snatched memories, and I wake drained and weary. I'm certain Summer knew something was off this morning. I hope I reassured her somewhat with my claims of a headache and impending perimenopause. It's not a complete lie. Disturbed sleep has left me nauseated and with a heavy head.

I take a seat on the sofa with a direct line of sight to the kitchen. I'm going to wait right here until he appears. Never have I tried to summon the guests. They have always materialised unwelcome, but today, I have a purpose.

Closing my eyes, I breathe in and out, slowly and deeply, focusing on the movement of my chest and stomach. There is a shift in the room, and then a sharp coldness that starts at the nape of my neck and slithers down my spine. Before I even open my eyes, I know he is there.

He is standing, clutching the phone and holding it tightly to his chest. Pulling it away and cursing me, his twelve-year-old daughter. I speak directly to him, never breaking eye contact.

"Why didn't you give me the phone? That was the first nail in your coffin."

His mouth doesn't move, but I hear his voice. "Would you have called if I had?"

I walk purposefully towards him. My visual field closes in, and there is only him.

"Honestly, I don't know." The words hurt, but they are the truth. "But that didn't give you the right to tell me to fuck off. I was a child. Your child."

He doesn't ask anything further. Next to come will be his predetermined fall and the sound of his skull smashing against the kitchen worktop. I take in every single second and do not flinch or look away as the scene unfolds before me.

Reluctantly, I crouch down beside his body. I know irrefutably that he is not physically here with me, but the clarity and detail with which I see him is so extraordinary that I struggle to comprehend how this could be a product of my mind.

I'm taken back to that day, and I feel the burning desire within me to do something, the desperation and helplessness I felt when Mum wouldn't come to his aid.

"I asked her to help you. She wouldn't move. I begged and pleaded with her."

I need him to know this. His face squirms with a mixture of pain and despair, and I'm not sure if he hears me. My eyes fill with tears.

"I did try to help you. I know I didn't do everything that I could. I should have called for the ambulance myself. But I was so very afraid and I wanted Mum to help me." My voice cracks, and I squeeze my eyes shut to stem the flow of tears. "I don't deserve this. I don't deserve to be held responsible for something that happened when I was a child. A child whose mother wouldn't help her."

I let my head fall, and my shoulders drop so my face almost touches his chest. The sound of him struggling to breathe is nauseating. He raises his right hand, and I flinch.

"Shhh."

He moves his fingers slowly towards me and caresses my cheek. Goosebumps prickle my face, but there is no other sensation, no pressure from his touch. His voice fills the inside of my head. I look down at his mouth, opening and closing but not making the movement of the words that I'm hearing. "I wasn't a good father."

"No, you weren't." I had never dared say this to Dad when he was alive, and there is a huge sense of release at being able to reveal it now.

"You wanted me gone."

A chill runs through me. He is right. Life was better when he wasn't there. I turn my head to face him. Life is slowly ebbing away from his eyes. I wish I felt differently. I wish I could tell him that I loved him and that I was heartbroken when he died. He doesn't have long left, and I have no idea what to say. His voice consumes my thoughts once more, and I stare unflinchingly into his eyes.

"You wanted me gone, but you didn't want me dead." My heart calms and I have a sense of understanding as Dad says his last words. "None of this was your fault."

His words echo inside me as I watch him take his last breath. I let my tears fall freely, somehow knowing that this is it. This is the last time I will ever get the chance to see or speak to him again.

"Thank you."

I'm not sure whether he disappears slowly or suddenly. I am simply aware of a moment when he is no longer with me. I have carried the guilt of wanting my father to disappear and then watching him die for so long.

That guilt has muddled my grief, and I have never accepted how I actually felt about him. He was not a good father. He was uncaring, aggressive, and selfish. I wanted him to go away and would have been perfectly happy to never see him again. But now I know, I know with absolute certainty that I did not wish him dead. I wanted him to leave Mum and me alone and live his life elsewhere. Not once did I hope that his life would be extinguished. I had my part to play in his death, but I am not accountable for it, and now I understand his presence was to show me that. To help me let go.

I inhale deeply and use the handles of the kitchen drawers to help me up to my feet. My whole body is jittery, and I take a moment to readjust to being upright. There is one more guest I need to confront. My feelings about my dad were uncomplicated. I didn't like him, and I think he deserved that I felt that way.

As I look out of the window at the shadow of my mother, my emotions swing like a pendulum. I can't piece together how all her actions can belong to the same person. How could she have done something so evil yet also be so caring and thoughtful? I've been fractured in two by her duplicitous actions, acknowledging only the life where she is good and kind. If I want to live as one happy, whole person, I need to make my peace with who she is. I grab my phone and stride purposefully out into the garden.

The grass is soft underfoot from last night's downpour. Treading carefully around boggy sections of mud, I make my way towards my mother. I choose a spot in front of her, close enough to see the detail of every feature on her face but far enough away that we couldn't touch each other unless one of us moves. My body shudders at the memory of Dad's icy dead fingers.

It takes me several attempts to dial Mum's number correctly, my quivering fingers refusing to comply. The thought of combining the past and present in this way is terrifying. I hadn't originally planned to do it this way, but something inside tells me this is how to set my guests and myself free. Mum answers the phone.

"Hello." The air in the garden is still, and I can hear her clearly.

"Hi, Mum. It's Tamsin." I sound forceful, bordering on aggressive. It's not how I want to come across, but I need to get through this in any way I can.

"Are you okay? You sound–"

"I know how I sound, Mum, and I know I told you that I wasn't planning to do anything, and I'm not going to, but…" I stop and try to gather my whirlwind of thoughts. "I'm sorry, but I really need to say some things to you, things that aren't easy. So could you just…" I have to stop to breathe, and I take two big gulps of air to fill my lungs back up. There is a moment of silence before Mum's small, feeble reply.

"Okay... Yes, whatever you need."

I look at the woman before me and study her face. What I had once assumed was serenity now appears much more like detachment. She seems absent, as though her mind has ventured to a more comfortable place, leaving her body behind. This is a look I understand well. I have been there myself many times. I haven't prepared what order to say everything in, and my first thought spills out of my mouth unbidden.

"You let Dad die." I hear Mum's sharp intake of breath. "I asked for your help, and you did nothing." The figure in front of me does not move a muscle. I stare at her ferociously as I continue to speak. "You just stood there, staring. I pleaded with you."

My eyes are blazing hot, and I want to reach out and shake her, just as I did all those years ago. Make her react, make her do something. Anything.

"You threw the phone away!" My chest heaves, and an enormous sob escapes from my mouth. I let the pain flow out of me, crying freely and vigorously, never taking my eyes from my mother's face. There is a peculiar noise coming through the phone. It sounds as though Mum is shivering. Eventually, she speaks.

"I knew this day would come. When you called and told me you remembered, I knew you wouldn't be able to leave it in the past. I knew you would need it to be out in the open." I watch my younger Mum's face, imagining her lips moving as I take in the words. "I shouldn't have let this go on for so long. I knew this was coming. When you talked about seeing a flashback of me in the garden, that was the moment for me to help you through this resurfacing. I'm so sorry."

My temper sparks as I recall the details of that conversation. I had been so focused on the message of "you need to leave him" being related to Alex abandoning us, and Mum went along with my assumption willingly. Selfishly. This only fuels my anger and disgust further.

"How could you? He died because of you. You played God. What on earth gave you that right?"

I hear Mum clear her throat. A wet, sickly sound. "I have thought about this for years. And I still believe in what I did that day."

Disbelief almost knocks me off my feet. I have to put my hand over my mouth to stop myself from screaming at her.

"Just listen, Tamsin. Please." I don't trust myself to respond with anything but bile and vitriol, so I stay silent. "Before I went out into the garden, your father had his hands around my throat." I look from the woman's eyes to her neck, and I can see small pink marks that I hadn't paid attention to before. "He told me that he'd had enough and he was going to kill me. I managed to throw my head back and somehow get free to the garden."

Her revelation knocks all the air out of my lungs, and dark spots begin to cloud my vision. I squeeze my toes until my feet cramp, trying to keep the blood pumping to my head.

"I can remember standing there as though it were yesterday. I was making a promise to myself. I knew he was never going to leave. He would see that as a failure. It was only a matter of time until I ended up dead, and I was so terrified that if I wasn't there to protect you, he would hurt you and your sister." Mum is sniffing and choking on almost every word.

My heart aches, and I want the ground to swallow me up and take me to a place where none of this is happening. It is all far, far too much for me to take in. I feel as though I may shatter at any moment.

"Should I come over, Tamsin? I'm not sure this is right over the phone."

"No. That won't work. I'm with you in the garden. I'm looking at you right now. This is the way it has to be." I'm shocked at my dictatorial tone and my total lack of care for her opinion about what I have just revealed.

"Okay." I hear her blow her nose noisily and wait for her to continue. "I had been hoping he would get sick or have an accident for a very long time. I thought it would be a way out for us. I waited, but everything stayed the same, and he became more and more threatening with every day that passed. Standing there in the garden, I had decided that enough was enough. I knew that if I hadn't managed to break free from his hold on my neck, I would be dead. I had made a decision, a sacrifice of sorts. I was going to go inside and kill him."

I take a step closer to Mum's shadow, trying to get a glimpse of what is going through her head, but there isn't a single movement. She looks to the horizon, completely immersed in her own world, a world where I now know she is planning a murder. Mum's voice startles me.

"I was seconds away from going inside and grabbing a knife to stab him with. At that moment, it seemed like the only way to protect you girls. I wasn't going to try and hide what I'd done; I was going to call the police and tell them he had tried to strangle me. I had the marks on my neck to prove it. When you ran out and told me you thought he'd had a heart attack, I couldn't believe it. Well, that's not strictly true. He'd become so unhealthy, and I'd never seen him so red-faced and enraged. I saw it as a sign, a gift from the universe to save us all from the trauma of what I was about to do. I barely remember you being there. It's like I was glued to the spot, and I don't think I could have reacted if I wanted to. I don't remember throwing the phone. I must have done it on pure instinct."

As Mum explains, I feel all the pieces of the puzzle coming together in my mind and joining to create a complete picture. A horrific picture. The truth of my childhood. Both of my parents had been willing to kill the other.

Our household was beyond dysfunctional, a far cry from the

mildly tumultuous marriage that I had remembered. Dad was not just cruel and selfish; he was violent and murderous. Mum was not purely weak and deceitful; she was a victim and had nearly paid with her life. Not only that, but she was willing to sacrifice her own freedom to take what she saw as the only available course of action to protect Hetty and me. Whether I agree with her actions or not, and at this point, I'm not sure. I do understand them. And for the first time in my life, I think I understand my mother in her entirety.

I look at the frail woman standing before me. She may appear that way, but I now know that her mind is full of strength. My eyes stay fixed on her as she collapses to her knees. I kneel beside her, the wet grass soaking through my trousers. Craning my neck, I study her face, her hands covering her eyes and shoulders shaking so violently it looks like she is having a seizure. I take in the pure, unadulterated relief that is radiating from her tiny, convulsing body. I long to hug her, but I need to leave this moment as it was.

"I did what I thought was best. I didn't have a choice." I hear Mum's voice through the phone, and I feel the desperation and absolute belief in what she is saying.

It's time to put an end to this. I stand and lose my footing as my slipper squelches through the sodden ground. Regaining my composure, I clamber to my feet, before speaking very clearly, addressing both versions of my mother, past and present.

"I didn't want to leave Dad to die that day. I hated him and wanted him out of our lives, just not that way." My body is trembling with the exertion it takes for me to say this to her. "But now I know, I understand why you did it, and I'm so sorry that you found yourself in that position." I hear Mum begin to cry.

There is one final thing to say to her, and I mean it with all my heart.

"I don't blame you for what you did. I love you, Mum."

Violent sobbing fills my ears, and I close my eyes. When I

open them, I know the woman in the garden will be gone. She will be gone because I will make it that way. I no longer need to fracture Mum into two different people.

She is one.

One flawed, damaged human being.

I hear her whisper, "Thank you."

I slowly open my eyes and there is nothing but mud and grass at my feet.

34

TAMSIN

Everything is still and tranquil in the house. There is a sense of resolution in the air. In my bedroom, I strip off my muddy clothes and walk to the bathroom to take a shower. I concentrate on the feeling of the hot water bouncing off my skin. I breathe in the smell of my shampoo, noticing and naming every feeling that it gives me. I can feel the depth in every moment, every sensation that has been marred and blurred by my inability to live a full life.

Mum and I will move on from this and we will be stronger. I will build back bridges with my sister and her family, and they will be strong and held together by trust and honesty.

Summer and I will continue to invest in our relationship, and we will tackle any obstacles together, as a family should.

Alex may be back in the country. He may make contact, and if he does I will handle it in accordance with Summer's wishes. I will never let him hurt her again.

We are all ready to be a family now.

There are no more secrets to uncover.

35

SUMMER

It's our second full family gathering this month. Hopefully, this is the start of something more regular for us. Don't get me wrong, I love spending time with Mum alone, especially now she's so much happier, but there's something about the noise and chaos of us all being together that I love.

This time, we're at Grandma Arabella's instead of ours. Her house is beautiful and exactly the sort of place I'd love to have when I'm older and have a family of my own. It's colourful and quirky, and although it's bursting with ornaments, plants, and collectables, it still feels ordered somehow. Grandma has a penchant for nude sculptures and artwork, which used to embarrass me when I was younger, but now I can appreciate their beauty.

Mum and Grandma are sitting close together on the sofa, each smiling and sipping a glass of Prosecco. I'm so proud of Mum. I no longer have to worry that a single glass will turn into a dozen. There's a sense of closeness and ease between them that is new and fascinating to watch.

Auntie Hetty and Uncle Gavin are bustling around in the kitchen. Despite Grandma's protestations, they brought all the food and are busy trying to find everything they need. They bump into each other intermittently and laugh. Auntie Hetty comes into the living room to make an announcement. She is rosy-cheeked, and her hair is sticking to her forehead.

"Dinner will be about thirty minutes. Anyone want another drink?"

Mum and Grandma both put their hands over their glasses and answer in unison. "No, thanks."

I chuckle at their new-found synchronicity before catching Auntie Hetty's eye and shaking my head.

Luca and Kai are huddled together on an armchair and hovering over a handheld video game. They've barely interacted, only occasionally letting out a cheer or a groan to indicate how their game's going. Neither of them acknowledges their mum, and Auntie Hetty rolls her eyes before returning to the kitchen and playfully tapping Uncle Gavin on the bottom.

Scanning the room, I feel nothing but gratitude. No family is perfect, and mine is far from it. But we are all here, making time for each other, and to me, that's all that really matters.

We congregate around the dinner table. Auntie Hetty and Uncle Gavin have prepared a huge variety of Spanish tapas dishes. They are dotted around the table in earthenware bowls. I breathe in the incredible garlic and paprika aromas. It all looks incredibly delicious. Predictably, the younger boys turn their noses up. Any food that isn't beige is usually frowned upon by them, but I can't wait to dig in.

Grandma Arabella looks suitably impressed. "Well, this is very special, I must say!"

Grandma and Auntie Hetty smile at each other, and Hetty waves away the compliment. "Thank you. I hope you all enjoy it. Dig in."

We pass bowls around and pile our plates with the delicious, vibrant-looking food.

Auntie Hetty points towards the cooker. "That oven is a

dinosaur, Mum. You should get it replaced. It'll be costing you a fortune."

Grandma lowers her brow. "In that case, I think it matches me perfectly. We are both old and expensive to keep." We all laugh. "I'm in no rush to change anything in the house. I hate having builders or anything in, and I like everything just the way it is."

Grandma seems a little nervous and defensive, and I can't quite figure out why. She's not making eye contact with anyone and is overly focused on the food on her plate. I look over at Mum, and I can see from her curious expression that she has noticed Grandma's odd mannerisms, too. Hetty is clearly oblivious as she follows up with another question.

"Would you ever think of moving? Maybe a smaller, more modern house would be nice."

Grandma's mouth fixes into a straight line and she doesn't look up. "No, dear. This is my home, and I'll be staying here until the end."

The atmosphere around the table has changed. Grandma's prickly behaviour is out of character, and everyone has noticed now. We all exchange quick glances and a silent agreement to change the subject.

The bread I had been dipping in balsamic dressing has turned to mush. I put it to one side and ask Uncle Gavin to pass me the prawns.

Mum tries to rescue the situation. "I never make tapas at home. You must give me these recipes, Hetty."

Auntie Hetty and Uncle Gavin take the cue and start talking about various Spanish restaurants they have visited. Grandma is still in a world of her own, agitated and occasionally muttering to herself silently. I can understand why she might feel that way. Auntie Hetty's question about the cooker was purely innocent, and actually a perfectly good point. But I wonder if the second question about her moving made Grandma feel she shouldn't be living alone in a big house now she's getting older.

Grandma has always been very fit. She is surprisingly strong and flexible. In the last year or two though, I have noticed her becoming frailer. I suspect she's noticed that about herself, too. It can't be a nice feeling.

Eventually, Grandma stops being so inwardly focused and rejoins the room. The mood lifts, and by the time we move on to dessert, everyone is back in high spirits, the awkward moment long forgotten. Everyone stuffs themselves with churros and chocolate sauce, and the large carafe of red wine is empty. I quickly check Mum's glass and feel immediately guilty for doing so. She still has the half-drunk glass of Prosecco in front of her.

Mum and I offer to clean up, and everyone else goes to the living room to relax in front of the TV. I stand next to Mum, and after a furtive glance over my shoulder to make sure nobody can hear me, I decide to see what she thinks about Grandma's behaviour.

"It was weird, right? I've never seen her act like that."

Mum nods thoughtfully. "I think your grandma's just got to that age where she's worried people think she can't cope on her own."

"But nobody said that. Auntie Hetty only said the oven was old."

"I know, but I think she took it personally." Mum raises her hands before I can speak. "I'm not saying she should have; I'm just saying that I get it. It's nice that people offer support when you live alone, but I think she feels she has to defend herself for wanting to stay in a house that's too big for her."

I nod, realising that Mum probably feels some of that same pressure, too, since Dad left. I decide to leave it at that and Mum and I finish up the cleaning.

36
TAMSIN

Summer and I wave our goodbyes and get into the car. Mum seems to have shaken off whatever bothered her earlier. I agree with Summer. It was bizarre behaviour from her. Hetty definitely hit a nerve that I don't think can be entirely explained away by how I justified it to Summer. I'll mention it to Mum next time I see her.

I'm glad and proud that I can drive us home. I barely had a glass of Prosecco and so much food that I feel fit to burst. Being sober is wonderful. As I drive through the winding roads, Summer drifts off, the warmth of the car and the gentle humming of the engine lulling her to sleep.

I let the peacefulness of the moment wash over me, embracing the fact that I'm no longer controlled and tortured by my past. Everything that has happened has brought me to this moment in time. I finally accept myself as I am, and I'm looking forward to telling Dr McCabe about Dad. He doesn't have to know exactly what happened, but I think it would be good to work through some of my guilt about wishing Dad would leave and him then dying.

Summer lets out a small snort, and her eyelids flutter. I'm not even particularly concerned about Alex being back in the country. I doubt he's coming back for either me or Summer. If, indeed, he has returned, it will be for something that will benefit him, perhaps a job offer or a new relationship. There isn't a single part of me that cares to know. I'm genuinely happy for him to live his life. Alex and I were not the right fit, and I still don't think he is entirely to blame. Maybe he will be a much nicer person in a different relationship.

The wrong relationship can have disastrous and even deadly consequences. Who knows what could have happened if we'd stayed together. I look over at Summer, softly snuffling, and I smile.

Everything is exactly as it should be.

I am finally happy.

EPILOGUE

ARABELLA

Two years before

"I'll have to go. There's someone at the door." I say goodbye to my good friend, Nora, and end the phone call. Quite frankly, I'm relieved. I love Nora to pieces, but she would quite happily talk for hours about absolutely nothing, and there are things I should be getting on with.

I'm not sure who it could be. I'm not expecting anyone, not that I can remember anyway. I open the door and freeze, mouth agape. He is the last person I expected to see standing on my doorstep. A flash of irritation hits me. I stare at Alex and make no invitation for him to come inside. He's supposed to be halfway across the world, and that's exactly where I hoped he would stay. If he's expecting a warm welcome, then he has come to the wrong place.

"What do you want?" I close the door a fraction and place my body in the gap between the door and the wall.

"Well, nice to see you too, Arabella."

I'd love to close the door in his smug face. His blatant sarcasm is beyond rude. He takes a step forward, and I hold my position. I notice a large bag and a suitcase behind him. We are uncomfortably close now, but I will not show this man any weakness. He broke my daughter's heart and assaulted my granddaughter. I owe him absolutely none of my time.

"I want to go home. But I wanted to see you first. Find out what's been happening."

"Home?" I laugh sardonically. "You gave up the right to call my daughter's house your home when you walked out. And don't even get me started on what you did to Summer."

Alex runs his hands through his hair. He is squirming, and it's satisfying to watch. I've never seen him look anything other than sickeningly confident.

"Look, Arabella, I know what you think of me, and you're probably right."

"Pfft, probably?"

"Okay, you are right. I know I shouldn't have left like that, but I didn't know what else to do. Come on, you know how weird Tamsin had become. I got... well, to be honest, I got scared. I didn't know what she was capable of."

If he thinks he can win me over with his lame excuses, he's got another thing coming. Plus, he's clearly ignoring my comment about Summer. There is absolutely no excuse for raising your hand to a child.

"Yet you felt perfectly happy to leave your young daughter behind after slapping her across the face?" Alex's eyes widen.

"No! That is not true. I would never hurt Summer, and I wasn't happy at all. I tried to make Summer come with me. I wanted her to be safe, too. But she wouldn't come. So I panicked, and once I'd left, I knew I couldn't go back. Summer wouldn't take my calls, and time just passed, I guess."

I know full well he is lying to me about striking Summer. She would never make something like that up. But even so, this is a very different Alex than I have seen before. Whilst not strictly giving an apology, he's definitely coming across as more self-deprecating than I have ever seen.

"So what you're saying is you took the coward's way out?"

Alex rests his arm on my doorframe. "No. Not exactly."

I make to close the door, not caring if I squash his fingers.

"Wait. Yes, okay. What I did was cowardly, but I'd reached the end of my tether. I didn't know how to deal with something like that. Does anybody?"

I pause for a moment. Alex has a point, one that resonates with me strongly. It's easy to make poor choices in bad situations.

"Can I please come in? I just want to talk to you. I have nowhere else to go."

I look at his pleading face. Tamsin is still not in a great place, but Summer is doing so well – flourishing and growing into a lovely young woman. Perhaps if I talk to him, I could convince him to leave them be. I open the door and sigh loudly.

"Not for long, and I'm not interested in hearing any sob stories. If you've come looking for sympathy, then you'll be sorely disappointed."

Alex puts his palms together as though in prayer before grabbing his luggage and squeezing past me into the hallway. "Thank you."

"Go and sit down in the living room."

He does as I ask, and I take a seat directly opposite him. "Go on then." I sit back in the chair and fold my arms across my chest.

"The thing is, Arabella, I made a huge mistake leaving. I ran halfway across the world thinking I could start again, but I can't." He sighs and rubs his face. I watch him, my face stony. "I miss my wife and my daughter. We went off track, and I deserted them, which I know is unforgivable, but I'm going to do everything I can to win them back."

He looks genuinely sorry. He appears so authentic that I

know without a shadow of a doubt that Tamsin will welcome him with open arms.

"I don't believe you."

I see intense anger flash across his face for a split second before the false show of repentance returns. That is the real Alex right there, in that tiny moment before he pastes lies all over his face again. He can't fool me. I spent too much of my life with a man like this.

"Honestly, I mean it. I'm so sorry for everything, and I think that with time, Tamsin will find it in her heart to forgive me. She's wonderful like that, so understanding, and I feel terrible for taking her for granted for so long."

He is watching me intently as he vomits out his utter bullshit, looking for the micro changes in my face, checking if he is winning me over.

"I think you're right."

His eyes brighten, and the corners of his mouth twitch. I am watching you, too, Alex, and I'm a much better player at this game than you could begin to imagine. I lean forward and put my palms on my knees.

"I think that she would probably forgive you and let you back into their home. I think you would play nice for a while, get your feet back under the table and then slowly but surely revert back to your selfish ways."

"You make it sound as though I was a terrible husband throughout our whole marriage. I made them happy once, you know."

He's attempting to play the victim now. I hate this so much.

"Be honest with yourself, Alex. You don't actually care about Tamsin or Summer. You liked the idea of a perfect family, and when it turned out to be less than perfect, you bolted."

"I do care. I wouldn't be here asking for forgiveness if I didn't."

I roll my eyes and stand up. "They are just starting to get back on track." This is not entirely true, particularly for Tamsin, but I need him to think they are better without him. "There is no reason other than pure selfishness for you to insert yourself back into their lives. They don't need you, Alex, and I know for a fact that they don't want you either. Leave them alone."

He looks at me, flabbergasted. "How can you say that? At the very least, Summer should be allowed to see her father."

I stand over him. "You're not listening! Never at any point has Tamsin said you are not allowed to see Summer. Summer decided not to take your calls. Why on earth would she want to see you after what you did to her? She's fifteen now, more than old enough to make her own decisions."

Alex's mask of civility falls, and I suddenly feel less than safe. An ominous heavy cloud is in the air. An air of menace that I lived with for decades. I need to dial down the tension if I'm going to convince him to reconsider his actions.

"Look, I'm sorry. I'm incredibly protective of Tamsin and Summer. I'll make us some tea, and maybe we can talk a bit more sensibly."

I raise my eyebrows at him, and he nods in agreement. On my way to the kitchen, I look over my shoulder and see him rubbing his hands together, smiling. My blood boils.

As I busy myself making tea, Alex continues to plead his case, and I make the occasional nod or murmur to show that I'm listening. Everything he says only further convinces me that he must stay away from my family.

"I've done a lot of things I'm not proud of. But surely you don't want your daughter to be alone? I know I can make us a happy family again. I just need you all to give me a chance to prove it to you."

He is an excellent performer; I'll give him that. He's using all the right words and putting all the blame on himself. What Alex doesn't know is that I'm more experienced at deception than he could ever be. I know for a fact that everything he is saying is only to serve his purpose, to get him towards the outcome he wants. I can smell his lies a mile away. Painting a genial look on my face, I carry a wooden tray with two cups of tea and a plate of digestive biscuits through to the living room. I put the tray down on the coffee table and gesture for him to take a cup. He shuffles forward so that he's sitting on the edge of the armchair and reaches out. I perch on the edge of the coffee table and watch him. He takes a sip and puts the cup down.

"Look, I know this is a lot to ask, but could I stay here? Just for a few days."

I smile at the audacity and bare-faced cheek of this request. There is not a snowflake's chance in hell that I will let him stay with me.

"You must be kidding."

He puts on his best downtrodden, woe-is-me act. "Please, Arabella. I've been out of work for months. I'm broke, and I have nowhere else to turn."

I roll my eyes. "Ah, so that's why you're back. Money." I fold my arms. I couldn't care less if he ends up on the streets.

"No, of course not. I can't expect to walk straight back in with Tamsin. I need some time. If I could just stay here for a little bit, then I know I'll get things sorted. And I'll pay you back, I promise."

I stand slowly, turning away and calmly taking a few steps away from him. This meeting is over. I want him out of my house. Now.

"Get out, Alex. Leave."

He looks flabbergasted. I have no idea why. Alex is not my family, and more than that, he hurt my family. Why he thinks he deserves my hospitality is mind-boggling. He stands up, arms out wide.

"Come on, Arabella. Don't be like that."

I can't contain my anger anymore. I've been civil far longer than he deserves. Letting him in was clearly a mistake and one I plan to rectify right this minute.

"Like what exactly? I want you to get out of my house right now. I don't want you here and I don't care if you have nowhere else to go. You made your bed, and now you're going to have to lie in it." I stomp out of the room and grab his bag and case, flinging them towards him. "Take your shit and get out. Now!" I stand in the living room doorway, breathless but determined.

Alex looks at me and smirks before sitting back down very slowly in the chair. He crosses his legs and examines his nails, completely nonplussed by my outburst. His mouth curls into a menacing snarl.

"I am not going anywhere."

We stare at each other for a moment. Psyching each other out. He knows full well I can't physically remove him. But there is more than one way to skin a cat. I shrug and walk towards the telephone.

"Fine. I'll call the police."

Alex waves an arm towards me. "Please do." He holds out his mobile phone. "Here, use mine. When they get here, I can tell them that my psychotic bitch of a wife is unfit to take care of my daughter. Then I can have my house back, and you can all leave me the fuck alone."

A sickening dread falls over me. The look on Alex's face tells me he knows he has me over a barrel. I know without a doubt that he would do precisely what he is threatening. He is a predator, and will take down anyone and anything in his path. I sigh and look at the ground before returning to my perch on the edge of the coffee table. I run my hands through my hair and look him straight in the eye.

"Please, Alex. Just go. I will give you money to start again. Just please go away from here and leave me and my family alone."

He leans forward and pats me on the knee, his eyes never leaving mine. "Not a fucking chance."

Without hesitation, I reach into my back pocket and pull out the small kitchen knife I hid in there whilst making the tea. I plunge it directly into the side of his neck. His eyes go wide, and he reaches his hands out to try to touch the knife. Taking no chances, I pull the knife out and immediately plunge it into the exact spot on the opposite side. Blood begins to spurt from the first wound, covering both of us, and spills onto the brown leather of the chair.

Alex is gurgling and choking. He won't last long. I push the coffee table away from me and towards the sofa before dragging his twitching body onto the floor. I am a lot stronger than people give me credit for. Raising two children on my own and having to do everything in the house myself has kept me agile and fit.

I run to the window and check both ways down the street before closing all of the curtains. There's not a soul to be seen. Alex is no longer moving, his mouth wide, red, and gaping. There'll be no more lies tumbling from it. I run upstairs and grab some towels to soak up the blood and throw one over his deceitful face, noticing that one of the teacups has been spattered with blood, so I grab the other cup before I sit back down on the sofa and drink my tea.

I have everything I need to sort this mess out, and I don't need help. Nobody knows Alex was here and I shan't be telling anyone. If anyone comes looking, or if the worst happens and the police discover what I've done, then I will gladly go to jail with the knowledge that I protected my family.

I made that decision once before with Harold, and I'll stand by it again. But I won't be offering myself up on a plate. I'll be able to clean this place up so no trace of Alex's presence remains, and I'll stuff his luggage in the attic. Nobody ever goes in there. My family will never know. Although, the police, with their fancy forensics, are another kettle of fish entirely. If they ever suspect me, I know full well I'll be done for.

There is a large freezer downstairs in the basement, yet

another thing that my girls have been trying to convince me to get rid of. Why does my life have to be small just because I live here by myself? If I want a big freezer, then that's nobody's business but my own.

Scanning the room, I create an order of how I'm going to sort this considerable mess out. Alex first, I think. I open the door to the basement and prop it open with a chair. I find a large tarpaulin that we used to take camping and spread it out on the floor. It smells musty, and there's a variety of creepy-crawlies escaping from its folds and crevices, but I'm sure Alex won't mind.

I make my way back upstairs quickly. It's easy to drag Alex across the wooden living-room floor, but he is making a hideous mess. I pull him by his feet and watch as a slick red trail follows his head. This floor will have to be job two. If that blood soaks in, I'll need to rip it up.

Alex bumps noisily down the basement stairs. I have to nudge him with my foot a few times when he gets stuck at weird angles, but soon enough, he's at the bottom, and I drag him onto the tarpaulin. I wrap him up like a Christmas present and rest my toolbox on top so he doesn't unravel. I admire my handiwork and head back up the stairs.

The living room is an absolute bloodbath, and there is no time to waste. I'm grateful for my choices of hard flooring and leather sofa and chairs. They make my task much less arduous. Still, it takes me hours, many buckets of soapy water and an entire bottle of bleach to get the room clean so there is no visible trace of blood. I'll need to go round every inch of it with a torch many times to ensure I haven't missed anything until I get the chance to repaint.

The floor looks faintly discoloured, and I think a new mat is in order. I've always wanted to splash out on a handmade Turkish or Persian rug, and this seems like the perfect excuse. I'll drag the cheap one down from the spare bedroom for now in case of visitors. Although I'm planning on an imaginary bout of something infectious to ensure I'm left alone for the next week or two.

There is a bin bag filled with soiled cloths and towels that I'll need to add my own clothing to shortly. There might be room for the bag alongside Alex in the freezer, and if not, I'll burn it or dump it somewhere that can't be connected to me.

I've done as much as I can handle for now, and I crash down onto the sofa, completely exhausted. Alex should really go into the freezer today, but I'm not sure he is going to fit in one piece, and that's not a problem I have the energy for just now. I'll deal with it later, or at worst, first thing in the morning. My hands are red raw, and the skin is dry and starting to flake in places.

Killing someone is not in my nature, and I suppose Alex didn't really deserve to die, but it was the only way to stop him. He left me no choice. Sometimes things must take place in order to keep life moving in the direction it needs to. I learned my lesson with Harold. You can't sit around waiting and praying that something will happen. You have to make it happen. Swapping Harold's pills worked a lot quicker than I could have imagined, and I would have found another way if it hadn't.

I don't consider Alex's death to be murder. It is simply a mother following her most basic instincts. Tamsin and Summer's safety must be protected at all costs.

My daughters and their children are my life, and everything else comes a distant second. My love for them is fierce and cannot be extinguished. I let them both down when they were smaller by being weak and compliant, but I will never let that happen again.

Without question, I would die for my family.

But I'd rather kill for them.

THE END

ALSO BY CHARLOTTE STEVENSON

The Serial Killer's Son

ACKNOWLEDGEMENTS

Firstly and most importantly, I want to thank everyone who has read and supported me with my debut - The Serial Killer's Son. Without its success, The Guests wouldn't be here, and I am truly grateful.

I can't thank everyone at Bloodhound Books enough. Betsy, thank you so much for all your work on the cover and the title, and I am beyond delighted with the end result. To Abbie, editor extraordinaire, working with you was an absolute pleasure, and I hope I get the chance to do so again. And Tara, who to me feels like the heart of the team, you are simply wonderful. Special thanks to the very talented Patricia Dixon, whose advice and expertise I will always be grateful for.

Thank you to my amazing family. To my husband and our three wonderful children, who encourage me and celebrate every milestone and new success along the way. Thank you for believing in me! And to my amazing friends, who continue to support, share my work, and be excited for me. It means the world.

I have been so lucky to meet many wonderful authors and readers who are passionate about supporting and sharing the books they love. I've found and been welcomed into the most wonderful book-loving communities from all over the world. Huge love to all my fellow Gagents (yes, even Gage). You guys are THE BEST. Also... Red pop tart!

Finally, I hope you enjoyed Tamsin's story. I loved writing her and how she demonstrates that you can indeed be broken, brave, and strong all at the same time.

A NOTE FROM THE PUBLISHER

Thank you for reading this book. If you enjoyed it please do consider leaving a review on Amazon to help others find it too.

We hate typos. All of our books have been rigorously edited and proofread, but sometimes mistakes do slip through. If you have spotted a typo, please do let us know and we can get it amended within hours.

info@bloodhoundbooks.com

Printed in Great Britain
by Amazon

46467691R00142